Forbidden Claim

A Forbidden Series Novel

R.L. Kenderson

Also By R.L. Kenderson

Novels in The Forbidden Series
Paranormal Romance

Forbidden Blood

Forbidden Heat

Forbidden Temptation

Forbidden Addiction

Forbidden Claim

Novels in The Naughty Series
Contemporary Romance

Kinky

Dirty

Sexy: Luke & Elise's First Night

Nasty

Forbidden Claim

Forbidden Claim
A Forbidden Series Novel
by
R.L. Kenderson

PUBLISHED BY:
R.L. Kenderson

ISBN-13: 978-0-9988770-9-9

Editor: Jovana Shirley, Unforeseen Editing, www.unforeseenediting.com
Cover Designer: Viola Estrella, Estrella Cover Art,
www.estrellacoverart.com

For our dads and fellow bibliophiles.
Please don't ever read our books. We don't have to give you CPR.

ACKNOWLEDGMENTS

Thank you to everyone who waited patiently for Zane and Isabelle's story! The two characters needed a little time before they got together, and it was definitely worth it for both of them in the end.

Thank you to our Facebook friends who are hockey fans, Kara Schoenecker, Shauna Clonkey, Raven Lais, and Heidi Sohler. You supplied Isabelle with her verbal ammo at the end of the book.

Thank you to our editor, Jovana Shirley, our cover designer, Viola Estrella, and our PR rep Nazarea Andrews. You all do awesome work, as always.

Thank you to our beta readers, ARC readers, and bloggers. Our books wouldn't be the same without all of you!

And thank you to our families for being supportive and understanding.

Chapter One

Isabelle Rand kissed her boyfriend, Bram, on the cheek and exited his vehicle. As she walked to the front of the school, she took a deep breath. When she reached the doors, she turned around and waved at Bram, knowing he wouldn't leave until he saw her walk into the building.

She made no move to look and see if he drove away as she walked down the hall to her classroom. But, instead of going to the end of the corridor, she took a right into the school's office.

"He's gone," her coworker, Jessica, said.

Isabelle breathed a sigh of relief, but it didn't last long. She was only a fourth of the way through her plan.

Two more teachers, Danni and Alice, with their arms full, came from the back office area along with their principal, Noah.

Danni and Alice dropped the huge, mismatched luggage at Isabelle's feet.

"Here are most of your clothes," Danni told her.

"And here are the rest of your clothes and toiletries," Alice said.

Jessica came over from where she'd been watching the window and took Isabelle's hand, placing a set of car keys in it. "Here's your new car. It's nothing great, but it's bought and paid for."

"Give me the keys," Noah said. "I'll pull the car around."

Isabelle handed them over.

Noah looked at Jessica.

"It's a black Kia," she told him.

Isabelle swallowed hard as she tried not to cry. "I don't know what I'd do without you guys."

Jessica hugged Isabelle first. "This is what friends do for each other."

"Help them go on the run like a criminal in the night?" Isabelle joked as the first tear fell.

Alice embraced Isabelle next. When she pulled away, she squeezed Isabelle's arms. "No, we're helping you escape an abusive boyfriend who doesn't deserve to call you his."

Isabelle smiled as best she could.

Danni enveloped Isabelle last.

"I'm scared," Isabelle said in her friend's ear.

Danni drew away and looked into Isabelle's eyes. "I know. I would be scared, too. But we've been planning this for a month. Minneapolis is less than two hours away. You will make it before he even knows you're gone."

"Honey, are you sure you don't want to go to a shelter? Are you sure your friends in Minneapolis can keep you safe?" Alice, twenty years Isabelle's senior, asked.

There was no way Isabelle could tell these wonderful humans that she was going to the safest place in the world for her. Not only was Damien her friend, but he was also the alpha of the Minnesota Wolf Pack. And her other friends whom she was seeking solace from were the wolf-shifter sentinels. Once she told Damien about Bram, he would do everything to help her. And Bram wouldn't dare take on the alpha of their pack. Not if he wanted to live to tell about it.

"I'm absolutely sure. I just need to get there."

"Okay, honey. We trust your decision."

"We'd better go. I'm sure Noah has pulled the car to the side door by now."

Isabelle took one of the handles to wheel the bag outside, and Danni took the other.

Once they walked outside, Noah popped open the trunk and then got out of Isabelle's new car. The bags were loaded into the trunk, and then Noah hugged Isabelle.

When he stepped away, he held out his hand. "Phone."

"What?"

With his other hand, he reached into his back pocket. "Your phone."

"Oh. Yeah. I almost forgot."

The four of them had discussed the unlikelihood of Bram tracking her phone since he wasn't on her plan, but they didn't think it was a risk she should take. Plus, she didn't want to deal with the numerous phone calls he was bound to make once he realized she was gone.

She opened her purse and took out her phone. With a silent good-bye, she handed it over, and Noah gave her a new prepaid phone.

"I programmed all our numbers into it, just in case you need anything. And please let us know when you make it there safely."

"I will." She looked around at her friends. "I don't know how I'll ever repay you."

"I do," Alice said. "You can repay us by getting yourself to safety and staying there."

Isabelle smiled. "I will. I promise."

"You'd better."

Isabelle walked around to the driver's side of her new car but stopped before getting in. She'd almost forgotten. "Please be careful. Bram is not a good guy, and he's not what he seems. He's very strong and very dangerous."

She wished she could come out and warn them that Bram was a wolf-shifter, stronger than all of them combined, and capable of turning into a wild animal that could rip them to shreds. But she couldn't. They were her friends, but she couldn't give away her species.

"Honey, please don't concern yourself with us. It's a teacher in-service today, so no students to worry about, and we'll just tell everyone else you called in sick. We know nothing."

Noah waved the phone. "As soon as you leave, I'm going to call my office with your phone. It'll show up on your statement that you called in. Like Alice said, don't worry about us."

Isabelle closed her eyes. "You know that's never going to happen. But I will try to worry less. As long as you promise to be careful."

"We promise," Alice said for all of them.

And, with one last good-bye, Isabelle took off for Minneapolis…and for freedom.

Chapter Two

Zane Talon lay in bed, staring up at the ceiling, and threw his tennis ball in the air. It went up, almost touching the ceiling, and then back down. He caught it and threw it up again. Down it came again.

He'd been throwing the ball and catching it for a half hour now because there was simply nothing else to do. So far, this new ambassador program sucked donkey balls. They were supposed to learn from each other, but in the two weeks since he'd moved in with the wolves, their shifter communities had been practically perfect. It was like they were all planning to run for office someday. There hadn't even been any minor arrests. It was hard to learn or teach if there were no opportunities.

Hence the ball throwing. Because that was better than staring blankly at the wall.

"If you throw that ball one more time, I'm going to come over there and shove it down your throat," one of Zane's new housemates said from his bed in his room directly across the hall from Zane's.

Ever the nice guy his new roomie was.

"Damn, dude, you could just ask politely. Haven't you ever heard that you attract more flies with honey than vinegar?"

A deep sigh came from the other room. "I just need to get some sleep."

"Sorry. I didn't think I was making much noise."

The guy was turned away from Zane, and he'd assumed the guy was sleeping the whole time.

"Just because I'm not a shifter doesn't mean I have the hearing of a human."

"Why don't you just shut your door if you're trying to sleep?" Zane asked.

"I can't because someone turns the heat up during the day, and then I feel like I'm suffocating in here. I need the circulation. Why don't you shut yours?"

"Because I'm waiting for Payton to get here. This way, I can listen for her. And I'm not the one trying to take a nap."

Hunter rolled over and looked at Zane. The vampire's blue-green eyes looked sad. "I'm sorry. It's not your fault I'm stuck here."

"You didn't volunteer to switch spots with one of the wolves?"

Hunter laughed without humor. "Just the opposite. I adamantly opposed it, but Dante sent me here anyway."

"Why?"

"None of your business."

O-kay. Just when he'd thought the guy was going to be nice.

"Did you volunteer to be here?"

Zane shrugged. "Kind of."

He hadn't asked, but Vaughn had offered it to him, and Zane hadn't protested in the least.

"Why?"

Because Zane was pathetically pining away for a female wolf-shifter who didn't want anything to do with him, and he hoped that, by living with the wolves, he'd get to see her again. Even though, as far as he knew, Isabelle had never set foot in Minneapolis since she ran out on him almost two years ago.

"None of your business."

Hunter smirked and rolled away from Zane again. "Touché, cat. Touché."

Zane wanted to laugh, but when it came to Isabelle, he was very serious.

Almost two years ago, she'd entered his life when he least expected it.

The wolf-shifters had been exiled from Minneapolis for years, but the pack alpha at the time, Dwyer, had wanted revenge on the Minnesota Pride's alpha, Vance. Dwyer had tried to kidnap Vance's children. Damien, Dwyer's son, had stepped in to rescue Payton and sent his friend Isabelle to let Vance know his daughter was safe.

Except no one had been able to confirm if Isabelle was telling the truth, and Zane had been ordered to guard her until Payton and Damien could be found. It had been just the two of them, and after days of being stuck together, they had become less prisoner and guard and more like friends.

Then, one night, Zane had woken up right before Isabelle slammed her body down over his and used his dick as her personal dildo.

He often thought of that moment fondly.

They'd slept together a few more times, but after Payton was safely home and Damien was in the clear, Isabelle had hightailed it back home to Mankato. He hadn't heard from her since.

He'd never thought he'd be the type of guy to pine over a girl, but no matter how many other women he dated or had sex with, he'd been unable to forget the sexy little wolf-shifter.

Coming here and living with the wolves gave Zane hope he'd see her again. Maybe, just maybe, if he could see her and realize that he'd built her up in his head and that she was just another chick, he'd be able to purge her from his mind.

He wanted to move on with his life. After seeing some of his fellow sentinels settle down, he knew that it was something he wanted for himself in the future. Maybe not today or tomorrow, but someday.

Zane was drawn from his thoughts by the sound of commotion downstairs, the front door opening and shutting, and the hint of a female voice that didn't belong to Raven, one of the female wolf-shifter sentinels. Kendall, the other wolf-shifter female sentinel, had been the one to take Zane's place with the cat-shifters.

Finally. Payton was there.

Payton and her mate, wolf-shifter alpha Damien, had their own bedroom in the big house the wolf-shifter sentinels lived in, but they also had their own house, which was where they usually stayed. They only had a bedroom here in case it got too late or Damien felt like it was safer here.

That sucked for Zane. He didn't really know any of the wolf-shifters yet, so his only friend was Payton. With her being the cat-shifter alpha's daughter and Zane a sentinel, he'd known her for years.

He hoped that he wouldn't feel like an outsider forever, especially since he didn't know how long this liaison thing would last.

Zane got up and paused at his bedroom door to look at Hunter. At least Zane had Payton, and at least Zane was a shifter even if he was a different animal. The poor vampire was a different species entirely and had to feel very alone here.

Zane made a mental note to shift his sleep schedule, so he could spend more time with Hunter. After all, they did have the whole outsider thing in common. Maybe Zane could break through Hunter's prickly demeanor and offer to be his friend. It would suck not to be able to go out during the day when everyone else was awake, and Zane felt for the guy.

But later. Right now, he needed to go find Payton.

Except, the closer Zane got to the bottom of the stairs, the more he realized the new female voice was not Payton.

"Is Damien here?" said the exact female voice he'd been waiting to hear for two years.

As unprepared as he was to hear her voice, the smell of her knocked the breath right out of him.

He took a seat at the bottom of the stairs while he collected his emotions.

Until now, he truly hadn't thought he'd see her ever again.

Isabelle wrung her hands together as she waited to see Damien.

"Sorry, Damien's not here yet," the sentinel, Quentin, told her.

She'd met him before, but she didn't know him well. He had beautiful, dark skin and short, dark hair on his head and his face.

She'd arrived at the wolf sentinels' home in a little over two hours. She'd run into some rush hour traffic that delayed her trip a bit, but she'd made it safely.

She'd been white-knuckled the whole drive, and she'd glanced in the rearview mirror and over her shoulder too many times to count. Her fingers were stiff and her neck hurt, but it was worth it.

Now, if only she could talk to Damien. She'd assumed he would be at the sentinels' house, but she should have gone to his home instead.

"Would you like to sit? I can get you something to drink."

Isabelle spun at Quentin's question. "What?"

She needed to remember that just because Damien wasn't here didn't mean she was in danger. The sentinels would keep her safe.

"You're pacing. I thought maybe I could offer you a place to rest until Damien got here."

"What?" She'd spaced off again. "I'm sorry. Um…no, thank you. I've been sitting in the car for a couple of hours. I'm good."

He raised an eyebrow, and she looked around. He was right. She'd been pacing. She was almost so far from the front door that she was in the kitchen. She turned and walked back to the sentinel.

As she reached the front door, she smelled him.

Zane.

She closed her eyes and leaned back against the door. His scent flooded her with memories of him being inside her.

Back then, she'd thought she was in trouble, but now, she knew she'd had no idea what trouble was. If only she could go back to that time, she'd be safe.

"Are…you okay?"

Isabelle opened her eyes and shook the cobwebs off her brain. "Yeah. I just thought I smelled someone I haven't seen for a long time, and I wasn't prepared."

"Oh, if you mean—"

The sound of a vehicle coming up the driveway had her lunging for the window and ignoring whatever else Quentin had been about to say.

Chapter Three

Did Bram find me?

She'd told herself that he would never come here, looking for her, especially if Damien put her under his protection and the protection of the sentinels, but she didn't believe it one hundred percent.

She was pretty sure Bram was a sociopath. He'd been charming and every woman's dream when she met him. But, after a while, she'd begun to see the person underneath, and she wasn't sure if his pride would allow him to stay away. Bram hated to lose anything that was his. And he'd made it very clear that he saw her as belonging to him.

She shuddered as Quentin came up behind her. He put a hand on her shoulder, and she jumped.

"Hey, hey, it's just Damien," he said, his voice low and gentle.

Isabelle's shoulders sagged with relief, and she finally went and took a seat on the couch.

She heard the back door open, and someone said something to Damien before he came around the corner.

"Isabelle?"

She jumped up and rushed over to him. She wrapped her arms around him and began to cry. She didn't know what it was about seeing Damien, but it was as if, suddenly, all her strength was gone.

It was only when she saw Damien's mate, Payton, standing behind him with her eyes open wide did Isabelle let go and take a step back.

"Sorry about that," she said to Damien and Payton.

Damien grasped her biceps. "Hey, it's okay. Why don't we sit down, and then you can tell me what's wrong?"

Isabelle nodded in agreement. "It's probably best that you get everyone."

"I'll do it," Payton said.

Damien smiled at his mate. "Thanks."

Payton started back for the kitchen.

"Payton?" Damien said.

She turned. "Yeah?"

"For now, maybe we should leave the two new guys out of it."

She nodded. "Right."

Payton turned again, and Isabelle looked at Damien. "New guys?"

"Yeah. I'll tell you about it later. First, I need to know why you are here, why you are so upset, and why you smell like a Varg."

Isabelle winced. Of course Damien would know who the Vargs were.

The wolf sentinels filed into the room and took seats around Damien and Isabelle. She noticed they were two short. Kendall and Bowden weren't there.

Payton was the last to come in the room, and Damien held out his hand to her. She took it and sat on his lap.

Isabelle had hoped Payton would stay in the other room while she told her story. Not because she didn't like the female shifter, but because her story was embarrassing enough. The only reason she was telling Damien and the sentinels was because she needed their help and protection.

But Damien had made it clear that Payton was staying. He might be her friend, but he was still her alpha, and his word was law.

"Okay, Isabelle, we're all here."

She took a deep breath. "I need your protection."

"From whom?" Damien said as his spine straightened.

"My boyfriend. Well, now ex-boyfriend."

Damien clenched his jaw. "Why?"

"Because he's either going to force me to mate against my will or he'll kill me."

Damien swore.

Isabelle hung her head. "I know."

"Why don't you start at the beginning?"

"About six months ago, I met a guy, a wolf-shifter, name Bram Varg." She watched as everyone exchanged knowing looks. "He asked me out, and we started seeing each other. He was nice, respectful, and a gentleman." *Until he wasn't.* "I don't even know how it happened, but all of a sudden, I realized we were practically living together, which was fine, until he talked about getting mated. I told him I wasn't ready."

She paused to take another breath.

"He also started hinting about me quitting my job. I knew something wasn't right, so when he was out of town, I told him I needed some time apart from him and moved back home. At the time, I knew it was a cowardly move, and I told myself I had all sorts of reasons for doing it when he was gone. But, now, I admit I did it because I was scared of him. Turned out, I was right to be."

Damien closed his eyes. "What happened?"

"He broke into my apartment and dragged me out by my hair. Literally. He beat me so badly that, if I were human, I would have had to go to the hospital."

Damien moved Payton off his lap and jumped up from his seat. "Goddamn it, Isabelle."

"I know," she agreed.

She knew he was mad at the situation or at Bram, probably both, but she felt like crying again.

"Then, what happened?"

"I played along while I planned my escape." She rubbed her palms on her jeans. "It was embarrassing, but I asked my coworkers for help. Every day, I would sneak in an article or two of clothing, and one of my coworkers would take it home. I did this until I had at least a suitcase full of clothes. They helped me get a cheap car to drive here. They also got me a burner phone."

She looked down at her watch.

"He won't know something's wrong until he comes to pick me up from work, and I won't be there. Then, he'll really know I'm gone when he gets home. He'll find the note I left him.'"

"Did you tell him where you were going?" Damien asked.

"No, but he knows that I am friends with you."

Bram also knew that she and Damien used to date. He'd forbidden Isabelle from seeing or speaking to Damien ever again.

"Is this why you blocked my number?"

She hung her head. "Yes. I'm sorry."

"Isabelle."

She looked up.

"Don't be sorry. He's the asshole in this scenario, not you."

She nodded.

"You know we'll protect you, right?"

She nodded again.

Damien gave her a pointed look. "But you have to tell us everything. You said he's either going to mate you against your will or kill you. What are we missing?"

She lowered her head again and stared at the carpet. "He made a vow to take me as his mate."

There was a collective intake of breaths.

"Were you alone?" Damien asked.

Isabelle shook her head. "It was at a wolf-shifter-only event."

"We're screwed," the sentinel named Ranulf said.

They hadn't even heard the worst of it.

She swallowed hard. "He was also up onstage, making a speech."

Bram had everyone fooled. They all thought he was a good guy who wanted to give back to their community.

"That's where he made the announcement."

"Forget screwed. We're royally fucked," another sentinel called Chase said.

Isabelle looked up as Damien sighed and ran a hand down his face.

"How did you manage to stay unmated until now?" he asked her.

"My parents are out of state, visiting my sister in California. I convinced him they would want to be around when he made it official."

Isabelle had never liked that her sister moved so far away, but she was grateful it was keeping her parents away.

"You know that Bram Varg is the son of the Illinois alpha, right?" Damien asked.

Isabelle nodded.

"And you know that he lives in Minnesota because he got kicked out of Illinois, right?"

She nodded again. "I didn't at first, but I overheard him talking to someone else about it."

He'd almost found her in the hall, eavesdropping, and she shuddered at the thought of what he would have done if he had caught her.

"He's not a stable wolf," Damien said.

He didn't have to tell Isabelle twice.

"What are we going to do?" Raven, one of the female sentinels, asked.

Damien shook his head. "The only way we're going to really stop Bram from backing off on his vow is if someone else claims Isabelle."

"*What?*" Isabelle yelled.

Damien met her eyes, his gaze friendly and sympathetic but also stern. "It is the only way, Isabelle. From what you've said of Bram and from what I know about him, he's not going to just forget about you. The only way he can't claim you is if you're already someone else's mate."

The group of sentinels glanced around, exchanging looks and shifting in their seats.

"Sir, you do realize that, despite Bram's status with the Illinois wolves, we could be starting a war," Raven said.

Damien sighed. "I know."

"See, she gets it," Isabelle pointed out.

Damien narrowed his eyes at her. This look was from her alpha, not her friend, and she lowered her eyes.

"When he finds you—when, not if. *When* he finds you, we cannot stop him from claiming you. He took a vow in front of a room full of shifters, and shifter law says we cannot stand in his way."

"Even if I don't want it?" Isabelle asked.

"Did you say that?"

She sighed. "No." At the time, she hadn't wanted to start a fight. Now, she admitted to herself that she had been afraid of what he would do to her later.

"Then, everyone assumed you'd agreed. If Bram comes here and you don't go with him, he could say that we brainwashed you, that we changed your mind. He could challenge me for the right of alpha. I don't plan on losing. To anyone. But let's play what-if. Do you want Bram to be your alpha? Do you want him to be the alpha of your fellow wolf-shifters?"

This was why Damien was alpha. She hadn't even considered all the consequences.

"No. Of course not."

He breathed a sigh of relief. "Okay then. I know it's not what you want, but being mated to anyone else has to be better than being mated to him. Or him killing you."

"It is."

"So, boss, who is it going to be? It can't be you. You're already mated. Do you want it to be one of us?" Chase asked with a grimace. He looked at Ranulf, who returned his look.

"I honestly don't know," Damien said. "If we do this, we might have to be prepared to go to war."

There was a rustling over by the stairs, and then a voice that froze her to her seat said, "I'll do it."

Chapter Four

Quentin Rawling watched Isabelle freeze as Zane came into the room and offered to be the one to mate with her.

The tension surrounding these two was so thick; a knife could cut through it.

Quentin didn't know all the details about what had happened at the end of Dwyer's reign, but he did know that Isabelle had helped Damien out by going to the cat-shifters. It made sense that she knew who Zane was. But the unease between them didn't make sense.

"No, no. That won't do," Isabelle finally said, jumping from her seat.

This clearly raised Zane's hackles. "And why not?"

"Because…"

Zane raised an eyebrow, waiting for her to finish. When she didn't say anything, he said, "Would you rather mate with a wolf?"

"I don't want to mate with anybody."

"Well, Isa, that ship has sailed. It looks like you either mate with someone or move to Europe."

"You know, mating with a cat is probably a better option," Damien said.

"Oh, yeah? How so?" Isabelle asked incredulously.

"Several reasons. The worst-case scenario if you mate with a wolf is that Bram could challenge me for alpha."

This made the hairs on Quentin's neck stand on end. Bram Varg as their alpha would be terrible. He could see by the looks on everyone else's faces that they agreed with him, and Payton looked scared.

"If he challenges me for alpha and wins, he could void any wolf-mating you have."

"But that's not allowed."

"Isabelle," Damien said, "we are talking about someone who doesn't care what the rules are. However, he can't challenge Vance for his position. No matter what, a wolf cannot be the cat-shifter alpha. Also, when he comes after you, you will have the protection of the wolves and the cats. Bram is not going to win this thing."

Isabelle chewed on her lip and rubbed her temples with her fingers and thumbs. "This sucks."

Zane's face hardened. "I'm sorry the idea of mating with me repulses you, but this might be the best option."

Isabelle dropped her hands. "I never said you repulsed me. You're acting like a child."

Zane took two visible breaths but didn't say another word.

"You know, if I were going to be backed into a corner like this, I would want it to be with someone I at least liked," Raven said.

"You don't know what you're talking about," Isabelle said. "And I thought you were on my side?"

"I'm on the side that keeps everyone safe. Besides, it's obvious you two have history. A blind man could see it."

Isabelle blushed, and Zane smiled.

"She's right, Isa," Zane told her.

She scowled back at him.

"Okay, everyone, let's take a break," Damien said, holding up his hands. "Isabelle has had a stressful morning. Let's give her time to process all of this. Ultimately, the choice is hers. We can't force anyone to mate with anyone else, and we'll do what we have to in order to protect her."

Lachlan stood. "I'll get on the computer and see what I can find out about Bram that we don't already know."

Damien nodded. "Thanks."

Lachlan left the room, and Ranulf got up as well. "I understand we took an oath to protect our citizens, but they should be protecting themselves as well."

He narrowed his blue-green eyes at Isabelle and stalked from the room. Chase got up and followed him.

Damien smiled at Isabelle. "Don't worry about him. He'll do what needs to be done."

Quentin wasn't as vocal as Ranulf, but it would be nice if Isabelle went along with this idea. It wasn't fair, but life wasn't fair. He looked up the stairs. He knew all about life being unfair, and sometimes, one just had to do what one had to do in order to survive.

"I'm not going to pressure you into anything," Damien told Isabelle. "But I would really like for you to think about the situation and the options we have available."

Isabelle looked down at her hands and nodded.

Payton got up from the couch. "Isabelle, we don't have any more bedrooms because Zane and Hunter are staying with us. Why don't you go lie down in our bedroom?"

Isabelle's eyes widened, and she waved her hands in front of her face. "Oh no, I can't do that."

Payton chuckled. "No, it's fine. Damien and I have a room, but we rarely stay here. The sheets are clean, and we'll be going home tonight."

Isabelle clasped her hands together. "Are you sure?"

The female looked beat and was obviously barely hanging on.

"Of course." She elbowed Damien in the side.

"Oh, oh. Yeah, Isabelle, it's fine."

Isabelle grabbed her purse and practically ran from the room.

"Okay, let's call the meeting for now," Damien said. "We'll give Isabelle some time to sort things out."

The unofficial meeting broke up, and Quentin got up from his chair. Payton went over to Zane as Quentin left the room. He padded slowly up the stairs and turned down the hall. He told himself to keep going, to walk past the open door as fast as he could, but instead, he stood outside it with his back to the wall.

Quentin took a deep breath in and closed his eyes.

The vampire's scent was both wonderful and devastating at the same time. He reminded Quentin of black licorice. It wasn't the same, but it was close.

Images of the two of them kissing flashed in his mind.

Quentin had known he was gay his whole life, but Hunter hadn't. Quentin was the first man the vampire had kissed. The chemistry between them was explosive, but in the end, it hadn't mattered. Hunter had been too afraid of other vampires finding out and delivered his Dear John message in person.

How ironic that Hunter would be living with the wolves just months later.

"I can smell you, you know," Hunter said from the bedroom.

Quentin sighed. He opened his eyes and swung around the corner. "I'm sorry."

Despite the fact that they lived together now, they hardly ever spoke to one another. It was torture for Quentin.

"What's going on downstairs?" Hunter asked—maybe because he was curious or maybe because he didn't want to talk about the obvious tension between them.

Isabelle and Zane had nothing on Hunter and Quentin.

"One of our wolf-shifters got herself into a difficult situation with a bad male. Everyone's trying to keep her safe, but the best solution isn't ideal for her."

Hunter put a hand behind his blond head. "Oh, what is that?"

"They think she should mate with Zane."

Hunter lifted his head, his blue-greens wide. "Seriously?"

"Seriously."

Hunter dropped his head back down. "Wow. It's been weeks of nothing, and now, it's like a soap opera."

Quentin laughed. "I suppose." He cleared his throat. "Who are you going out with tonight?"

So far, Quentin and Hunter hadn't been paired to go out on patrol at all.

Hunter shrugged. "I don't know. You?"

Quentin shook his head. "Damien hasn't said anything yet."

The silence stretched on between them, getting more awkward by the second.

Quentin rubbed the back of his neck. "Well, I'd better go."

"Yeah."

"It was nice talking to you."

"You, too."

Quentin kept moving and walked to his room. Once there, he flopped down on his bed. That had been super uncomfortable. It was hard to imagine that he'd had Hunter's dick in his mouth and vice versa. It was like they barely knew each other.

It was almost worse than when they'd first met.

At the time, Quentin had thought Hunter had a problem with him being a wolf, gay, or both. It'd turned out that Hunter hadn't known what to make of his attraction to Quentin.

Quentin rolled on his side.

Anger and animosity Quentin could deal with. This unfeeling robot of a vampire he couldn't. He had no idea what would have happened between the two of them if Hunter hadn't broken up with him, but he didn't want Hunter to be alone. Of course, Hunter was never truly going to be happy if he tried to pretend a part of himself didn't exist.

Quentin closed his eyes and tried to sleep. He had an hour before he had to work that evening. He was a police officer and was on second-shift duty that week. Then, once he got off work, he had to go out as a sentinel.

One job was to be on the lookout for humans behaving badly, and the other was looking out for shifters behaving badly. He really should have found more variety in his two jobs. But it did help the wolves to have a connection on the inside of the police. And, if something weird or non-human came up, Quentin was usually able to fix it. It wasn't legal, but humans couldn't know about them.

Right now, Quentin was really hoping that he'd have one long and boring night.

Chapter Five

Bram Varg impatiently tapped his fingers against the steering wheel while sitting in front of Isabelle's school. He looked at the clock again. It was five minutes after five. She was five minutes late. She knew better than that.

He tried her cell again for the fourth time. It went straight to voice mail.

Bram shoved his door open and got out of his car. He slammed the door shut, marched into the building, and went straight to Isabelle's classroom.

Empty.

Bram took a couple of deep breaths before going to the school's office. He needed to rein in his temper. He'd let Isabelle know how much she'd disappointed him when they got home.

There were two secretaries in the office when he got there.

"Where's Isabelle Rand?"

"Excuse me?" the young brunette said.

Calm breath.

"Isabelle. Rand." He looked at his watch. "She's late. I came to pick her up, and I can't find her." Bram forced a smile.

"Oh." The brunette looked confused. "Isabelle called in sick today."

"She couldn't have called in sick because I dropped her off this morning." *You dumb cunt.*

She shook her head.

Bram put his nose in the air and took a deep breath. The brunette wasn't lying, but she and the older gray-haired secretary were both afraid. *Dumb bitches had better be if they know what's good for them.*

"What time did she call?" he asked through teeth he was fighting not to clench.

Young bitch went to a stack of papers and began flipping through them. Old bitch flew out of her chair and went to the back of the office, down a hall.

"She called at seven forty-eight."

"But I dropped her off at seven."

Young bitch shook her head in a panic. "I'm sorry. I didn't show up until seven thirty this morning. It was an in-service day. There weren't any students."

I am going to kill Isabelle.

Old bitch came back to the main office with a man. Bram immediately sized the human up. He could snap the skinny prick with one hand.

Skinny prick held out his hand. "Hello. I'm Principal Calder. May I help you?"

Bram wanted to punch him in the face, but he knew, if he did, he wouldn't stop until the stupid human was a bleeding mess on the ground.

"I am looking for my girlfriend. Isabelle Rand."

Skinny prick looked puzzled. "I'm sorry. I was told Ms. Rand called in sick today." He looked over to the young bitch, who nodded.

Bram wasn't going to get anywhere with these losers. "Fine. If you see her for some reason, let her know I'm looking for her."

As Bram stalked back to his car, he tried Isabelle again, and once more, he got her voice mail.

He raced to their home. It had originally been Isabelle's apartment, but he'd slowly begun spending more time there and leaving more stuff there, and before she had known it, he had moved in.

He still had his apartment. He couldn't bring random bitches home and fuck them in front of Isabelle. He managed to push her around a lot, but he knew that would be the end of their relationship.

As he went through every room in the apartment, he began to panic. He had searched for months for the perfect mate to bring home to his father, and Isabelle fit the bill.

He needed someone who wasn't gorgeous, so his father couldn't say he'd married for looks. But she had to be good-looking enough to fuck. He'd shuddered at some of the ugos he'd considered.

He needed someone with a wholesome image, and who was better than a schoolteacher? No one.

And he also needed someone with a backbone, so his father couldn't accuse him of manipulating the situation. But he didn't need one of those feminist bitches. He still wore the pants in the fucking relationship.

The icing on the cake was that he'd found out Isabelle would be going through her mating heat soon. It was perfect. He'd knock the slut up, and his father would see he was a family man.

He wished he could go home to Chicago and challenge his father. But his father had warned Bram that, if he came back and challenged him for alpha, he had put safeguards in place. Ones that included Bram's death. Bram might not like his old man, but he respected his tenacity. If his father wanted him dead, Bram would be dead.

That was why he needed to show his father he'd changed. Isabelle was the key.

Bram went through the apartment one more time. Everything was in place. No clothes were missing. No luggage was missing. But Bram knew the bitch had left him.

He picked up the vase of flowers that Isabelle always kept on the dining room table and threw it across the room. It shattered against the wall, a piece coming back to hit his face.

There was no way his father wasn't going to find out that his girlfriend had left him. That she had snuck away like she was some prisoner.

The fucking bitch was dead. She had better run far away because, if he found her, he was going to make her suffer for making him look like a fool.

Chapter Six

Zane knocked on the bedroom door. It was almost dark outside, and he would be heading out for the night. He needed to talk to Isabelle before he left.

He heard movement on the other side, and then she swung the door open. Her scent, which reminded him of lilacs, deepened.

"Oh, it's you."

Zane put a hand to his chest. "Ouch." He was trying to make light of her comment, but it did sting a little. He didn't know what he had done to make her not like him. He'd thought they'd parted on good terms. For the most part.

Okay, he was lying to himself. The day she'd left, she'd been planning to sneak away without saying good-bye to him. He'd confronted her, they'd had hot sex, filled with anger and resentment, and then he'd let her go. So, maybe things hadn't ended well. But he'd been upset and hurt. He'd thought that maybe they had the start of something good together, but she hadn't wanted to have anything to do with him.

It seemed like she still felt that way.

"Look, Isabelle," he said, purposely not using her nickname so that she would understand how important this was, "I know I'm not your ideal mate. I know I'm not the one you want."

Isabelle opened her mouth, but Zane grabbed her hands. He had a feeling he wouldn't like what was going to come out of her mouth.

"I know this is not the situation you pictured when you dreamed of a happily ever after, but you're in a bad state, Isa." Zane closed his eyes and tried not to picture Bram hurting Isabelle. Zane had immediately Googled the wolf-shifter, and his image alone had put Zane on edge. He opened his eyes. "I don't want to see you hurt. I'm not trying to trap you into anything. I don't want to force you to be my mate. I just don't want this guy to hurt you."

He dropped her hands and stepped back.

"And I know you're tough, but I saw his picture, and the guy is huge. And it looks like he has a couple of goons with him wherever he goes."

"Yeah, they're his 'bodyguards,'" Isabelle said with air quotes. "They're really his muscle and the ones who do his dirty work."

"I don't get it. How did you end up with someone like him?" An asshole, a girlfriend beater, and Zane hadn't seen a single picture with a smile on the dick's face.

He was the opposite of Zane. And maybe that was why Isabelle had dated Bram. Maybe a class clown like Zane wasn't what she wanted. Even if he'd made her come like nobody else.

Her words, not his.

He shook his head. Now was not the time to think about sex or feel sorry for himself. He held up his hand. "I'm sorry I asked," he told Isabelle. "Why you dated him is none of my business."

"Thank you," she said, looking surprised. "But I'm still not exactly on board with this plan."

"I get it. But I want you to remember, it's not just you that's involved. It's the sentinels, possibly your whole pack."

"So, I should just involve your pride, too? Add more people to the mix?"

Okay, so she had a point, but the answer was obvious. "Yes. My pride and your pack together are no match for Bram. If his father got involved, it could be the Illinois Pack against the Minnesota Pack, but he couldn't take on the Minnesota Pride as well. And, if we got the vampires involved…" Bram's father wouldn't want to mess with them.

"So, should I mate with a vampire, too? I know one of them is staying here. We could have a lovely ménage à trois going on. How would you like that?"

Zane snapped his fingers and smiled. "Now, that's an excellent idea. I've never done it with another dude, but what the hell?"

She put her hands on her hips. "I was being sarcastic."

Zane mimicked her. "I know."

She threw her hands up in the air, and her hazel eyes rolled toward the ceiling. "You're so frustrating, you know that?"

He shrugged. "It's part of my charm."

It was part of his charm. There was just something about this cat that Isabelle couldn't explain when she told others about him.

She hadn't seen him in two years, but he hadn't changed much. His dark blond hair was a little shorter on the sides, and there was a little more seriousness in his sea-green eyes, but that could be the situation.

She sighed and sat on the bed.

She knew she was being a little selfish about the situation, but she had so many thoughts and emotions running through her head. When she thought about Bram and the danger he presented, the obvious answer was to mate with Zane. It was the safest and smartest option. She didn't want to put her life in danger. That was why she'd left in the first place. But she certainly didn't want to endanger anyone else either.

But her heart. Her heart was the one struggling.

There was a part of her, way down deep, that wanted Zane to be her mate. It was the silly, fantasies-come-true part of her.

But Zane wouldn't be mating with her because he loved her. He would be doing it to keep her safe. It was the sentinel in him.

If only they'd never had sex. If only she didn't feel like they had a connection because of the past. Then, her head would be clearer. She could think and assess more rationally.

Zane came and sat next to her. She secretly hoped he'd put his arm around her and comfort her, but he didn't. He kept a proper distance. Besides grabbing her hands earlier, he hadn't touched her. She loved that he respected her, yet she wanted to pound her fists against his chest and ask why he wasn't more affected.

"I'm not trying to push you into anything," he said. "But, if it helps, I would never force myself on you. We will be mates in name only. No sex."

She felt even more depressed. Of course, she didn't want him to expect her to sleep with him, but it seemed like he wasn't even interested while she'd never forgotten their time together. Nobody made her feel things the way Zane had.

She was a mess of contradictions.

"Thanks for your sacrifice." She couldn't quite keep the bitterness out of her voice.

He narrowed his eyes. "What the hell does that mean?"

She looked away. "It means that you're in the same situation I am. You're doing this because it's the right thing. You're not doing it…" *Because you want to be with me. Because you love me.*

"Don't worry about me."

"Of course. Zane the martyr."

He jumped up. "I'm not a fucking martyr. Jesus, what is up with you?"

She wished she knew.

He swiped a hand down his face and took a huge breath. "Look, no one is making me do this. I'm not doing this for the greater good. I'm doing this because I want to."

"But why?"

"My reasons are my own, okay? You wouldn't understand." He pointed a finger. "But I'm not a fucking martyr."

"Okay. I'm sorry I said that."

He nodded his head. "Will you just tell me when you decide? I need to let my alpha know if we're going to go through with this."

She tilted her head to the side. "You're not going to ask his permission?"

He sighed. "I probably should since it involves the whole pride, but no. This is my decision."

Wow. Isabelle had no words.

"You're looking at me funny."

She shook her head to clear it. "Sorry."

He raised his brow. "So, you'll let me know when you decide?"

She stood. "Yes."

He turned to go.

"Zane?"

He swung back around.

"What happens if I tell you no?"

He stiffened but only for a moment, and then he shrugged. "I don't know. I suppose that's for you, Damien, and the wolf sentinels to decide."

"Will you still be around if I mate with a wolf?"

Zane's jaw tightened, and he looked away. "Yes. I'll still be a part of the liaison program."

Payton had explained to Isabelle why Zane and the vampire were here when she showed her to the room.

Zane looked her in the eye. "Just don't expect to see me much." He turned once again.

"Zane?"

He stopped but stayed facing away from her this time.

"I've made my decision."

He swallowed. "Yeah?"

"I'm going to do it."

He didn't say anything. He didn't move a muscle. But his rich sandalwood scent flooded the room, and Isabelle knew she'd made the right call.

Chapter Seven

Tegan Leonard reached out her arms and squeezed her hands. "Gimme, gimme, gimme," she said to her friend and co-sentinel Phoenix. "I want to hold Ash."

Phoenix kissed her baby boy on the top of his head and then ever so slowly handed him to Tegan.

Dante put his arm around Phoenix. "She's a little overprotective," he explained.

Tegan laughed. "I can see that." It had taken almost two months to convince Phoenix to bring the baby to the bunkhouse. "Who would have thought?" Not her. Of the two female cat-sentinels, Tegan had always assumed that she would mate and have a baby before Phoenix. Life sure was funny sometimes. She looked down at the baby in her arms. "Your mommy loves you, doesn't she?"

Ash yawned in response, and Tegan laughed.

Tegan looked at Phoenix. "Where did you get his name?"

Phoenix blushed, surprising Tegan. The female was tough and didn't do blushing.

Dante laughed at his mate. "It's a play on fire. Dante's *Inferno*, Phoenix rising from the ashes."

Tegan smiled. "Pretty clever."

"It's cheesy," Phoenix said.

Tegan barked out a laugh, which caused the baby to scrunch up his face.

Tegan bounced him up and down in her arms. "No, no, don't cry. I'm sorry I laughed." She rubbed her cheek against his soft, dark hair, and the baby calmed.

There was a noise from the hall, and Ram walked out. "Hey, Dante. I thought I'd heard your voice."

Ram was one of Dante's Guardians. He had basically taken Phoenix's spot with the cat-shifter sentinels. She and Dante had come up with this liaison program to help them get to know each other better and work together more. Tegan thought it was an ingenious way for Phoenix to stay with the Guardians.

Ram was huge. A few inches over six feet with large muscles. He looked like he could crush anyone with his bare hands. But watching him with Dante and Dante with Phoenix had Tegan's mind wandering.

What was so special about Dante that Phoenix had given up her self-imposed celibacy to mate and have a baby with the vampire? Tegan had tried to get information out of Phoenix, but it would be easier to break into Fort Knox. Phoenix was not a gabber or a gossiper.

The only thing Tegan had been able to discern was that there was something to do with blood and feeding. To say it made her curious was an understatement. She'd always been sexually open. She dated whoever had caught her fancy. Men and women, although she always found herself coming back to men. There was just something about a big, hard dick that a dildo could never replace.

Ram walked over to Tegan. His hair was short and dark blond or light brown, depending on the light. His yellow eyes were his best feature though, and they lit up as he looked down at the baby. "Cute kid."

"Thanks," Dante said.

Tegan held out her arms. "Do you want to hold him?" she asked, fully expecting him to say no.

He shrugged. "Sure."

As Tegan handed the baby over to Ram, she looked over at Phoenix, whose eyes were as big as the plates in the cupboard.

"Don't worry; I won't drop him," Ram said even though he was looking at the baby.

Dante laughed.

Tegan noticed that Ram smelled sweet, like honey, and when their fingers touched, she noticed how warm his skin was. There wasn't a zing or spark, but it didn't stop Tegan from wondering what it would be like to have sex with Ram. And this wasn't the first time the thought had crossed her mind since the male moved in.

He looked up and met her eyes, the look in them knowing. He couldn't possibly have guessed what she was thinking, but even if he had, she wasn't shy about her interest. If he were game, she'd totally give him a ride. Or let him give her one.

Ram took the baby in his big, meaty hands and went to the living room. They'd been sitting at the kitchen counter, and Phoenix was the first one to get up and follow the big vampire. Dante and Tegan trailed along, and Tegan sat next to Ram because she hadn't gotten her baby fill yet.

Tegan heard the front door open, and the other sentinels poured into the bunkhouse, including Kendall, the wolf-shifter who'd taken Zane's place with the cats, and Vance, the cat-shifter alpha.

Everyone crowded around the baby to look at him and ooh and aah for a few minutes. Tegan moved to the opposite side of the couch from Ram to give the others more room since she'd already had a turn.

The group slowly stepped back after holding and talking to Ash, and Reid came to sit beside Tegan. She turned her back to the side of the couch and propped her legs up on Reid's lap. He drew her legs close to him, and she ran her fingers through his shaggy reddish-brown hair and tucked some behind his ear.

"Your hair's gotten long. Are you growing it out?"

He shook his hair out, obviously not liking where she'd placed it, and shrugged. "I don't know." He looked at her. "What do you think?"

She tilted her head to the side and studied him. She'd known Reid for years, and she didn't often think of him as a sexual creature. He was her friend, but she looked at him to see how other females might see him.

His eyes were a yellow-green and really stood out among his hair, especially now that it was longer and there was more of it. She'd often thought of Reid as kind of a geek because he was always on the computer, but she didn't really know why. He worked out as much as the next sentinel and had the body to show it. His form-fitting white T-shirt showed off his strong pecs, and she even saw a hint of his six-pack from where the fabric rested on his stomach. And his biceps and triceps strained against the fabric as he massaged her calves.

Damn. When did Reid get so sexy?

Heat began to travel up her thighs to that special place between her legs. She was suddenly hot all over.

She needed to get ahold of her libido, stat. She was in a room filled with all her coworkers and her alpha.

"I think it looks good," she said as casually as possible.

Vance clapped his hands. Tegan sent a silent thank-you to anyone who was watching over her upstairs.

"I have some developing news," the cat-shifter alpha said. "You all probably remember Isabelle Rand?"

Everyone nodded their heads, except the two vampires.

"Isabelle helped us when Payton went missing," Phoenix explained to her mate and Ram.

"Ahh," Dante said.

"It turns out that Isabelle has gotten into some trouble."

This news immediately put Tegan on alert, and all sexy thoughts flew out of her head.

"She got involved with a guy who was bad news. She managed to leave him yesterday and has gone to the wolf-shifters for help."

Poor Zane.

It probably had hurt him to hear that Isabelle was dating someone else even if that someone wasn't a great guy.

"The male Isabelle was dating is a wolf-shifter named Bram Varg. His father is the alpha of the Illinois Pack, but it seems he has exiled his own son from Illinois."

"Oh, shit," Reid said.

Tegan had to agree. If your own flesh and blood kicked you out, you were bad news.

"It also seems that he made a vow to mate with Isabelle," Vance continued to explain. "So, our very own sentinel Zane has offered to step in to be her mate so that Bram has no claim on her."

"Holy shit," Tegan said. This was like a soap opera.

"I told Zane that we would help protect Isabelle, no matter what, after everything she did to help get Payton back to us, but he's determined to go through with this."

Of course he is.

Zane had been going through Isabelle withdrawal since she left. He would never let anything bad happen to her, and if he got to mate with her in the process? Bonus.

"So, you're saying, we might have an angry, unstable wolf-shifter sniffing around us?" Saxon asked.

Vance put his hands on his hips. "Pretty much."

The front door opened, and Vaughn and Naya came in along with their eleven-month-old son, Aidan, and daughter, Victoria. Behind them were Sawyer and Kenzie, who was just beginning to show.

"Hey, guys. What's with all the grim faces?" Vaughn asked after setting Aidan down on the carpet.

Vance filled his son and Sawyer in on the news as Naya put Victoria next to her brother. She sat on the floor next to them and took them out of their car seats. Victoria walked over to her daddy, and he immediately picked her up despite the deep conversation he was having with his father.

Aidan crawled over to Saxon and pulled on his leg. Saxon rolled his eyes but picked the infant up and set him on his lap. Only Aidan knew why he liked Saxon so much.

"Everyone," Vance said to the group again, "I will keep you up-to-date on anything I discover. Until then, Reid, can you find out whatever you can on this guy and send his picture to everyone's phones?"

Reid set Tegan's legs aside and stood. "I'll get my computer."

"Great." Vance nodded. "Once you get the info Reid will be sending you, take a good look at it and be on the lookout. I know the wolves will be on high alert, but it doesn't hurt for us to have some extra patrols around their homes." He clapped his hands. "That's it for now. Let's get out there, and report anything you see back to me."

Vance turned to Vaughn. "Now, give me my granddaughter. You're on watch tonight, too, son."

Chapter Eight

Early the next morning, while the moon was still in the sky, Isabelle dragged her butt out of bed and down the stairs. She'd barely slept a wink all night long. The first and only person she saw was Damien.

"Hey, Izzy. How are you?" he asked when he saw her.

"Okay, considering." She looked around the room and into the kitchen. "Where is everyone?"

"They should be here soon. The ones who just got back from patrol are showering, and the others should be up and getting ready. They don't usually get up this early."

Isabelle had been told that, sometimes, they were on patrol all night, and sometimes, they did half the night, so they would all be sleeping during the day. Most of the crime happened at night, but it didn't mean that nothing happened during the day when the sun was out. Damien had cut last night's patrol early, so they could all be here in the morning before the sun came up.

"Are you ready to do this?" Damien asked, his face full of concern.

Isabelle rubbed her hands together. "As ready as I'll ever be."

A couple of minutes later, everyone began filing into the living room. The wolf-sentinels, Payton, and even the vampire named Hunter. But no Zane.

"Where's Zane?" Isabelle asked the room, hoping someone had seen him.

"Uh-oh, the groom got cold feet."

"Be quiet, Chase," Damien told his sentinel.

It couldn't be true. Had Zane decided to back out?

There was the sound of at least two vehicles coming up the long driveway. Everyone went to the windows and watched as the first SUV pulled up, and Zane got out.

"When the hell did he even leave?" someone asked.

"Fricking cat," somebody else said.

Isabelle ignored their comments and watched all the cat sentinels empty out of the two SUVs along with the cat-shifter alpha, Kendall, a couple of other vampires, and a human. One she knew was the cat-shifter alpha's daughter-in-law.

"So, he didn't bail after all. He brought his people." Chase was nodding, as if he admired Zane.

Relief came over Isabelle. Now that she had decided to mate with Zane, she definitely didn't want him to change his mind.

Zane walked through the front door. "Hey, I've brought a few guests. I figured, if we were going to do this, then my alpha should be here as well. I don't want there to be any question as to the validity of our mating."

"Good thinking," Damien said as the living room became very crowded, and everyone greeted one another.

Payton hugged her father and sister-in law and bumped fists with her brother.

"Isabelle," Zane said, "you remember all the cat-shifter sentinels."

She wasn't quite sure she recalled everyone, but since it was a statement and not a question, she nodded.

"And you met Naya."

She nodded again.

"That big vampire over there"—Zane pointed to where the vampire stood next to Hunter—"is Ram. He took Phoenix's place with the cats because Phoenix is mated to this guy." Zane put his arm around the shoulders of another vampire. Not as tall or as wide as Ram, but there was an air of authority about him. "This is Dante, and he is the leader of the Guardians." He then walked over to the only human. "And, last but not least, this is Kenzie. She is Sawyer's mate."

Isabelle nodded to everyone around the room. "Hello, everyone. New and old. Thanks…for coming."

It felt weird to thank them for coming to watch a mating that needed to be done out of necessity. Most matings took place behind closed doors. They were so unlike human weddings. But this mating needed as many witnesses as possible.

She rubbed her temples. *Oh, Isabelle, what have you gotten yourself into?*

Zane stepped over to her and grabbed one of her hands. He squeezed it. His little bit of reassurance meant a lot, and she dropped her other arm from her forehead.

"So, how are we going to do this?" the cat-shifter named Vaughn asked. He was the cat alpha's son.

"Well, I promised Isa there wouldn't be any sex, so for those of you expecting a show, you're outta luck."

Isabelle practically choked on her tongue, and the room erupted with laughter.

Zane squeezed her hand again. "I was kidding. It was a joke. To lighten the mood."

She gave him a shaky smile, but she was still too nervous to laugh.

"I have an idea," Kenzie said. "Since we don't have an officiant like at a human wedding, what if each of you are asked if you accept this union of free will? Maybe by each of your alphas because it's someone you trust. And then, instead of exchanging rings, as it were, you bite each other?"

No one said anything at first, and the human looked at her mate.

He put his arm around her. "It's a good idea, mate."

She smiled up at him. "Thanks."

Zane looked at Isabelle. "Sounds good to me."

As good as it could be. "I agree."

Zane grabbed her hands, and they faced each other.

Nobody said anything, and everyone exchanged looks.

"Who goes first?" Damien asked.

"You go," Vance said.

"Okay." Damien cleared his throat. "Isabelle Rand, do you take Zane Talon as your mate, free from force and coercion?"

She took a deep breath and swallowed. "I do."

Zane grinned at her, and despite her anxiousness, she smiled back.

"Zane Talon," Vance said, "do you take Isabelle Rand as your mate, free from coercion and force?"

"I do."

The two alphas looked at each other and then at her and Zane.

"You may now bite each other," Vance said.

Zane looked around the room, obviously looking for something. When he didn't find what he was looking for, he dropped her one hand and pulled her toward the kitchen.

He sat on the stool at the kitchen island. "That's better. Now, we're closer in height." He pulled his T-shirt over his head and laid it on the counter. He drew her close to him and tilted his head to expose his neck. "You first, Isa."

His skin was smooth, and she could smell him. She suddenly wished they were alone. She wished she could do what she wanted to him, which was trail her nose up and down to take in his scent. Then, she would lick him and suck on his skin.

But they weren't alone, so rather than doing all the things she wanted, she shifted her teeth, so her sharp wolf canines emerged, and she sank them into Zane's neck.

His grip tightened around her, and she felt him get hard against her belly. The area between her legs answered the call, and she grew wet.

Someone shifted behind her, and she just then realized everyone had followed them and that they were far from alone. She let go of Zane's neck and stepped back.

Her mark was there for everyone to see, and he even bled from a couple of spots. They were already beginning to heal, and he made no move to wipe the blood away.

"Your turn," she said in a low voice, meant only for him. Thankfully, she'd put on a shirt with a wide neckline that morning, and it was her turn to face away and expose her neck to him.

As she bared the vulnerable part of herself, she knew she trusted Zane not to hurt her, and she relaxed in his arms.

He had no reservations in doing what he wanted to her. He nipped her ear and slid his lips from her lobe to the hem of her shirt and then back up to the top where her shoulder met her neck. He flicked his warm tongue out and then sucked her skin into his mouth.

She was abruptly transported back to the last time they'd had sex. Zane had sucked on her so hard; it had been as close to leaving a mark on her without actually doing so. What if she had told him to do it that day? To mark her?

Zane pressed his erection into her belly, bringing her back to the present, and she grabbed on to his shoulders before her knees gave out and dropped her to the floor.

All too soon, he released her neck, and she swayed.

She'd been claimed.

Zane stared at the area he'd just had his mouth against, and he rubbed his thumb over it. It was tender there, but she liked it.

He shifted his eyes to hers, and she licked her lips.

Zane stood, keeping his eyes on hers. "We're going upstairs."

Isabelle's breathing quickened.

Someone cleared their throat.

"Sorry, son, but we need to go over what the next steps are in this plan," Vance said.

Zane looked over her head to his alpha and nodded.

Isabelle closed her eyes for a moment. She was disappointed but also relieved. Having sex with Zane right now could be a mistake. They didn't need any more complications.

Chapter Nine

Zane was disappointed, but Vance was right. There were more important things to do than have sex with his mate.

He looked down at Isabelle.

He had a mate.

The thought made him dizzy, and he had to sit down again.

"Are you okay?" Isabelle asked him.

He smiled. "Yes. Just had a surreal moment; that's all." He looked past her to the two alphas. "What else do you have in mind?"

"Well," Vance said, looking at Damien, "we talked last night and had a couple of thoughts."

He could feel and smell the tension filling Isabelle's body again. "What were you thinking?"

"First," Damien said, "you need to go down to the courthouse and legally marry. It'll be another way to keep Bram away. He can't take on the human laws."

Isabelle started chewing on her lip.

Zane grabbed her hand. "Hey, we can always get divorced. Humans do it all the time."

She nodded.

"What else?" he asked.

"You two are going to be spending every minute together," Damien said.

"As of right now, you're out of the rotation," Vance added.

Zane narrowed his eyes. "Why?"

"Because you two need to spend as much time together as possible. You need to smell like each other," Damien told them. "We don't know when Bram is coming, and he needs to believe this claiming is legitimate."

Vance cleared his throat. "This means, sleeping in the same bed together." He held up a hand. "Isabelle, you don't have to do anything you don't want to do, but you need to sleep next to each other. That will only strengthen your mating bond."

"What about me?" Zane asked. "Do I have to do anything I don't want to do?"

This earned him a few, "Yeah, right," and some, "Whatever," but Isabelle smiled, so it was worth it.

"I think you can handle Isabelle," was all his alpha said.

Raven cleared her throat. "Might I point something else out?"

"Sure," Damien said.

"Correct me if I'm wrong, but are you close to your mating heat, Isabelle?"

Isabelle blushed, and it hit Zane. "Is this why you chose to escape now? You didn't want that asshole getting you pregnant?"

She slowly nodded, and Zane clenched his jaw. He was starting to hope Bram showed up sooner rather than later.

"How-how did you know?" Isabelle asked Raven.

Raven gave Isabelle a sympathetic look. "I can smell it."

"Raven is our best tracker," Damien explained. "She's a super smeller."

That explained how she'd known Zane's laundry needed to be done last week. He hadn't thought it was that bad until Raven barged in his room, demanding he get to work.

"You're probably not going to like this idea," Raven said, pushing her long black ponytail over her shoulder, "but, if you were to let Zane service you during your heat, it would only make it that much harder to break you up."

Isabelle turned red again, and Zane smiled.

"But what if I get pregnant? That's not fair to the child."

The way she'd said that made Zane think she wasn't against the idea of letting him take her during her mating heat. He had to fight very hard not to think about it, or everyone in the room would know how turned on he was. They'd see and smell it.

"Would you love the child?" Raven asked.

"Of course."

"Would Zane love the child?"

Zane opened his mouth to answer, but Isabelle beat him to it. "Of course."

Raven shrugged. "Well then, I don't see a problem. There are so few of us as it is."

"But what if Bram did something to the baby?" Isabelle put her hand over her lower abdomen, as if she were already with child.

"Shit, that's a good point," Zane said. He put his arm around his new mate. "But, if you do get pregnant, we will have eliminated Bram as a threat by the time you have the baby."

Isabelle put her head on his shoulder. "I can't believe we're actually talking about having a baby. All I wanted to do was break up with the guy."

Her words were low and quiet, but Zane still heard them, and he couldn't help but feel a little punch to the gut. He knew she hadn't asked for this, but it still hurt.

Quentin knew he was supposed to be paying attention to what was going on with the Isabelle and Bram situation, but he couldn't keep his eyes off Hunter.

The minute the big vampire, Ram, had walked into the house, Hunter's eyes had lit up.

The jealousy running through Quentin's veins was inconvenient as hell. He was supposed to be working. And there was nothing he could do about how he felt.

What he really wanted to do was march over to the two males, push Hunter up against the wall, and take his mouth. Let everyone in the room, not just Ram, know that Hunter belonged to him. Then, he would drag the vampire upstairs and push him down on the bed and show him how he made love.

Fuck. Now, he was sporting a throbbing erection in a room full of shifters and vampires.

Quentin looked around before he turned to face the wall for a second to adjust himself. He hoped that nobody noticed because Damien, Vance, Isabelle, and Zane were still talking.

But, when he turned back around, Hunter was staring at his crotch.

Quentin almost crossed his arms in front of himself to cover up Hunter's effect on him, but at the last second, he changed his mind and scratched his leg instead. Right before he pulled his hand away, he ran his thumb down the outside of his length.

That's right, Hunter; look at what you do to me.

Quentin pretended that he was paying attention to the main conversation in the room, but out of the corner of his eye, he saw Hunter. Quentin was practically holding his breath to see what the vampire would do.

Hunter narrowed his eyes and then looked at Ram and said something. Ram leaned his head down closer to Hunter and smiled.

Quentin told himself to look away because, if Hunter left the room with Ram, he might do something he would regret.

All the other sentinels knew that he was gay. After Damien had taken over as their alpha, he'd felt comfortable with coming out. Turned out, most of them had suspected anyway. But they didn't know Hunter was gay. Hunter barely knew he was gay. He was so far in the closet; he couldn't even see the door.

And, as much as Quentin hated that Hunter had broken it off with him, he would never reveal Hunter's secret. And, right now, he might just go after Hunter if he left with another male.

But Ram nodded toward one of the cat-shifters and shrugged.

It was soon apparent that the two vampires weren't conspiring to leave the room together or anything like that. When Dante walked over and joined their conversation, Quentin was sure of it.

That was when Quentin knew he was in over his head. He had never felt unjustified jealousy over someone. He rarely ever felt justified jealousy. He had dated a guy a few years back who spoke to his ex all the time. Everyone had told Quentin that he should be worried, but he'd shrugged it off.

It'd ended up that his friends were right, but the point was, he had never been jealous of his boyfriend's ex, even when he obviously should have been.

But, now, he was jealous that Hunter was just talking to his fellow Guardian. Someone who obviously liked the opposite sex by the looks he'd been giving the blonde cat-shifter and that she had been giving him in return. Not to mention that Hunter had told him that none of the other Guardians knew about him.

Quentin shook his head and searched for the nearest wolf-shifter sentinel. Chase and Ranulf were leaning against the wall, looking bored, and Quentin headed in their direction.

"Hey," he said when he reached both of them.

Chase picked up his dark head. "Hey."

Ranulf nodded in greeting.

"I'm going to head out."

Chase narrowed his citrine eyes in concern while Ranulf just tilted his head, as if he was studying Quentin.

"I forgot I had a department meeting."

Understanding dawned on Chase's face. "Oh. Yeah, go. I'll tell Damien you had to go to work for a little while."

Quentin smiled his appreciation. "Thanks."

Chase resumed his bored posture. Ranulf had never lost his. Quentin went to the front door. It took everything in him not to turn around and look. It was a good thing he had some solid willpower.

Chapter Ten

After the awkward mating in front of everyone and returning to the bunkhouse from the wolf-shifters' home, Tegan kicked off her shoes and grabbed something comfortable to wear.

She'd worked most of the night, so she was going to try to get some sleep while things were calm and quiet in the shifter world.

Her ears perked up as she heard the heavy tread of Ram's boots coming down the hall. She fully expected him to walk past without saying a word to her, but the footsteps stopped, and a throat cleared behind her.

Tegan turned. "Yes?"

Ram had an arm braced on the doorjamb and one leg crossed over the other. He looked behind himself, presumably to make sure the hall was clear, and then looked back at her. "So, are we going to do this?"

"Do what exactly?"

"Fuck."

She wasn't surprised he had approached her, but she was a little surprised that he had been so blunt about it. Some females might be offended by his candor and lack of romance but not Tegan. She didn't need romance from Ram. She wasn't looking to start a relationship with him. She just wanted to have sex with him.

"Sure," she told him. She tilted her head in his direction. "Shut the door," she said and pulled her shirt over her head. Her white-blonde hair landed in her face, and she quickly pushed it away to watch Ram pull his own T-shirt off over his head as he stalked toward her.

When he reached her, he put a finger under her bra strap and rubbed his digit up and down a few times. "Nice bra. But I think it has to go."

She grabbed on to the waistband of his jeans. "So do these."

Ram stepped back and grinned. "Ladies first."

If he was expecting her to be shy, he got the wrong girl. Tegan took off her bra and then pushed her underwear and pants down in one swoop. She kicked them off her legs and put a hand on her hip. "Your turn, stud."

Ram laughed, and soon, their outfits matched.

Tegan reached out to grab Ram's huge cock. She should have known, with his size, that he'd be packing something like this in his pants.

"I want you to feed from me," she said.

He opened his mouth and thumbed a fang. "Whatever the lady wants."

She smiled at him. *This should be fun.*

It had been okay. But a little disappointing.

Tegan grabbed a handful of soap and scrubbed away any remains of Ram from between her legs.

She felt bad for thinking the sex had been just okay, but it definitely hadn't made her world tilt or made her want to mate with the male. She didn't even want to sleep with him again. Whatever Phoenix had with Dante, Tegan had not experienced it with Ram.

Sure, he had a big dick, and he did know how to use it. A fumbling idiot he was not. But there was just something…missing.

And, when he'd fed from her, she hadn't really liked it. It hadn't hurt or anything, but it had almost annoyed her. She'd just wanted him to stop. It was only because she had plenty of experience in the bedroom—with a partner and on her own—that she knew her body well enough to get off. She couldn't remember the last time she'd worked that hard for an orgasm.

Part of her thought she had done it more for him than for herself. She hadn't wanted to hurt Ram's pride.

She winced as she scrubbed her body for the third time. She felt a little coldhearted. Thankfully, it had been obvious Ram didn't want a relationship from her either, and hopefully, they could pretend like it had never happened.

Tegan shut off the water and grabbed her towel. After drying off, she put on her sweatpants and T-shirt and combed out her hair. She wiped off the condensation from the mirror and inspected her neck. Two small wounds were quite noticeable, but her shirt covered them up.

She looked at her face. Her brown eyes looked the same, except her blonde eyelashes were matted together from the shower. Other than that, she appeared normal, which was a relief. She didn't look like she'd just had okay sex.

She lifted her arm and sniffed. She smelled like the body wash she usually used, but it didn't comfort her. She didn't know why she didn't want Ram's smell on her, only that she didn't.

She actually felt bad because he was a nice guy. They could probably be friends. And they probably would be if he was with the cats long enough and as long as they put the sex behind them.

Judging by how quickly Ram had left her room once they were done, it would be easy for him, too. He hadn't run out of there, but he hadn't stuck around either.

Tegan grabbed her dirty clothes and took them to her room to put in her hamper. She had planned to lie down, but she didn't want to be in her bed. She went back out to the hall and went down two rooms.

The door was slightly ajar, so she knocked.

"Come in," Reid said.

Tegan slipped through the half-open door and shut it behind her. Reid was sitting at the huge computer setup that took up half of his room.

He turned when she shut the door, and even though she'd just had sex, she felt a slight pull between her legs.

Reid was sitting in his computer chair without a shirt, without socks, and his jeans were unbuttoned, and it was apparent he wasn't wearing boxers or briefs. His chest was tan and sported very little hair for a shifter. His abdomen showed off his eight-pack. When he'd gotten an eight-pack, she didn't know. She really needed to pay more attention. And the treasure trail going from his abdomen to inside his open pants was very tempting.

"Hey, what's up?"

Tegan shook her head to clear her wandering mind. "Do you care if I lie in your bed for a while?"

He shrugged. "Sure."

That was just like Reid. He hadn't asked her why. He hadn't thought she was weird to ask to sleep in a friend's bed. He just let her do it.

That was one of the reasons she loved him. Like a friend, of course.

Tegan climbed into his queen-size bed and buried herself under his covers. She inhaled his woodsy smell and cuddled up with his pillow. Hopefully, by the time she woke up, she'd smell like Reid.

She fell asleep to the sound of his keyboard clacking, feeling safe and content.

Sometime later, she heard Reid curse. She opened her eyes to see him shake out his hand and stick his thumb in his mouth. She would have laughed, but she was only half-awake.

As she closed her eyes, she heard the sound of clothes moving, and then Reid slid into bed beside her.

"Do you want me to leave?" she asked him. She didn't want to encroach on his space.

He lay on his back. "No." He turned his head and looked at her. "I know you need something. You're more than welcome to stay here. I just hope you find it."

Tegan smiled at him. "I think I already have."

He leaned over and kissed her forehead. "Good. Now, I'd better get some sleep in case Vance needs me to work on something soon." He yawned and shifted. His leg touched hers. "Sorry," he said and rolled over, putting his back to her.

"Can I ask you a question, Reid?"

"You already did."

She rolled her eyes. "Okay, another one then."

"Shoot."

"Are you naked?"

"As the day I was born," he said as he yawned again.

"Okay."

"Why do you ask?"

"Just curious, I guess."

"I'd ask more about this curiosity, but I'm tired."

Tegan smiled and rolled to face away from him. She wasn't sure why she'd asked. Maybe it was to see how much he trusted her. Maybe she'd asked to see if he would answer. Or maybe she'd asked, hoping his answer would be yes, to see what her response would be.

It was kind of crazy though. He was her friend. She'd just had sex with another male. She didn't understand why she was thinking about Reid in a different way than how she'd known him for years.

Maybe her early morning sexcapade had shifted something in her. Maybe she had reached a point where she couldn't do one-night stands or casual sex anymore.

She was in her early thirties. Hardly a teenager anymore. Maybe she was just getting older.

She grimaced. She hoped not. She had a lot of years left to live. Hopefully, a lot of sexual years.

Reid shifted behind her, and his breathing was deep and even. Feeling content once again, having Reid beside her, she decided she'd worry about her sex life later.

Right now, it was time to go back to sleep.

Chapter Eleven

Isabelle tried to smile at the lady behind the counter to make it look like she was happy and excited to be applying for a marriage license, but she was nervous.

"How can I help you today?" the clerk asked in a monotone voice.

Zane grabbed Isabelle's hand. "We want to get married."

"Great," Monotone said. She slid a packet of papers over to them. "Fill these out."

Zane grabbed the packet. "Thanks." The two of them turned to find a place to sit and fill out the paperwork, but Zane paused and looked back. "How long do we have to wait for the license?"

"It should be in the mail in about a week."

Zane spun around. "A week? I thought it would be, like, thirty minutes."

The clerk laughed, her first sign of any real emotion. "Sorry, but this isn't Vegas."

Zane sighed with frustration and walked past Isabelle. She ran to catch up to him.

Once outside, he pulled out his phone, hit a couple of buttons, and put it to his ear. "Boss, we have a problem. We have to wait a week for a marriage license. That gives Bram way too much time to find Isabelle."

"That's not good," Vance said on the other line. Isabelle was close enough to hear everything. "I forgot about that."

"Yeah, well, shifters don't get legally married that much."

"Let me talk to Damien, and I will get back to you."

Zane looked at Isabelle, and his mouth dropped open as his eyes widened.

"What?" she asked.

He pulled the receiver away from his mouth. "The clerk said this wasn't Vegas."

She shook her head. "So?"

Zane brought the phone back to his lips. "Boss, Isabelle and I are going to Vegas."

"What?" she said in a high voice.

The other side of the line was silent.

"Boss?" Zane asked.

"I'm thinking," Vance said. "That isn't a bad idea, but there will be a ticket in Isabelle's name."

"Shit," Zane said. "Bram could track her."

"But the marriage license is going to be in my name. Couldn't he track that, too?"

Zane hit the heel of his hand on his forehead. "Damn, how did we forget about that?"

Isabelle narrowed her eyes. "I didn't forget. I just assumed it wasn't something you were concerned about."

Zane scowled back. "Next time, say something. Don't just assume."

"Zane."

"He could have tracked you here, Isabelle. We're not ready for him."

"Zane."

Zane ran a hand over his face. "I don't even want to think about that."

"Zane!"

He pulled the phone away from the side of his head and looked at it like he'd never seen a phone before. He put it back to his ear. "Sorry, boss. What are you thinking?"

"This Vegas thing might be for the best. You can fly there and be back home before Bram would even discover Isabelle went. Also, this way, he won't know where Isabelle is staying. With the marriage license, he could narrow it down by county."

"Won't he know where she is because we'll be flying in and out of here?"

"Hmm," Vance said. "I think that is less of a concern. The Minneapolis-St. Paul airport is an international airport. People drive from out of state to fly from there. I think we should be okay on that angle."

"Okay."

"Take Isabelle back to the shifters. I will talk to Damien, and we'll figure out who we're sending with you."

"How many?"

"I'll let you know after I talk to Damien."

Zane nodded. "Sounds good." He hit End and looked at Isabelle. "We're going to Vegas, baby."

"I'll go," Quentin immediately volunteered.

They were having yet another impromptu meeting since Isabelle had shown up.

Damien shook his head. "I can't have you going to Vegas. I need you at your job here. You're the only one who can legally access the police department database. If we're going to stay one step ahead of Bram, you can't go to Vegas."

Fuck.

Quentin gritted his teeth in frustration. Not at Damien. His alpha was right. He was needed here. He was frustrated because he'd thought going to Vegas would be the perfect opportunity to get away from Hunter. Instead, there were going to be less shifters around as a buffer.

"Who's going?" Raven asked. Her eyes lit up.

"Not you," Damien said.

Raven grimaced. "Damn it."

"I need you here, too. I need your nose. And you and slot machines don't get along." Damien tilted his head. "I take that back. You and slot machines get along too well."

"Not true."

"I practically saw dollar signs in your eyes a second ago."

Raven looked at Quentin, and he just lifted his eyebrows. Damien wasn't wrong.

"Fine," Raven said, crossing her arms over her chest. "Who's going?"

Damien swung around and pointed both forefingers. "Ranulf and Chase."

The two males jumped up from their seats.

"Why us?"

"I don't want to go."

"This is not right."

"Why can't someone else go?"

The two had already expressed their distaste for Isabelle bringing danger to their doorstep. It wasn't surprising that they didn't want to go to Vegas to guard her.

Damien swept his hands in a slicing motion. "*Enough.* I can't go. I need to be here in case Bram shows up. Bowden is with the vampires, and Kendall is with the cats. And I need Lachlan here on the computer. You already heard why Quentin and Raven are staying. That leaves you two. There will be no arguing. You understand me?"

"Yes, sir," they both said and dropped in their seats. They looked like petulant children who hadn't gotten what they wanted.

But Quentin was impressed with Damien. He had a softer heart than some alphas, but he knew how to put his sentinels in line.

A car came up the driveway.

"That'll be Zane," Damien said. He looked at Chase and Ranulf. "You two had better not slack off while you're in Vegas. I know you're excited, but Isabelle is a wolf-shifter. You took an oath to protect all wolf-shifters. And she's my friend. If I find out you let her get hurt…let's just say, you don't want to know what I'll do to you."

Chase scoffed, "I can't believe you would even doubt us."

Damien turned his back to them and rolled his eyes.

"At least you get to be together," Raven told them.

Ranulf and Chase grinned and bumped fists.

"Vegas won't know what hit it," Chase said.

This time, Raven rolled her eyes. "Please. You two are a waste of space."

Ranulf raised a brow. "That's not what you said last night."

"*Ohhh*. Burn," Chase said.

Quentin looked at Raven. She wasn't embarrassed, nor did she give any other indication that Ranulf's statement was true.

"Actually, I think you two just proved my point."

The door opened, and Zane and Isabelle walked in.

"Things didn't go as planned," Damien said to Zane.

"Yeah, nobody seemed to know that there was a waiting period. I take it, Vance called you?"

"Yeah. We were just discussing the trip. Lachlan?"

Lachlan stood and handed Zane a piece of paper. "Your flight leaves at three forty this afternoon."

"What, no private jet?" Zane asked.

Lachlan laughed. "It's not in the budget." He walked over and handed papers to Chase and Ranulf.

Chase narrowed his eyes at Lachlan. "Does this mean, you already knew we were going?"

"Yep. Kind of hard to buy your tickets if I didn't know." Lachlan's mouth was twitching. It looked like he was trying really hard not to smile at Chase's misfortune.

Chase opened his mouth, but Damien turned and shot him a look. Chased snapped his mouth shut.

"I take it Dumb and Dumber are going with us?" Zane asked.

Quentin bit his lip but couldn't hold in his laughter. Zane always seemed to make him laugh. The cat had only been living with them a couple of weeks, but Quentin had already gotten used to him living here. Unlike the other new person in the house.

Damien sighed, as if he were in a room full of children instead of adult sentinels. "Yes, Ranulf and Chase are going with you. I'm not going to discuss why. My word is final."

Zane held up his hands. "I wasn't going to say anything. I'm fine with it."

He looked back at Isabelle. Quentin saw the look on her face. She didn't seem as okay as Zane was.

"Who's going for the cats?" Quentin asked. *Could you take a certain vampire with you?*

"I don't know yet. Vance didn't say."

Chapter Twelve

There was a knock at Tegan's bedroom door.

"Yeah?" *Please don't be Ram.*

There were too many shifters and vampires going in and out of the bunkhouse all the time that she couldn't clearly sense who was outside her room.

"Tegan, I need to speak with you," her alpha said.

Her whole body relaxed, and she pulled open the door. "Yes?"

"I need you to start packing a bag."

She was confused. "I'm sorry, but why?"

"You're going to Las Vegas. You're going to help Zane and Isabelle. They are going to elope in Vegas." Vance explained the problem the two new mates had run into that morning. He looked at his watch. "Your flight leaves in a little over three hours, so you don't have much time to get ready."

Tegan went to her closet to look for luggage among her pile of clothes and other belongings. "How long are we going to be there?"

"The plan is for only overnight, but you might want to pack an extra outfit or two, just in case."

She looked over her shoulder. "I'm guessing there will be no time for gambling or seeing a show?"

The corner of Vance's mouth ticked up, but he shook his head.

"Do the Nevada Pride and Pack know we're coming?"

"Yes, but unless you need them, they're staying out of Las Vegas."

The Nevada wolves didn't live in Las Vegas itself because there were too many people, and it was hard to let your animal free to run and play. It was why the Minnesota shifters didn't live in downtown Minneapolis. Not enough rural area.

"I'll make sure you have their contact numbers before you get to the airport."

"Thanks," she said and turned back to her closet. "Am I the only one going?"

"No. Chase and Ranulf are going."

Tegan didn't know the wolves well, but it would be nice not to be the only one on sentinel duty. She had to eat and sleep sometime. "Okay, thanks." She pushed aside a pile of old clothes she had sitting in the corner and found her small suitcase. "Yes! Success."

She yanked the piece of luggage out of the back when Vance added, "Oh, and Reid will be going with you. I decided it would be helpful to have someone along who knows what they're doing with computers."

She turned to look at her alpha, but he'd already walked away.

A moment later, Reid walked in. "What's got you so happy?" he asked her. "You're looking forward to going to Vegas?"

At Reid's words, she realized she'd been grinning when he walked in. *No, I'm looking forward to going to Vegas with you.*

She shrugged. "I don't mind going to Vegas. And it's only March, so it won't be as hot as if it were July." She got up from the floor and brought her suitcase to her bed. "How do you feel about going?"

"I'm already packed. I haven't gone out of town for a long time," Reid said as he sat on her bed.

Tegan went through her clean clothes, trying to decide what to bring. She made a quick trip to the bathroom to grab the essential toiletries. When she came back, Reid had flopped back onto her bed.

She grabbed the three outfits she wanted to take and stuffed them into her suitcase while Reid watched her. "Actually, this trip has come at the most opportune time." She hadn't planned to tell him anything, but he was lying there, silent and watchful, as if he were giving her the chance to talk about whatever was bothering her.

He raised an eyebrow. "Yeah?"

"Yeah…" She winced. "I slept with Ram." She opened one eye to see Reid's reaction.

He lifted his head. "Really? How was it?"

She hadn't known what to expect, but his curiosity was not it.

She finished packing and put her bag on the floor. With her luggage out of the way, she now saw that Reid's T-shirt had ridden up, so there was a nice slice of skin showing above his jeans, which were riding low on his hips.

"Tegan."

She looked at Reid's face as her face heated from being caught checking him out.

"Hey, you don't have to be embarrassed. You're not the first person to have sex with a vampire." He laid his head back down.

Oh, thank God. He thought she was embarrassed for having sex with Ram, not for practically drooling over his abdomen muscles.

"I've often wondered what it would be like," Reid said, staring at the ceiling.

Tegan frowned. "You have?"

"After Vaughn and Phoenix mated with vampires, I've often wondered if they have something special that we don't have."

Tegan eyed Reid's patch of skin. She had the sudden urge to bite him. Right above his V. That way, any woman, vampire or otherwise, would leave him alone.

Tegan spun and plopped down on her bed and put her head in her hand. She felt a little like she was going crazy. Why the sudden possessiveness over Reid? He was her friend. Why did the sight of some skin turn her on? She'd seen him in the buff on countless occasions because, as shifters, it was hard not to see each other naked, and at the time, it had done nothing for her. Plus, she'd just had sex last night.

Shake it off, Tegan.

She turned, putting a knee up on the bed.

"So…how was it?" Reid asked again, meeting her eyes.

"Honestly, it was…meh."

Reid grimaced. "Meh, huh? That's kind of a bummer."

She shrugged. "I suppose."

"Is this why you want to leave? So that you don't have to face Ram?" Reid picked his head up again, his face showing concern. "Are you afraid he's going to do something bad, like force you to have sex again?"

Tegan actually laughed at this. "No. I don't get the vibe from him. And I think he was as unimpressed as I was. Maybe you're right. Maybe there is nothing special about having sex with us." She gasped facetiously. "Or maybe there's nothing special about having sex with me."

Despite her joke, Reid got up on one arm so fast, she almost jumped.

He put a hand on her cheek and met her eyes. "Tegan, if a male had sex with you and doesn't enjoy it, that's on him. There are some men who would love to be with you."

A flash of heat flared in his eyes. It only lasted a second, but it was enough for her to feel a pull between her legs, and within seconds, her bedroom was filled with the slight scent of her arousal.

"Fuck," Reid whispered but didn't move. "How could any man not get hard at the smell of you?"

She didn't answer because it seemed like a rhetorical question. Yet his words took a second to sink in, and Tegan looked at his crotch.

While she'd seen Reid naked plenty of times, she'd never seen him naked and *hard*. He was practically bursting from his jeans.

She wanted to touch him.

Without warning, Reid jumped up from her bed. "I don't think so."

She was still staring at his crotch, and she had to force her eyes up to his. "What do you mean?"

"You," he said as he covered himself, "can't touch this until you're sure it's what you want."

Tegan felt like she was in the twilight zone. "I don't understand. I'm so confused."

Reid got down on his haunches and grabbed her hand. "You want me," he said. The corner of his mouth ticked up. "And you don't know what to do about it." He squeezed her fingers. "It's okay. I've been waiting for over five years. I can wait a little longer."

"You've been waiting for me?" she squeaked out. *How did I not know this?*

He reached up and pushed her hair behind her ear. "Yeah, Angel. Can't you tell?"

She leaned closer, putting her nose on his neck, and inhaled. God, he smelled like the jungle and sex, and she felt it when he groaned.

She wanted to taste him.

Again, he quickly backed away.

She stared at him in wonder. "Can you read my mind?"

Reid laughed. "No, Angel. I just know you really well."

That was the second time he'd called her that. She kind of liked it.

"Why won't you let me touch you?" she asked him.

"While I love that you came and slept with me this morning, you just had sex with Ram less than twenty-four hours ago. I'm all about supporting you in whatever you do and decide to do with your life. But I don't share." He shook his head. "When you decide to lie down and open those sweet legs for me, I'm going to be the only male between them."

Holy shit. She needed a fan and new underwear.

"Fuck, babe, you make it really hard to say no to you," Reid said with a smile.

"Reid, Tegan…you two ready to go?" Saxon yelled from down the hall.

"Be there in a second," Reid yelled back. He stood up, kissing her on the forehead along the way. "Come on, Angel. Let's go."

Chapter Thirteen

Isabelle, Zane, Chase, Ranulf, Tegan, and Reid followed the bellhop into their three-bedroom suite at one of the major hotels in Las Vegas.

"Holy shit," Zane said. "No wonder we couldn't afford a private jet."

Zane was right. The suite had to have cost a fortune.

"Would you like a tour?" the bellhop asked.

Isabelle exchanged looks with everyone else. It seemed like they all just wanted the human gone, so they could discuss things.

"No, thank you," Isabelle said.

The bellhop nodded. "Please call the front desk if you need anything."

Zane shut the door behind the man, and the six of them exchanged looks and then took off running in different directions with grins on their faces. Sure, they were there for a reason, but it didn't mean they couldn't enjoy their accommodations.

They all ended up outside in the back of the suite.

"Holy crap, we have a pool," Isabelle said.

"And a putting green," Chase added.

"This place is awesome," Tegan said. "I want to live here."

Ranulf put a hand over his eyes to block the sun. "So, who is sleeping where?"

"We'll take the master suite," Zane said, pointing to the two of them.

Chase raised an eyebrow. "Who died and made you alpha?"

"No one, but I'm the groom, and this is my bride. It only makes sense that we get the master suite. Plus, the other two rooms each have a bathroom, so no one needs to share."

"Okay then, who is sharing the other two rooms?" Ranulf asked.

"Tegan and I will share," Reid said.

Tegan looked at Reid and licked her lips. Too bad Reid missed the look she had given him.

"So, you're saying, the two of us have to share?" Chase pointed to himself and Ranulf. "What if I wanted to room with Tegan?"

"Not happening. Ever," Tegan said, and Isabelle laughed.

"What's the big deal?" Zane asked. "You two are butt buddies anyway."

Chase took a step toward Zane with his fists clenched, and Reid stepped in between the two males.

"Whoa, whoa, whoa," Reid said. "Let it go."

Reid was probably used to Zane and his sarcastic comments since they lived together. Or they had until Zane went to stay with the wolves.

"Theoretically, we're going to be sleeping in shifts anyway, right? So, when you're sleeping, Ranulf will be on watch. You don't have to share a bed with a dude."

Chase frowned. "I don't care about that. Although I do prefer sleeping alone. I'm offended that he thinks I would date someone like Ranulf. I am clearly out of his league."

Ranulf punched Chase in the arm. "Fucker. If we were gay, I would be the one out of *your* league."

Chase pretended to throw hair over his shoulder. "In your dreams."

"Hey, hey," Zane said. "It's settled. Isabelle and me, Reid and Tegan, and Chase and Ranulf. Okay? Okay. You four can fight over which rooms you're taking." He picked up Isabelle's hand. "But, right now, we're going to get some rest before we head to the chapel tonight."

Oh, thank God. Isabelle was tired. The flight had been three hours long, and despite not sleeping much last night, she hadn't been able to get comfortable on the plane. Too much noise and too many smells. It was not an ideal place for a shifter to get rest.

When they reached their room, Zane shut the door. "Sleep or shower first?"

"Shower." She always felt gross after getting off an airplane.

"Okay. You go ahead. I'll grab our bags from the entrance."

"Would you mind handing me my shampoo and conditioner when you come back?"

"No problem."

Zane left the room, and Isabelle went into the big bathroom. She could get used to having a bathroom this luxurious.

She removed her clothes and threw them into a pile on the floor. She wouldn't be wearing them again until they got washed. She'd have to look into the hotel's laundry accommodations.

She'd just gotten under the hot spray when she heard Zane come in the bathroom. While she waited for him to find her stuff, she got her hair wet. With her head and ears under the water, she yelped when she felt something cold hit her arm. She backed her head out and reached for the object. It was one of her bottles, and she took it from Zane.

He chuckled. "Sorry, I didn't mean to scare you."

Isabelle pushed her sodden hair from her face and wiped the water away with her free hand. She opened her eyes to see Zane, naked, standing in front of her.

"What are you doing?"

He looked baffled. "Showering."

"You couldn't wait until I was done?"

He shrugged and looked like he was trying not to smile. "We were told to do everything together."

She swiped the second bottle from his hand. "I don't think they meant showering."

He tilted his head. "Do you want me to leave?"

She scanned his body and really looked at him for the first time. She hadn't seen him without clothes for two years. His chest was peppered with light-brown hair, and she could be wrong, but it looked like he'd gained more muscle. When she reached the area between his legs, she felt an answering clench between hers.

Zane had been flaccid when he first got in, but now, he was growing in length and thickness before her eyes. She couldn't believe that one appendage could bring her so much pleasure. Of course, part of it was whom it was attached to.

She wanted to feel him inside her again, and suddenly, she didn't know why she'd been fighting this mating so much. Yes, they weren't in love, but they liked each other, and they definitely enjoyed each other's bodies. She should be looking at the positives of this situation. Like really good sex.

She hadn't had good sex in...well, two years.

Sleeping with Bram had been okay, but the longer the relationship had gone on, the more she'd avoided sleeping with him. She hadn't had sex with him for over a month. She'd suspected he was getting it elsewhere, which was one of the first red flags to her in the relationship. Not because he was cheating though, but because she didn't care that he was cheating as long as she didn't have to be the one to have sex with him.

Isabelle raised her eyes until they reached Zane's.

"If you keep looking at me like that, you're not going to get very clean."

She wiggled her eyebrows, but Zane just shook his head and laughed.

He picked up her shampoo and told her to turn around.

Isabelle let Zane wash her hair and her body, and she let herself enjoy being taken care of. It didn't stop her from sneaking in some suggestive touches though. She trailed her fingers down his biceps and up his inner thigh. Sometimes, she pretended it was an accident, and sometimes, she let him know she had done it on purpose.

When he was finished washing both of them, he threw the washcloth in the corner and pushed her up against the side of the shower, holding her arms beside her head. "You are a tease, Isabelle Rand."

"Don't you mean, Isabelle Talon?"

He lifted his brow. "You're going to take my name, huh? Even though you plan to leave me as soon as possible?"

"When did I ever say that?"

"It's one thing to tease my body, but now, you're teasing my heart."

Isabelle didn't get a chance to ask what he meant because he dropped down to his knees. He pulled her ass toward him and one leg over his shoulder. She spread her fingers against the side of the shower to stay upright.

Zane opened her as wide as possible without her falling and put his mouth between her legs.

Isabelle's head dropped against the wall with a thud as she moaned.

Zane didn't tentatively touch her; he pushed his whole face into her. He sucked her clit into his mouth and rolled it between his teeth, the little bite of pain making her slick with her desire.

He shifted down and licked at her entrance. He swept his tongue in as far as possible and everywhere he could reach, as if he couldn't get enough of the taste of her.

She let him do what he wanted with her. She let him do what made him happy.

If they were having sex and all he cared about was his pleasure, it would piss her off, but because he was going down on her, it turned her on that he was getting so much out of the act. Some guys didn't like it, but Zane obviously did.

When he groaned so loudly that she could hear him over the spray, knowing that it turned him on that much to give her head was what pushed her over the edge.

A silent scream was torn from her throat as she came and exploded all over Zane's face. He didn't stop sucking and licking, even after her orgasm waned, and she had to gently nudge him away.

He questioningly looked up at her.

"I came."

He snorted. "I know."

"You don't have to do that anymore."

An eyebrow went up. "I know."

He moved to put his mouth between her thighs again, and she pulled the leg on his shoulder down.

"Get up," she said.

Zane stood up and stared into her eyes. They were full of heat, and his cock rubbed against her stomach.

She draped her arms around his neck and kissed him. He tasted like her, but it didn't deter her. She just kissed him deeper.

Zane reached over and shut off the water, never taking his lips from hers. He picked her up, and she wrapped her legs around his waist. As he carried her from the bathroom, she rubbed her wet pussy over his hard length, but he didn't enter her.

When he got to the bed, he laid her down and pulled away. "Get under the covers. I'll be right back."

She nodded and quickly pulled the thick comforter and five-thousand-count sheet down, not caring that she was wet. She lay back on her elbows to see what Zane was going to do.

He went to the bathroom and shut off the light.

Isabelle's mouth practically watered as she watched his tight ass walk away, and then his thick cock bounced against his six-pack as he came back toward her. But, instead of going to the side of the bed she was on, he went to the other side and slid under the covers.

"What are you doing?"

He punched the pillow under his head. "Taking a nap. Wasn't that the plan?"

Isabelle dropped onto her back. "Yeah, that was before you went down on me," she said incredulously. She turned away from him.

He snaked an arm around her waist and yanked her over to him. "Don't worry. We'll have plenty of time to consummate this relationship later."

"That's what you think."

Zane laughed. "That's what I *know*."

Chapter Fourteen

Tegan watched as Isabelle shook her head at Zane.

"No way. No Elvis wedding."

Zane gasped mockingly. "But we're in Vegas. We have to do an Elvis wedding."

She laughed. "We don't have to do anything."

He sighed. "Fine. You win."

Isabelle grinned.

Zane looked over at the gentleman helping them. "We're going to do a traditional wedding."

"Outside," Isabelle chimed in.

"Outside?"

She nodded. "Outside."

Zane looked at the man helping them again. "I guess we're getting married in your outside chapel."

"Sounds excellent, sir. Do you need any additional services? Hair, makeup, dress, tux?"

"No, we're good," Isabelle said. "We just want to get married."

The man looked at Zane.

He shrugged. "What the lady wants."

They had to wait fifteen minutes or so for another wedding to finish up and for Zane and Isabelle to fill out the paperwork and marriage license.

Then, the group of them was escorted to the outside chapel. Tegan could see why Isabelle wanted to get married out there. It was beautiful, and it was an excellent night for a wedding. Clear sky, only a slight breeze, and the perfect temperature.

Tegan watched the bride and groom as they stared at each other. They might have gotten mated and were getting married to protect Isabelle, but the heat between them was real. Everyone, at least the cat-shifters, knew how disappointed Zane had been after Isabelle left. He'd moved on, but he'd never quite stopped carrying a torch for her.

The surprising thing for Tegan was how much Isabelle seemed to be into Zane. She wondered why the she-wolf had left town so fast. Sure, Zane liked to make jokes and was a smart-ass, but he was a nice guy and a hell of a sentinel. Isabelle could do way worse, which she obviously had.

But she was here with Zane now, and those two were going to have one hell of a wedding night.

Tegan looked at Reid next to her. He was leaning forward, his elbows on his legs, and she wished she were having one hell of a wedding night.

She'd practically had an orgasm back in her room, just hearing Reid talking filthy to her. But she didn't forget the actual words he'd spoken either.

"I don't share. When you decide to lie down and open those sweet legs for me, I'm going to be the only male between them."

She'd had no idea the alpha-male, possessive thing would do it for her. Tegan didn't normally date men like that, but maybe it was because, in everything else, Reid wasn't an alpha male. He wasn't cocky, he followed Vance's lead, he was supportive of his fellow sentinels, and he never tried to show off or put himself in danger just to prove himself. Plus, he was kind of a computer nerd.

Computer geek by day, sexual alpha by night.

Tegan stifled her laugh so as not to interrupt the nuptials.

Reid looked up and over at her with a questioning expression on his face.

She shook her head. There was no way she was going to tell him her tagline for him.

Reid sat up, put his arm around her, and nuzzled her behind her ear.

"I would love to know what you're thinking in that big brain of yours."

Tegan pulled away to look him in the eyes. "I think we should get married, too," she whispered.

Reid opened his mouth and then closed it. He tilted his head to the side, and Tegan tried not to laugh at his confusion.

"You want to get married?" he asked, his voice low.

"Yes." She nodded.

"Why? Where is this coming from?"

Tegan glanced toward the front of the chapel and across the aisle at the two wolves before turning back to Reid. She put her mouth by his ear, and Reid put a hand on her thigh.

"Because I can't stop thinking about what you said. About how you want to be the only one between my legs."

Reid squeezed her leg.

"I want you to fuck me, Reid. You and nobody else."

Reid pulled away and looked at her. "You know that marriage is not a mating, but it's still a big deal."

She nodded. "I know."

"You're a little crazy, you know that?"

"Crazy fun." She nudged him with her knee. "Come on. We're in Vegas. Let's do what people in Vegas do. When in Rome. If we change our minds, we'll do what people who leave Vegas do. Get an annulment."

Reid shrugged. "Okay."

"*Really?*" she said way too loudly, and everyone turned to look at her. She cringed. "Sorry," she told the room.

To say she was shocked at his response was an understatement. Reid was very left-brained, which was probably what made him so good with computers. But she was very right-brained. She didn't like labels or to do things the way they were "supposed to be done" just because society said so. She followed the laws—she was a sentinel after all—but laws and rules were different than society's expectations. Like getting hitched in Vegas. Her mom was going to flip her lid.

"Really," Reid said, "let's get married, Angel."

Once Isabelle and Zane were officially married, Tegan and Ranulf signed the marriage license as witnesses. Then, Tegan told everyone the announcement that they had one more wedding to do before they left.

Zane and Isabelle looked surprised, but Chase and Ranulf looked bored. But that was their problem.

After Tegan and Reid filled out the paperwork and went to stand in front of the officiant, she expected the thrill of doing something wild to go through her. That feeling that what she was doing wasn't quite right, but she was going to do it anyway.

Instead, she felt a calmness settle over her. As if she was doing the right thing.

She looked up into Reid's eyes. "Are you okay with this? I know you're not the type of person to normally do something like this."

He smiled at her. A truthful smile. "I'm more than okay." He looked at the officiant. "Let's do this."

The words were spoken, and the wedding vows were exchanged.

Tegan said, "I do," and held her breath as Reid said it, too.

"I now pronounce you husband and wife. You may kiss the bride."

Whoa.

It just occurred to Tegan that she had never even kissed Reid, and she was getting human-mated to him.

Reid stepped closer to her and put a finger under her chin. He tilted her head up and gently kissed her. It was a little too sweet for her taste, but Reid wasn't the type for public displays of affection, so she didn't mind.

Just when she thought he was going to pull away, he bit her lip—and not gently.

Tegan gasped, and Reid took the opportunity to deepen their kiss. He tilted his head, and his tongue swept into her mouth.

She wrapped her arms around his neck as he took complete control of their kiss. She basically hung on for the ride.

It was only after Zane yelled, "Get a room," that Reid broke their embrace.

He stepped back, and Tegan had to catch her breath.

If that was the way Reid kissed, once they had sex, there was a strong chance she was going to want to stay married.

Chapter Fifteen

$\mathcal{Z}$ane stood with Isabelle and Tegan outside their hotel suite while the other three shifters went inside to make sure everything was safe before entering.

"So…you and Reid decided to get hitched? Just like that?" Zane asked,

Tegan pushed her white-blonde hair over her shoulder. "Pretty much." She batted her eyes, her white-blonde eyelashes a contrast to her brown eyes.

"You two are crazy."

Isabelle smacked him in the stomach. "Be nice. We're not much better."

She was wrong about that. He and Isabelle had been intimate before. Tegan and Reid were just friends.

Aren't they?

Jeez. He must have missed a lot the last few weeks while he had been living with the wolves.

"I beg to differ, Isa. We got married for your safety. These two did it for shits and giggles."

"Actually, I did it to get laid."

"Seems like an extreme measure to get laid." Zane leaned closer to Tegan. "You heard about Reid's monster hog, huh?"

Tegan gasped. "No." She greedily rubbed her hands together. "Do tell."

Isabelle made an odd sound, and he and Tegan looked at her. Her eyes were wide, and she looked like she was in shock.

"What's wrong?" he asked, suddenly concerned.

"I can't believe what you two talk about with each other."

That's it? He'd thought something was wrong.

Tegan shrugged. "Zane and I have known each other a long time. We're more than friends; we're like brother and sister. You don't talk to your friends about sex?"

"Yes, but not any guy friends. Isn't it weird?"

Zane and Tegan looked at each other and back at Isabelle. "No," they both said at the same time.

"All clear," Reid yelled from inside the suite.

"Finally," Tegan said and went inside.

Zane held out his arm to indicate that Isabelle should go next before he brought up the rear. There was no indication that Bram knew where Isabelle was, but it was always best to play it safe.

Zane shut the door behind him as Isabelle turned around.

"Are you all like that together?" she asked.

"More or less. Why?"

"I can't imagine being so close with a group like that."

"It's kind of hard not to be. We live and work together." Zane felt bad that she didn't have relationships like he did with his fellow sentinels.

"Will we live with the sentinels now that we're mated?"

Zane froze, not wanting to react too much. He didn't think she knew what she had said.

He had assumed Isabelle would go right back to Mankato once she was safe, but now, she was talking about staying with him.

He needed to play it cool. "I don't know. I suppose it depends on what happens with Bram. And, right now, I'm living with the wolves anyway."

Isabelle chuckled. "Oh, yeah. That's a little easier of a transition for me."

"Zane?" Reid called out from the living room area. "Get in here, so we can discuss shifts."

Zane nudged her forward. "Let's go talk to them."

"How do you want to do it?" Zane asked when he entered the room.

"Who's up first?"

"I'll go first," Chase said. "I took a nap earlier. Then, Ranulf can sleep."

"Works for me," Ranulf said. "I'm beat. I'll see you all in the morning." And, with that, the wolf turned and went to his room.

"I'm going to bed, too," Isabelle said.

Zane watched her walk away. He looked at the remaining shifters, and Reid knew exactly what he was thinking.

"We checked your room to make sure it was safe."

Zane sighed with relief. "Thank you."

Reid looked at Tegan. "Why don't you sleep? I'll stay up tonight."

Tegan looked like her dog had just died. "But...but...I thought..."

Reid kissed her on the forehead. "All in good time, my dear."

She pushed him away. "All in good time, my ass. You're a tease, Reid Spencer." She huffed as she walked to her bedroom.

"Good luck with that," Zane told Reid.

Reid smiled, looking like the cat that had eaten the canary. "I'll be fine. She just needs to learn that patience breeds pleasure."

"Whatever you say. Night, dude." Zane left Reid to go to his own room.

He didn't know if he agreed with Reid's philosophy. Zane had been waiting to have sex with Isabelle again for two years. And, after going down on her this afternoon, he was hornier than ever. It had taken all his willpower not to fuck her after their shower.

After she'd made him wait, he was making her wait. Even if a few hours had no comparison to a couple of years.

Zane quietly pushed the bedroom door open.

Isabelle was facing away from him in just her bra and panties. A matching set. White lace.

How was he supposed to torture her with multiple orgasms before he pushed himself inside her when she was dressed like that?

She was in front of her suitcase, and she pulled something out that looked an awful lot like pajamas.

Hell no. She wasn't wearing anything to bed on his watch.

Zane walked up behind her and buried his nose in her blonde hair.

"What are you doing?" she asked with a satisfied sigh as she relaxed into him.

"Making a memory of your scent," he said next to her ear.

"Why?"

"Because I want to remember what you smelled like before."

"Before what?" she asked and rubbed her head against his chest.

"Before I finished marking you as mine."

Zane put his arm around her waist and moved her off to the side, so she faced the wall.

"Hands on the wall."

"Zane?"

He picked up her wrists and placed her palms where he wanted them. "Shh…it's okay." He nuzzled her cheek. "You know I would never hurt you."

She nodded even though he hadn't phrased it as a question.

"Don't move, Isa."

He trailed his hands across her arms, over her shoulders, and down her back until he reached the waistline of her underwear. He gently nudged her legs apart before pulling the crotch of her underwear away and pushing two fingers inside her.

Isabelle whimpered and pushed against his hand.

Fuck.

She was scorching hot and almost dripping with her pleasure.

Zane turned his fingers away from him and rubbed them against her G-spot.

He could feel her swell underneath him. Around him. She was already close.

Zane pulled his fingers from her body, and Isabelle made a sound of protest. He ripped the crotch of her panties in two and unbuttoned his jeans. He wrapped a hand around her neck and an arm around her waist and slammed into her.

"Oh, shit!" Zane yelled. He was never going to last. "Fuck me, Isabelle."

When she hesitated, he showed her how he wanted her to move against him.

She moaned as she pulled her body away and pushed back against him. "Yeah, Isa, just like that. Fuck me."

Isabelle picked up speed, and soon, she was almost slamming her body against his. That was when Zane tightened his hold and began to fuck her in return. He eyed her vulnerable neck, loving that she never tried to escape his grasp.

She was his for the taking.

Right before he knew it was over for him, before his orgasm hit, he bit down on the side of her neck, sinking his teeth in so far, she was going to be in pain. Yet he was unable to stop himself from marking her so deeply.

He roared around her body as he exploded inside her, and Isabelle followed him over the edge. Her pussy sucked his cock in as far as it could go as his barbs extended from his head to scrape the inside of her vagina.

Isabelle swallowed against his hand around her neck, but Zane didn't release his teeth. Instead, he pulled his still-hard, barb-covered dick from her body.

Isabelle came again, so hard that she collapsed against the wall, and Zane was forced to let go of her neck with his mouth.

They were both breathing hard, and he slid his hand from her throat to rest on her hip.

"Isabelle..." he started, but he was unsure of what to say. He'd never fucked anyone so violently before.

His mate turned around in a flash, extended her claws, and ripped his shirt in half. She jumped into his arms and sank down onto his body. At the same time, she pushed her teeth into his neck, and with that move, Zane knew he hadn't done anything wrong.

Chapter Sixteen

$\mathcal{E}$arly the next morning, Damien slipped from his bed, leaving his mate naked and sated. Payton had fallen back asleep after they made love, and he didn't want to wake her as he got up for the day.

He'd tried to go back to sleep, but the whole Isabelle situation was weighing on his mind. He wasn't sure if he'd made the right calls and done the right things. This was his first big dilemma where he'd had to make sole decisions as an alpha, and he hoped he wasn't screwing things up for everyone.

Damien quietly closed the bedroom door behind him and headed downstairs. Payton and he had reclaimed their room after Isabelle left for Vegas. She would be staying with Zane now that they were mated, and Damien didn't want Payton alone at their house.

He'd been thinking about having them move in permanently with the sentinels, but he knew his mate really liked her own space. Once they had children, his family would be more vulnerable, but at the same time, he wasn't sure having kids in the house would be for everyone.

They had several acres of land on their property, and he had been considering building a second house there for him and Payton and their future children. Or building a good-sized mother-in-law suite onto the main house for them to live in.

Either way, he'd better decide soon because Payton had told him she wanted to try to get pregnant during her next heat. And just thinking about that made him hard as hell despite having just had sex with his mate less than a half hour ago.

He hadn't taken her during her heat after that first time. They'd gotten lucky that she didn't get pregnant then, so they had stayed away from each other all the times after. It killed him, knowing she was miserable without him during her heat time, but they were both adamant that she should finish her master's degree first.

She was done now and had settled into her job at L & L Construction, and she was finally ready to try. And so was he. He would never admit it to his sentinels, but he couldn't wait to see what Payton looked like while carrying his child and who their children would favor. And would they be wolves or cats? Only time would tell.

Damien started the industrial-sized coffee pot. He was the only one up so far, and the ones on night duty hadn't arrived home yet. The sun hadn't begun its ascent into the sky, so he had a little time to himself.

He grabbed his first cup of coffee and was making his way to his office when there was a knock at the front door. Damien paused and looked at the clock on the wall.

It was about five in the morning. *Who the hell is knocking at the door?*

Damien stiffened.

Bram.

It had taken Isabelle's ex two days to find her, but that wasn't surprising. Isabelle had told him that Bram knew she was friends with Damien. She had mentioned it in passing, but Bram had probably remembered it. He was an asshole, but he wasn't stupid.

It was a good thing Isabelle was in Las Vegas.

Damien calmed himself, not wanting his scent to give anything away. There was a second knock right before he reached the door, and he knew what he needed to do not to give anything away.

"I'm coming; I'm coming. Did you forget your keys again?" Damien pulled the door open and feigned surprise when he saw that it was indeed Bram on the other side. "Oh, hello. I'm sorry. I was expecting it to be one of my sentinels."

Bram was on the shorter side, but he was stocky. He clearly worked out. Maybe a little too much, going by the size of his neck. His blond hair was slicked back, and his hazel eyes were narrowed. And the chip on his shoulder was the size of Texas.

What the hell was Isabelle doing, dating this guy?

"So, you're Damien, the Minnesota Pack alpha?" Bram looked Damien up and down, evidently unimpressed.

Damien had to calm his wolf. His wolf didn't like the disrespect Bram was displaying and wanted to show him who his new alpha was because, if Bram lived in this state, then Damien was his alpha.

But the human side of Damien wanted to play this cool. Bram was the kind of guy just looking for a fight. And, even though Damien would kick the asshole's ass, he didn't want to fight Bram. He didn't want to give Bram any ammunition to come after himself, his mate, his sentinels, or Isabelle. Bram was also the kind of guy who would and could spin situations to his advantage.

Bram might not be stupid, but neither was Damien.

Damien took a sip of his coffee, casual and cool. "I am he. What can I do for you?"

"I'm looking for my girlfriend."

When Bram didn't offer any more information, Damien raised his brow. "Okay?"

He wasn't going to let Bram know that he knew who Bram was or that Isabelle had told him about Bram. As of a couple of days ago, it had been true, so Damien was mentally going back in time.

"And you are?"

"I'm Bram Varg," Bram said, obviously thinking this announcement would mean something to Damien.

"Oh, yes. Your father told me you had moved to the area." Damien smiled into his cup of coffee as Bram gritted his teeth. Damien swallowed his drink. "Is there something I can help you with?" He pretended to be concerned. "Is someone causing you trouble? Usually, we don't have problems with shifters who move here from out of state, but you never know," Damien rambled on. "I'm sorry that Minnesota hasn't been the best place for you. Please tell me who is bothering—"

"Minnesota is fine," Bram said through clenched teeth.

Damien grinned. "Oh, good." Then, he frowned. "Then, why are you here?"

Bram took a deep breath and sighed, frustrated.

Damien tried not to smile, but he was having fun, pretending to be clueless.

"I'm looking for my girlfriend," Bram said again.

"Oh, yeah. Sorry. We got off track." Damien took another sip of coffee. "Who's your girlfriend?"

"Isabelle Rand," Bram said, studying Damien's face for a reaction.

Damien grinned again. "No shit? Isabelle's got herself a man." He shook his head. "And she's been keeping you a secret." Damien tilted his head and stiffened. "What do you mean, you're looking for her? Did something happen?"

Bram's eyes widened. He probably didn't know what to do. He had expected to find Isabelle there, but instead, he had put her alpha on alert. He raised his arms. "No, no. I don't think anything happened. She went out of town and didn't tell me where she was going." He backpedaled.

Damien relaxed a little and realized he hadn't invited Bram in the house. Even though he didn't want the asshole to set foot in the same house where his mate slept, it would look suspicious if he didn't.

Damien stepped back and opened the door wider. "I'm sorry. Would you like to come in? You just have to be quiet. I'm the only one awake."

Bram shook his head, but he did take the opportunity to stick his nose in the air and sniff.

It wouldn't do any good. They had hired a professional cleaning service to come and clean the whole house from top to bottom, and they'd left every single window open in the house. If there were any traces of Isabelle, it would be very hard to find.

"Can you tell me the last time you saw Isabelle?"

Damien gave Bram a guilty look. "Two years." Before two days ago, that had been true. "I'm not a very good friend."

"How about the last time you spoke to her?"

"Oh God. It's been months. I should really call her. It's been a little crazy around here."

"Don't bother. She didn't take her phone."

Damien stiffened. "What?"

Bram's eyes widened. "I mean, she doesn't have it on."

"Oh. That's weird. She must really want to be left alone." *Hint, hint, asshole.*

There was movement upstairs. Someone was up.

Please don't be Payton.

He didn't want Bram to meet his only weakness.

But Damien should have known the encounter with Bram wouldn't go so smoothly.

Feminine arms wrapped around his waist from behind, and Payton peeked her head around Damien. "Hello."

Damien put his arm around his mate and pulled her next to him. He squeezed her shoulder, giving her as much warning as he could.

"Hey, baby girl." He kissed Payton on the forehead. "This is Bram. He's new to the area."

Payton smiled and held up her hand in a wave. "Oh, hi. It's always nice to have new people move to the area."

Damien wanted to shut the door in Bram's face and kiss the hell out of her. She had caught right on and given nothing away. She was beautiful and smart. He was one lucky wolf.

Bram cleared his throat.

The scent of Damien's arousal was in the air. "Sorry, dude. She's just so irresistible."

Payton shook her head but laid it on his chest. "What brings you here so early?" she asked Bram.

"He's looking for Isabelle."

Payton raised her head. "Oh?"

"Yes. Bram is dating her, and she seems to have left town."

"Oh. Well, she's smart enough not to come here," Payton told Bram.

He raised his brow. "Why is that?"

Damien drained the last of his coffee as Payton said, "She used to fuck my mate."

Damien began coughing and had to pound on his chest a few times. *Holy crap.* He hadn't expected Payton to say that.

"You okay?" she asked him.

He nodded.

She looked back at Bram. "I'm kind of jealous and possessive. I like Isabelle well enough, but I don't like her here. She knows it's best she just stay away." Payton ran her hand down Damien's chest and past his waist, and when she reached his crotch, she grabbed. "This is mine and no one else's."

"*O-kay.*" Damien took his arm from around Payton's shoulders and removed her hand from his dick. "I apologize for my mate," he told Bram, but Bram was barely listening.

The wolf probably didn't like the idea of Isabelle and Damien having sex. It was ages ago, and Bram knew Damien was mated now, but Bram was obviously affected. That meant, he was going to be a little off his game.

Damien's mate was a genius.

"It's fine. I'd better go. If you find her, please let me know."

Damien nodded as Payton hugged him from behind again. "Will do."

Bram turned and walked back to his car, not even realizing that he hadn't left a number with Damien.

Damien made a mental note of the make, model, and license plate number, and then he shut the door and turned in Payton's arms. "You are diabolical."

She shrugged and batted her eyelashes. "Little ole me?"

He chuckled. "Yeah, little ole you." He kissed her. "I need to make a phone call. I want to tell Isabelle to stay in Vegas for now. And I need to speak to Quentin quick." He kissed her again. "But, after that, I'm taking you upstairs and fucking you again."

"Promise?"

"You can count on it."

Chapter Seventeen

Bram punched the window of his car door and shook off the sting of pain. *That fucking bitch.* He wasn't sure if he was talking about Isabelle or the stupid she-cat the alpha was mated to.

Bram got behind the wheel and slammed the door. He needed to cool his head before he drove. The last thing he needed was to get pulled over.

He should have brought Stan and Larry with him. He hadn't wanted his two bodyguards to seem like a threat to the Minnesota Pack alpha, but now, he had to drive himself.

He'd thought for sure that Isabelle would be here. When she had mentioned she was friends with Damien Lowell back when they started dating, Bram had forbidden her from ever speaking to him again. He didn't want her in contact with her ex, but since she left town this seemed like the most logical place to go.

He banged his hand down on the steering wheel. But she wasn't here.

He looked up at the house, imagining the Minnesota alpha having sex with Isabelle.

That wasn't going to calm him, and he couldn't sit in front of the house forever.

He started the car and slowly drove down the long driveway.

He had no idea where Isabelle was, but he was going to have to punish her for her disappearance when he found her, since she hadn't seemed to learn her lesson in the past.

First, he was going to force her into their mating. Then, once she was his, he was going to beat the living shit out of her to let her know who the fucking boss was in this relationship. He had wanted to raise his hand to her many times before, but, except for the stint where she tried to leave him, he'd always managed to rein himself in.

Not this time. That bitch was going to get what she deserved.

As Bram drove away, something nagged at him. At the back of his brain.

He glanced in the rearview mirror at the house and tried to replay the conversation over in his head.

The alpha hadn't seemed to recognize him by sight. And his name only triggered his father. Nothing about him dating Isabelle. And yet…

He snapped his fingers.

It was the alpha's mate. He had tried to play it casual, but his demeanor had changed. He'd gone stiff. And he never introduced his mate to Bram. It was true that they'd gotten off topic, but still…

Bram needed to look into this situation further.

If the alpha was lying to him, he was going to regret the day he did.

No one knew it, but one of the reasons his father had kicked him out of Illinois was because Bram had almost killed a shifter. He'd beaten the male with his bare fists. Bram's only saving grace had been that the male lived and had lost his memory of the night. No one but Bram and his father knew what had happened.

Of course, the male was dead now. It was a shame the brakes had gone out in his car. One day after getting out of the hospital. It was also a shame that his girlfriend had had to die with him.

But maybe the cunt shouldn't have left Bram for another male.

He shook his head.

Maybe he should tell Isabelle this story, too. Apparently, she needed a good fucking reminder not to cross him.

The whole situation was getting him riled up again. He wanted to punch something, someone, but he was trapped in his car.

Movement off the side had Bram looking to the left.

He rolled his window down to speak to the male walking up the driveway. Maybe he would give Bram more information than the alpha had.

But, as he got closer, Bram wrinkled his nose. It was a fucking vampire. *What the fuck is a vampire doing here?*

He'd heard rumors about the shifters and vampires coming together to form some kind of alliance. Apparently, it was true.

He curled his lip. It was another reason to get out of this stupid, godforsaken state and go home.

This only fueled his rage, and suddenly, Bram knew what would make him feel all better. If only for a minute or two.

He cranked the wheel and rammed the gas. The stupid vampire looked up as Bram neared, his face full of shock. He tried to jump out of the way, but he didn't make it.

Bram's car slammed into the male. The crunch of bones breaking and the thump of a body landing brought a tranquil peace over him. The icing on the cake was the vehicle tipping as he ran over the vampire on his way out of there.

If the bloodsucker lived, he'd know to stay away from the shifters now.

As Bram turned off the driveway and onto the road, he turned on the radio and began to whistle along.

Despite his dead end this morning, today was turning around. It just might end up being a good day.

But, as he pulled onto the main road and then the interstate, leaving the wolf-shifter suburb behind, lights began to flash in his rearview mirror. He had just passed the sign saying he was in the city of Minneapolis. He looked down at his speedometer. He was going the speed limit.

With a sigh, he pulled over.

He'd get rid of the stupid cop and be on his way. All he had to do was flash a little fang, a little claw, and his wolf eyes, and they always ran, screaming, for their cars.

Dumb, pussy humans.

His window was still down from earlier, so he leaned out of it as the police officer approached.

For the second time in twenty minutes, Bram was surprised by someone's smell. First, the vampire he'd thought was a shifter, and now, the wolf-shifter he'd thought was going to be a human.

This day was getting even better. A shifter cop. Bram laughed. He'd be out of there in no time.

"License and registration, please."

Bram smiled. "Hello, Officer"—he had to look at the cop's name tag—"Rawling."

The officer didn't return Bram's smile. "License and registration." No *please* this time.

"Okay." *What is this guy's problem?* Bram opened the glove compartment for his registration and his wallet for his license. He handed them over.

"Sir, I need you to step out of the car."

"What? Can't you just tell me what's wrong and send me on my way?"

"Your tags are expired, and so is your license. I can't let you drive anywhere until this is taken care of."

"Are you serious?"

"As a heart attack. Now, please step out of your car."

Fuck.

The day had gone from good to bad in less than half an hour.

Chapter Eighteen

Tegan kicked the covers off the hotel bed and sighed. She was still alone.

She swung her legs off the mattress and left the room. Chase was sitting in front of the TV with droopy eyes. He tried to smile at Tegan but yawned instead.

She directed a thumb over her shoulder. "Go to bed. I got this."

He shut off the TV and threw the remote on the couch. "Oh, thank God." He shook his head as he stood. "I don't know how your mate does it. He's been up all night, staring at his computer, wide awake." Chase stepped around her. "Good night."

"Good night," she said, her mind on how Chase had called Reid her mate. Sure, they'd gotten married under human law, but they weren't mates. The term made her anxious and giddy at the same time.

She left the living room and went looking for Reid. After stopping in the kitchen for a glass of water, she found him outside, sitting at the patio table. He was on his computer, just like Chase had said. It was sitting in his lap with his feet up on another chair.

Reid looked up as she neared. She hadn't said anything and was barefoot, but he must have sensed her anyway.

Reid smiled. "Hey, Angel." His shirt was unbuttoned, and he was barefoot in jeans. He looked way too good after staying up all night.

"Hey. Looks like your night wasn't very exciting."

"Not for us. But Bram showed up at the wolf-shifters' home this morning."

"No kidding?" Tegan pulled out a chair and sat down at this news. "What happened?"

"Not much, from what Chase said. Damien played dumb. It seemed to work. Bram left."

"That's good. Unless he's planning to come back."

"Yeah. Damien wants us to stay here for a while until it's safer to come home. I talked to Vance, and he agrees. So, it looks like we're staying here for a few days."

Tegan held her arms out. "In this dump? Darn."

Reid chuckled. "For now. We don't know when Bram will figure out that Isabelle came to Vegas."

All humor left Tegan. "What if he's doing that now? What if he finds us?"

Reid smirked. "Well, he's not coming here now."

"How do you know?"

"Quentin pulled him over this morning after leaving the wolves' home. The idiot has an expired license and expired tags."

"But both of those would just be fines, wouldn't they?"

"He might have thrown a punch when Quentin told him he couldn't drive anywhere until his license was renewed and that his car would be towed."

Tegan's good mood was back. "That is hilarious. Serves the asshole right."

"How did you sleep last night?" Reid asked, changing the subject.

"Pretty good. The million-count sheets are to die for." She looked him in the eye. "Of course, I would have slept better if I hadn't had to give myself an orgasm."

Tegan watched heat fill Reid's eyes as he sucked in a breath.

He visibly swallowed before he said, "That doesn't sound too bad."

She didn't know why he wanted to keep her waiting, but it was nice to know she affected him.

She pushed her chair back and stretched. She wore an oversize T-shirt nightgown, and she watched Reid stare at her legs as she put her arms over her head.

He wasn't the only one who could tease.

"I looked at the weather for today, and it's supposed to be over seventy. I think I'm going to go for a swim." She stood and stepped away from the table, and then she stuck a foot in the water. It was cool, probably too cool for a human, but it was fine for her.

"Did you bring a suit?" Reid asked.

Tegan pulled her pajamas over her head and threw it in his lap and over his computer. "Nope." She walked to the opposite end of the pool, making sure to put a little sway in her walk as she went. She didn't want Reid to miss checking out her naked ass.

Part of being a sentinel was knowing how to swim well, so when she reached the other side, she dived into the water with ease. She put Reid out of her mind and swam laps until she felt the burn in her muscles, and then she pushed herself a little more.

She swam toward the shallow end of the pool and stepped out of the water. She grabbed her hair and wrung out as much water as she could.

"You're cold."

Tegan looked up. "What?"

"You're cold," Reid said again.

She flipped her hair behind her and made her way over to him. "How can you tell?"

Reid pulled her in between his legs and traced one of her nipples with his thumb. "Your body is giving you away." He brushed his hand down her stomach and over her hip. "You're beautiful."

"So are you."

She wiped her hands on his sleeves and then picked up his laptop and set it on the table. Then, she grabbed her nightgown and placed it on the ground between Reid's legs. The front of his worn jeans were distended against his fly.

She took her forefinger and ran her finger up to the button of his pants. She took her time, waiting for Reid to stop her and ruin her fun, but the only thing he did was keep his eyes glued to her.

She unbuttoned his jeans and then pulled down the zipper. Black boxer briefs looked like they'd been painted on his impressive package.

"Did you really masturbate last night before falling asleep?"

She looked up into his face. "Yes."

"What did you think about while you touched yourself?"

"You." She wrapped her hand around him the best she could with his underwear still on and squeezed. "Are you going to stop me if I pull down your pants and put you in my mouth?"

Reid brushed his thumb across her lips. "I should say yes, but I have only so much willpower, and the thought of being in your mouth is past my limit. I won't stop you, Angel, if this is what you really want."

With his permission, she grabbed on to his boxer briefs and jeans and pulled them down as Reid lifted his butt up for her.

His cock sprang out, free and beautiful and huge.

"Wow," she breathed as she took him in both her hands. Zane hadn't been joking.

Reid groaned and closed his eyes.

"Hey," she said, and Reid looked at her. "Remember, you're still on duty, and Chase went to bed. You have to keep your eyes peeled for any danger." She swiped her finger over his tip. "We wouldn't want anyone sneaking up on us now."

Reid groaned again, but this time, it was out of frustration rather than pleasure. He grabbed her hand and pulled her up and onto his lap. "I have a better idea."

"Oh, yeah? What is that?"

He adjusted her on his lap, shocking her when he pushed his thickness deep inside her.

"Holy shit," she said, digging her nails into his shoulders.

She was turned on and ready for him, but he was big.

"I say that my shift is over, and you're on duty now."

Reid kissed her, and she melted into him, her pussy relaxing around his length.

He pulled his lips from hers. "How about you keep your eyes open while I fuck you senseless?"

She lifted her hips and pushed back down onto him. "I don't know if I can do that. You feel so good."

He gripped her hips in his hands and rocked her over him. "All I ask is that you try, Angel."

And Tegan did try.

Tried and failed.

Chapter Nineteen

Quentin returned home just as the sun was coming up into the sky. He went to his room to drop off his stuff and change. He should collapse into bed and sleep for a while, but he was a little amped up from his encounter with Bram. And Quentin knew that Damien wanted a full debriefing on what had happened.

When Quentin entered the living room, the room was full, and everyone started clapping for him. He hated being the center of attention, and his face heated. Good thing his darker skin hid it. He was embarrassed that he was embarrassed.

He waved away the praise. "Stop. I was just doing my job. If Damien hadn't given me a heads-up about Bram's expired tags, I wouldn't have known."

And Quentin was lucky that Bram had come within the Minneapolis city limits. If he had gone a different direction, Quentin wouldn't have been able to pull him over.

The group was still smiling at him, and that was when he sought out Hunter. Quentin hated to admit it, but he hoped that Hunter felt the same as the sentinels. Why Quentin wanted to impress the vampire so badly, he didn't know, but he did.

"Hey, where's Hunter?" Quentin asked when he didn't spot him.

"He was with me last night," Raven said. "When we got home, he said he was going to go for a walk."

Alarm bells began to go off in Quentin's head. "Did you see him come back?"

Raven shook her head and looked around at everyone else. Quentin scanned everyone's faces, and they all shook their heads.

He turned and took the stairs two at a time to Hunter's room. It was empty.

He ran back down to the main floor and looked at the sun peeking through the blinds on the front window. "If he's out there, it's not good."

Damien clapped his hands. "Okay, everyone, split up. We'll do a grid search of the property—"

Quentin didn't wait for his alpha to finish. He charged out the front door and stuck his nose in the air. He thought he might have caught a scent, but he couldn't be sure. He practically ripped off his clothes as he shifted into his wolf.

His sense of smell now stronger, he lifted his nose to the wind again. *There.* He sprang off the front steps as he heard the rest of the sentinels and Payton following him outside.

He found Hunter on the edge of the property. His leg was twisted in a way that wasn't normal, and there were tire marks on his clothes.

Quentin had come to a full stop upon seeing Hunter. Now, he slowly approached, afraid the vampire wouldn't be alive. Quentin sniffed around Hunter, relieved to find his heart was still beating. Quentin licked Hunter's face, but he didn't budge.

Quentin shifted back into his human form and put his fingers on Hunter's neck, just to be sure. His pulse was strong under Quentin's fingers.

"Quentin," Damien called from behind him.

"He's alive," Quentin yelled back. "We need to call someone. I don't want to move him without a neck brace."

Damien already had his phone out and was dialing as he reached Quentin. He threw Quentin's clothes at him as the other sentinels were behind him.

"Oh, shit," Raven said as Quentin pulled his jeans on. "I should have paid more attention to him coming home."

"Now's not the time to beat yourself up," Quentin said. "Go get the big tent out of the basement and something to cut the bottom off. We need to get Hunter out of the sun."

Raven nodded and ran back to the house.

Quentin looked at Damien. "Who are you calling?"

"The infirmary." Damien's face changed as someone answered the phone. "Yes, I need…" he said as he walked away.

"Payton, can you call your brother?" Quentin asked. "It's good that Damien is getting a doctor here as soon as possible, but Hunter should probably be seen by a vampire physician. Maybe Vaughn can figure out a way to bring one to us."

"On it." She pulled out her own phone and started hitting the screen. She stepped away as she began to speak into the mouthpiece.

"Why don't we just take him to the Vampire Clinic? Wouldn't that be faster?" Lachlan asked.

"Yes, but we don't know if he has a neck injury, and I don't have a neck brace," Quentin explained.

Vampires along with shifters were faster healers than humans, but they weren't immortal. They could be injured, and being paralyzed was a very real possibility.

"It's a good thing you're here," Lachlan said.

"It's a good thing I'm a first responder," Quentin countered.

Several hours later, Quentin sat by Hunter's bedside at the Vampire Clinic.

When the shifter doctor had arrived at their home, he'd decided it was best to bring Hunter to the clinic. They would have to X-ray Hunter's leg, and they couldn't do that from the house.

They had gotten the neck brace on him, put him on a stretcher, and loaded him in the back of the shifter ambulance to take him to the Vampire Clinic.

Once there, they'd decided that Hunter's leg needed surgery along with his spleen and liver. Both had lacerations that needed to be closed before he bled to death.

The only good news was that Hunter didn't have a spinal injury.

There was no doubt in anyone's mind that it was Bram who had hit Hunter. And they needed to figure out how to proceed with the situation. Quentin could call his captain and tell him everything—minus the shifter and vampire information—and they might be able to hold Bram in jail longer. But, if they did that, they wouldn't be able to exact shifter law on him. It would look pretty suspicious if Bram turned up dead after everything they reported to the police.

And that was just what the shifters wanted to do to him. The vampires were out for blood—from what Quentin had heard—and were ready to storm the clinic as soon as the sun went down.

Hunter began to stir, and Quentin jumped from his chair.

"He's waking up," he yelled. He panicked and looked around. There had to be some sort of button to alert the nurse that he was awake.

"I already pressed it."

Quentin looked at Hunter. The vampire's eyes were closed, but they were the only two in the room.

"I already pressed the nurse button," Hunter said, his voice low and gravelly.

Quentin crumpled in his seat and dropped his head into his hands, trying not to cry.

Damn you, Hunter. Damn you for making me care.

"Hey," Hunter said, trying to get Quentin's attention.

Thankfully, Quentin didn't have to show Hunter how much he was affected because the door opened, and the doctor and nurse walked in. Both females began to look over Hunter's monitors and check his vitals.

"Mr. Esmund, you gave us quite a scare," the doctor said. "Can you tell us what happened?"

"I got hit by a fucking car."

Quentin tried not to laugh, but it was better than crying.

"I understand this," the doctor said. "But do you know where you were impacted and what was hit? We have done a thorough examination, but we don't want to miss anything."

Hunter shook his head. "I don't know exactly. I remember hitting the windshield but not much else, except being in pain everywhere. Especially my leg."

"That is broken, so you'll be off your feet for about three weeks at least."

Hunter grunted at the news.

"But that's as long as you feed," the doctor said. "You've not only sustained injuries, but you were also out in the sun this morning. You need blood." She turned to the nurse. "Who is available right now?"

"I'll do it," Quentin said.

The doctor looked startled. "Oh, there's no need. We have vampires here just for this reason."

Quentin stood up. "I said, I'll do it."

The thought of *anyone else's* blood, male or female, in Hunter was too much for Quentin at the moment.

The females looked at each other, clearly confused by Quentin's tenacity, but he wasn't going to explain it to them. He appreciated all they had done for Hunter, but they could go fuck off for all he cared.

"Uh..." The doctor looked at Hunter, but Quentin kept his eyes on the doctor. He didn't hear Hunter say anything, but the doctor looked at him again. "Okay then. But he might need more than you can give at one time." She straightened her spine, ready for a fight. "I don't need a shifter falling down on me because he gave too much blood. If you pass your limit, you'll be done until you recover. Understood?"

Quentin nodded. "Yes, ma'am. Will you update my alpha on Hunter's condition?"

The doctor nodded and looked at Hunter again. "Call us if you need anything."

The females turned and left, and Quentin crumpled in his chair.

"I'm sorry. I know I had no right," he said as he stared at Hunter's feet. "I just...I just couldn't handle watching you drink from someone else."

Hunter grabbed his hand. Quentin looked up into Hunter's blue-green eyes.

Hunter smiled. "It's okay. I'm not mad." He closed his lids. "I want to feed from you."

Quentin didn't know if Hunter had closed his eyes because he didn't want to say the last sentence while looking at Quentin or because he was going to fall back asleep.

"Hunter, you'd better feed before you go unconscious again."

Hunter smiled again and opened his eyes. "Give me your wrist."

Quentin really wanted to give Hunter his neck, but it was too much for the both of them. "Do you need me to wash it or anything first?"

Hunter laughed. "No. Just give it to me."

Quentin held out his arm and placed his wrist near Hunter's mouth.

Hunter grabbed his fist and licked at his pulse. The vampire closed his eyes for a moment and sighed.

Then, Hunter struck, sinking his fangs into Quentin, and Quentin relaxed, knowing that he was the one who was going to help Hunter heal.

Chapter Twenty

Isabelle woke up, feeling warm. That explained why she hadn't slept that well last night. That, and Zane had woken her several times to fuck her.

She preferred the temperature to be cool, so she could snuggle under the covers all night.

But she'd been so hot last night that she kicked the covers off sometime while she was sleeping.

She looked over at Zane. He was still sleeping. He was under the sheet and comforter and didn't seem to be having any problems.

Of course, he'd been up a lot, screwing her brains out and marking her all over. But she'd been up just as much as him, yet she felt wired for some reason.

She might as well get out of bed. Maybe she'd be able to sleep on the plane on the way back to Minnesota.

She went into the bathroom, flipped on the switch, and practically screamed when she looked in the mirror. She looked like she'd gotten in a fight with a pack of dogs.

She had bite marks on both sides of her neck, on one breast, on the inside of both thighs—she turned around—and on one ass cheek.

There was no mistaking that she belonged to Zane now.

Despite the possessiveness of it, she thought it was hot as hell. She chuckled. Bram would flip his lid when he saw her.

Isabelle turned on the shower and emptied her bladder while she waited for the water to warm up. She was halfway through her shower when Zane stepped in behind her. She turned to tell him to wait his turn, but his eyelids were half-closed, and he looked exhausted. Her bite marks on his shoulders stood out against his pale skin.

She stepped closer to him. "Hey, what are you doing up? You look like you need three days of more sleep."

He shook his head. "I can't leave you. What if something happens?"

Her heart went out to him. "Okay, turn around. I'll wash you. You just stand there and let me take care of you."

The corner of his mouth tipped up, and he turned.

"*Oh my God.*"

Zane looked over his shoulder, a little more awake. "What's wrong?"

"Your back." She looked lower. "And your butt." There were slashes going up and down and left to right. "I scratched the hell out of you."

"Oh." Zane shrugged and looked forward. "I don't mind." She could hear the smile in his voice, but she still felt a little bad.

She took her time in washing his body, and when she was done, he did the same for her. They got dressed and headed for the kitchen. Zane got sidetracked by Ranulf and Reid, so Isabelle went in search of breakfast on her own.

When Isabelle got there, Tegan was already in the kitchen, standing in front of the coffeemaker. Her hair was wet, but she was still in her pajamas.

Tegan turned and saw Isabelle looking at her. "I went swimming," she explained.

Isabelle looked out the window into the back. "That sounds heavenly. I should have done that this morning. I've been hot since I woke up, and taking a warm shower didn't help."

"I'll go swimming with you later, if you still want to. We can go buy ourselves some suits this morning. We're all going to need more clothes, so we might as well go shopping early."

Isabelle grabbed a coffee cup from the cupboard. "But we're leaving today."

"Oh, you probably haven't heard yet. We're staying put for a bit. Bram showed up at the wolves' house this morning."

Isabelle dropped the cup, but Tegan caught it before it hit the ground.

Tegan set the cup on the counter and put her arm around Isabelle. "Hey, it's okay. He doesn't know where you are. You're safe here."

"Was anyone hurt?"

"Nah. He was sent on his way by Damien. He pretended like he hadn't seen you in a while, and it worked."

Someone cleared their throat from the doorway.

"That's not entirely true," a male voice said.

Isabelle and Tegan looked over to see Zane, Reid, and Ranulf in the doorway. All three males looked grim.

Zane stepped forward, and Tegan dropped her arm.

He picked up Isabelle's hands. "Uh, Isa...I just found out that Hunter was hurt. Bram had hit him and run him over with his car as he was leaving the property."

"Oh no," Tegan said.

A wave of incredible guilt washed over Isabelle, and her knees gave out. Zane caught her, but she wished he'd just let her fall.

"This is my fault. I'm the one who brought Bram to your doorstep. If it wasn't for me, Bram wouldn't have hurt anyone."

Zane raised her chin. "Except you. He would have hurt you, Isa."

"But that I could live with."

"Not if you were dead," Zane said in a stern voice. "And everyone took an oath to protect all wolf-shifters. Even ones with asshole boyfriends."

She knew he was trying to make her smile, but it wasn't going to work. "But Hunter's a vampire. He didn't take an oath to protect me. And it's my fault he's hurt." Something just occurred to her, and she grabbed Zane's shirt. "He's still alive, right? Please tell me he's still alive."

If Bram had killed Hunter...she didn't know what she would do.

Zane ran his hand down her hair. "Yes, he's still alive. Hunter is at the Vampire Clinic. He's conscious and feeding as we speak. His prognosis is good."

Isabelle sighed and fell against Zane.

He wrapped his arms around her, and despite everything, she'd never felt safer in her whole life. At that moment, she never wanted him to let her go.

Zane pulled her upper body away from his and met her eyes. "Right now, Bram is in jail. He had an altercation with the law this morning. We don't know how long he'll be there. He'll probably make bail. But Damien is staying on top of the situation. Bram will not escape punishment for what he did."

Isabelle wanted to believe Zane, but Bram had a way of always getting out of stuff.

About a month ago, she'd overheard a conversation he was having with his dad, and she'd found out the real reason he'd moved to Minnesota. It'd seemed like a punishment for Bram to get exiled from his own state but not enough of a punishment when he should have been convicted of attempted murder. That was when Isabelle had begun to plan to leave him.

She'd begun to see his true colors, and she'd always felt he was holding himself back with her, especially when he was upset. But to find out that he'd nearly beaten a male to death was the last straw.

"I don't think you understand how ruthless he can be," she told Zane.

He rubbed his thumb across her chin. "I've seen a lot of things, Isa. Please don't worry about us."

"That's impossible," she told him. Of course she was going to worry.

Zane smiled and pulled her into his arms again. "You need to eat something."

Isabelle curled up her nose. She couldn't possibly eat at a time like this. "No, thanks."

Zane turned the two of them, so they faced the counter. He poured coffee into the mug she'd dropped earlier. He let her go and handed the coffee to her. "You're eating. Now is not the time to not keep up your strength. I know you feel guilty, but, honey, you cannot let this prick win."

Tegan rubbed Isabelle's back. "Zane is right. I'm not saying you shouldn't feel guilty. You have a right to feel the way you feel, but you cannot let this guy ruin your life. Because then he wins. And I think we can all agree that we don't want him to win."

Isabelle took the coffee cup from Zane. "I see your point." She looked at her mate, pleading with her eyes. "Is Hunter really okay? You're not lying to me?"

Zane smiled, but his eyes were sad. "I wouldn't lie to you, Isa. Hunter is really okay. He can't do much with a broken leg for a few weeks, but he'll make a full recovery. I don't know the male well, but I'm sure he wouldn't want you beating yourself up."

Isabelle nodded.

"Good. Now, I'm going to get you something to eat."

She nodded again.

"And then we're going shopping," Tegan said.

Isabelle looked at her like she was crazy, which made Tegan laugh.

"Not for fun, silly. But I don't have much for clothes, and I'm guessing you don't either. It's shopping out of necessity, and it'll keep your mind occupied."

"You're right. I only have one other change of clothes."

"Good." Tegan poured herself a cup of coffee. "I'm going to shower, and we'll leave within the hour." She turned and left the kitchen. As she walked by Reid, she said, "I need to speak to you."

Reid smiled and followed.

Isabelle looked over at Ranulf. She knew he hadn't been happy when she showed up, looking for help. She expected to see contempt in his eyes.

Instead, there was sympathy.

"Tegan's right, Isabelle," Ranulf said. "Hunter wouldn't want you blaming yourself."

Isabelle took a deep breath. "Thank you."

Ranulf nodded and left.

Isabelle looked back at Zane. "All right, I'm ready. Feed me."

Chapter Twenty-One

Tegan and Isabelle walked into the next clothing store. The she-wolf was feeling a little better despite this morning's news. It had helped that Zane got Hunter on the phone to talk to Isabelle.

Isabelle felt a little less guilty after being able to apologize, and Hunter had reassured her that he didn't blame her in the least. She was not responsible for other people's actions. Isabelle still felt bad, but at least Tegan and Zane had gotten her out of the house.

Ranulf had stayed behind to watch the hotel suite, and Reid and Chase were sleeping.

"I just want to pick up a few things for Reid, and then we can go home," Tegan said.

"No problem. Take your time," Isabelle responded.

But Tegan could tell that she was eager to get out of there. They'd been shopping for over an hour, and Isabelle had been getting antsier with each store. She was too polite to tell Tegan that she wanted to leave.

"Thank *God*," Zane said. He was not polite at all and had no problems with bitching the entire time.

Tegan put her hand on her hip. "Do you want to walk around Vegas, naked? Or perhaps you'd prefer to wear dirty, smelly clothes?"

"I don't care as long as we get to leave soon." He scratched the back of his neck and curled his lip, as if he couldn't get rid of his itch. "I need to get out of here."

"That's easy for you to say. You found clothes at the second store we went to."

"It's because I'm not picky."

Tegan rolled her eyes. "Whatever. Neither is Reid. He knows exactly what he wants. I just saved this store until last."

"Seven-hundred-dollar shirts, and he's not picky?"

Tegan sighed. "They're not seven hundred dollars. Exaggerate much?"

"Fine," Zane said. "But I could buy a whole package at Target for one shirt here."

"And that's why you look like a bum." Tegan spun on her heel and walked away.

"I don't look like a bum," Zane called after her.

"Jeez, you two fight like brother and sister," she heard Isabelle say.

Tegan smiled. Zane was definitely like a brother to her.

Unlike Reid, who'd given her the best damn orgasm of her life this morning. Twice.

She shook her head as she went through the pile of T-shirts.

All those years wasted that she could have been having phenomenal sex.

She couldn't wait to tell Phoenix. She'd never believe it.

Tegan picked up two shirts that she thought would look good on Reid. A blue one and a black one.

Tegan went to the checkout, glancing over just to make sure Isabelle was okay and that no one was watching her or looked suspicious. And ten minutes later, she was finished.

"I'm ready."

Zane opened his mouth to say something smart-ass-like, she was sure, and Tegan shot him a look.

"Let's go," was all he said instead.

Once they walked outside of the mall, Isabelle said, "Why is it so hot?"

Tegan looked at Zane, who was fanning himself with his shirt.

"It is a little warm," he said.

She thought they were both crazy. "You guys, it's, like"—she pulled up the weather app on her phone—"seventy-one degrees outside. It's perfect weather."

Isabelle looked at Tegan. "It's hot. I don't think I can walk home."

It had taken them about twenty to twenty-five minutes on foot to get to the mall. It was not far to walk at all, especially for shifters.

"We'll get a cab," Zane reassured Isabelle, putting his arm around her.

Tegan had been looking forward to their walk home. They hadn't bought that much, and it was a gorgeous day outside.

"If we're taking a cab, then we're going to stop and pick up some groceries on the way home, so we can cook dinner."

They'd had airport food yesterday, then room service for dinner, room service for breakfast, and fast food for lunch. Tegan wanted something home-cooked.

"That sounds great," Isabelle said. "I'm too tired to go out to dinner, but I'm starved."

A cab pulled up, and all three got in the back after putting their shopping bags in the front.

Tegan stared out the window on the way to the closest supermarket. Vegas was so bright and beautiful, and she closed her eyes and took a deep breath.

An enticing scent filled Tegan's nose, and she turned to Isabelle, who was sitting in the middle of them. "When did you start smelling so good?" Tegan leaned close and inhaled.

Isabelle laughed. "I don't know." She lifted her arm and smelled herself. "I don't think I smell any different than normal."

Tegan moved closer. "Well, you do."

Zane reached behind Isabelle and pushed Tegan away. "Back off. She's mine."

Tegan gave him a dirty look. "I wasn't going to try anything. Sheesh. She clearly has a thing for you." *And I kind of have a thing for Reid.*

Isabelle put her hand on Zane's leg. "I don't think Tegan was going to try anything. She likes boys."

Tegan held a finger up in the air. "Correction: I like men. Not boys."

"And women," Zane added.

Isabelle looked at Tegan. "Really?"

Tegan shrugged. "I've dated a couple of women." That was probably another reason she'd thought she'd be mated before Phoenix. The potential for her to find a partner was double.

"Tell me, what's it like? Is being with a woman super hot?" Isabelle gasped. "What's it like when you're going through your heat?" She whispered the last word, so the driver didn't hear.

Tegan laughed. Isabelle was like a kid. "It can be super hot. I dated a woman for over two years. Toward the end, it got to be that our cycles synced up, and we would go into heat together. Let's just say, it was twenty-four hours of sex, sex, and more sex. The only downside was that there was no male there to give a...donation. After a while, we had to take medicine to dull the pain."

During a shifter's heat, the female body's goal was to get pregnant, and what the female body wanted was the male's seed. It was really the only way to relieve the burning ache for a significant amount of time. Single females or females without a male partner often took muscle relaxants, antianxiety drugs, or sedatives to help them through their mating heat.

"Have you been with a male during your heat, too?"

Tegan nodded. "Of course. But only with human men, so they could wear a condom and never for the whole time. I had to use medication then too, but that was also hot."

Isabelle bit her lip and stared off into space. "I bet."

Tegan narrowed her eyes at Isabelle and leaned closer. "Have you never been with anyone during your heat?" she whispered.

Isabelle quickly glanced at Zane and back at Tegan. She wiggled her eyebrows and shook her head.

Tegan fanned her face. "Ooh...girl..." She leaned forward. "Oh, Zane—"

Isabelle elbowed her in the arm.

"Ouch."

Zane rolled his eyes. "I can hear everything you two are saying, you know." He pointed to his ear. "I'm not deaf."

"So then, you heard me say that I was going to take Isabelle home with me?"

Zane growled. "Don't you dare."

Tegan sat back against the backseat and laughed.

The car stopped, and Tegan looked out the window to see they were at a grocery store. She met the driver's eyes in the rearview mirror.

The driver was staring at her with his mouth open.

She winked. "I'll be back in a flash. Don't leave."

The driver nodded.

Tegan went through the supermarket at record speed and was back at the car in less than ten minutes. She'd moved so fast, she'd started to sweat.

She pulled open her door to see Isabelle practically on Zane's lap. Tegan looked at the driver. From what she could see, his face was beet red.

"Will you two knock it off? You're going to give the young man a heart attack." To the driver, she said, "To the hotel, please. And you'd better get used to stuff like this. You work in Vegas."

The driver laughed. "It's my third week."

That made sense.

Ten minutes later, they were in the hotel and making their way to their room. It seemed to take forever because everyone stopped to stare at the three of them. That wasn't true. They all stopped to stare at Isabelle.

Zane finally picked her up, throwing her over his shoulder, and ran toward their room. The bags she was carrying from their shopping trip smacked the backs of his legs the whole way there.

In the living room, Tegan set her bags down and said hi to the three males watching TV. Isabelle and Zane were nowhere to be seen.

"You can look in the bags for the clothes I bought you. I left the receipts in there, so you can pay me back."

"Okay. Thanks, Tegan," Reid said, not looking up from the TV.

She took off her blouse, leaving her in a tank top, because the room was warm. She walked around, so she could see the screen. UFC. That explained why they were television zombies at the moment.

"I'm going to start dinner," she said to herself since no one else was listening. "I sure hope no one breaks in or anything," she said a little lower.

At least two of them shushed her.

She was halfway through dinner, sweating her boobs off from all the heat from the stove and oven, when Isabelle came into the kitchen. Her cheeks were flushed, and she smelled like she'd just gotten laid.

"Do you need any help?"

"I'd love some."

Tegan walked past Isabelle to grab the items out of the fridge when Isabelle's scent made her pause. She turned and looked at the she-wolf. "Isabelle?"

Isabelle was fanning her face. "Yeah?"

"When are you supposed to go into heat again?"

Isabelle shrugged. "Like a week, maybe two."

Tegan stepped closer and put her nose in Isabelle's neck.

"What are you doing?" She laughed, but then she put her nose in Tegan's neck. "Man, you smell kind of good, too."

Tegan stepped back. "What did you say?"

"You smell good." Isabelle frowned. "What's the big deal?"

Tegan shrieked and backed away. "No, no, no, no. Not now." She was on a job. It was hard enough, being a female sentinel without her body betraying her.

Yet all the signs were there. They'd been talking about mating heat in the fricking car, for God's sake.

Reid and Zane came rushing into the kitchen, panic all over their faces.

"What's wrong?" Reid asked.

"Is someone here?" Zane looked around.

"No," Isabelle said. "Tegan just started freaking out."

"What's wrong?" Reid asked again, taking a step toward her.

She moved back. "I don't know if I'd come any closer if I were you." She looked over at Isabelle. "Isabelle's about to go into heat." She looked back at Reid. "And she's taking me with her."

Chapter Twenty-Two

Isabelle looked at Tegan's panicked face and then over at Zane. "I'm not supposed to go into heat yet." But then she closed her eyes and shook her head.

"What?" Zane asked.

She looked at him and sighed. "It's the sex. It caused a jump in my hormones, speeding up my heat. Damn it." She'd known her mating heat was coming. She just wasn't prepared for it to be this soon. She still didn't know how she felt about Zane and having sex with him during her heat.

All the talk about it with Tegan had her very interested, but for Isabelle, it was a big step. She'd heard of human couples who wouldn't have sex without a condom or who would use birth control until marriage. For her, it was the same thing.

But she was married and mated to Zane. Yet she still wasn't sure.

Zane grinned. "So…you're saying, I caused you to go into your heat?"

If he could pat himself on the back and give himself a high five, he probably would. The pride coming off him was unmistakable.

"Do you not realize the enormity of the situation?" Tegan asked.

Zane rolled his eyes. "Of course. My mate and I are going to be doing a whole lot of screwing. But what better place than here? Bram is hundreds of miles away."

"Oh, *yeah*. So sexy," Tegan said sarcastically. "And who's going to be watching your back when Bram is free from jail? Me? Nope, because I'll be curled up in a ball, waiting for my own heat to pass."

"Shit," Zane said. "That takes you and Reid out of sentinel duty, doesn't it?"

"Why will Reid and Tegan be taken out of sentinel duty?" Chase asked as he and Ranulf came up behind Zane and Reid, pushing the two cats past the doorway.

The kitchen was probably the smallest room in the suite besides the two bathrooms, and it was getting very crowded in there.

"Tegan's going to go into heat soon, so she and Reid won't be around to help stand guard."

Isabelle watched Tegan and Reid exchange looks before Tegan glanced away and blushed. That seemed odd for someone who had been speaking about sex so freely in the car on the way home.

When Isabelle turned back to Chase and Ranulf, they were sniffing the air.

"It smells like she's not the only one," Ranulf said. "That means, you and Isabelle will be busy, too."

"We're fucked," Tegan said.

Zane laughed.

"Not like that. No pun intended." She scowled at Zane.

Reid inched closer to Tegan. "It'll be okay. We'll figure something out."

"We could call for reinforcements," Zane said. "They could be here in less than half a day."

Tegan tilted her head. "Have you ever been around a female in heat?"

Zane shook his head. "Not really. Maybe for an hour or two but never the whole time."

"What about you two?" Tegan asked Ranulf and Chase.

The two wolves looked at each other and shook their heads.

"And you?" Tegan said to Reid.

He uncomfortably rubbed the back of his neck. "Uh...once." He dropped his arm. "And I know what you're getting at."

Tegan stared at Reid a little longer. Isabelle had no idea what the she-cat was thinking.

But then she squared her shoulders and addressed the room, "Everyone in this suite is going to be affected, especially with two females in heat. *Everyone.*" She stressed the last word. "We're all going to be sitting ducks. Or sitting cats and wolves."

Ranulf and Chase looked at each other again.

Ranulf said, "So...either we leave or—"

"We get hookers," Chase finished.

Tegan made a sound of disgust.

"What?" Chase said. "Prostitution is legal in the state of Nevada, and those women have to earn a living, too."

"I don't care about that. I'm all for women making money the way they want to. I'm referring to how you two are only thinking about sex at a time like this."

"Angel, I'm pretty sure we're all thinking about sex."

"Yeah," Chase agreed. "Besides, *you're* the one going into heat. You're going to be having way more sex than Ranulf and me, combined."

"It's not my fault," Tegan said through clenched teeth.

Isabelle flinched.

"No, no, Isabelle. I don't blame you. I know us hanging out together caused mine to come sooner, but it's our stupid shifter biology to blame."

Isabelle still felt bad even if she hadn't meant for her hormones to rub off on Tegan.

"Tegan's right, guys," Reid said. "None of us are going to be free from this. And it doesn't matter how much backup we call. We'll all be in the same predicament."

A lightbulb went off in Isabelle's head. "What if we hired a human security team to watch over the room for a few days? Humans aren't as affected as strongly as shifters."

Zane put his arm around Isabelle. "My mate is a genius."

Isabelle was embarrassed by his praise, but she was proud of herself for thinking of a solution.

"Good idea, Isabelle," Tegan said. "There are probably a ton of security firms here with all the famous people who come and visit." She looked at the two male wolves. "Do you two think you can handle calling around and finding a good one?"

Chase put his hand on his waist. "And what are you going to be doing?"

"Trying not to stab your eyes out while I finish making your dinner."

"Sheesh. I thought mating heat was supposed to make you horny, not mean."

Tegan gave Chase the finger.

"Just go and do what the lady asked, will ya?" Reid said. "Let me know who you decide on, and I'll do a quick background check on them."

Chase and Ranulf made a few more grumbles but left the room.

Zane squeezed Isabelle's shoulder and grinned at her. "So…"

She pushed him away. "I'm not going through heat yet. Get out of here." She laughed. "I'm going to help Tegan finish cooking."

"Fine, but you know where to find me. Just follow the scent of red-blooded male."

"Oh my God. Go." She gave him another playful shove.

Zane laughed as he left the room.

Isabelle looked at Tegan and Reid. Neither of them was smiling.

"Do you want me to leave?" she asked them.

"No," Tegan said as Reid said, "Yes."

"Uh…" Isabelle didn't know what to do.

Reid clenched his jaw. "We'll talk later," he said to Tegan and then left.

Awkwardness was left in Reid's wake.

"Would you still like my help with dinner?" Isabelle asked. "I can go if you're worried I might have more of an effect on you."

Tegan sighed. "No. Stay."

Tegan didn't sound like she wanted Isabelle to stay.

"Are you sure?"

"Yes." Tegan went to the fridge where she grabbed a couple of vegetables and handed them to Isabelle. "You can cut these up if you'd like."

"Sure."

The two worked in silence for about five minutes with their backs to one another.

"I'm sorry if I came across like a bitch," Tegan said, surprising Isabelle.

"Oh. Uh…it's okay."

Tegan laughed. "I was hoping you'd say, *You weren't a bitch*, but I totally deserve that." She sighed. "It can be really hard to be a female sentinel. I feel like I have to prove myself a lot just because I don't have a penis. And my heat is just another reminder that I have a weakness that males don't."

Isabelle spun around. "You are looking at the whole thing all wrong."

Tegan smiled and looked over her shoulder at Isabelle. "I am?"

"You have the ability to give life, Tegan. To a society that doesn't have enough in the first place. Your heat is not a weakness. It is a strength. And those male sentinels should be singing your praises because you are going to help bring the next generation into this world. They need you to keep the species going. Don't ever let anyone tell you that you're weak."

Tegan leaned back. "Damn, girl, I didn't know you were such a feminist."

Isabelle laughed. "I have a lot of female students, and I hate when they think they are weaker than boys or not as good as boys. Differences don't equate weakness. Differences equate diverse strengths."

"Wow. Who said that?"

"Me. I did. I'm glad you like it."

Tegan chuckled. "It's a good quote. You should spread the word. You could be famous."

Isabelle laughed, too. "No, thanks."

Tegan touched Isabelle's arm. "Thank you, by the way."

"For what?"

"For what you said about my heat being my strength and not my weakness."

Isabelle smiled. "Well, it's true. What badass male wouldn't want you to be the mother of his offspring?" She nodded. "Remember that the next time they give you hell."

Chapter Twenty-Three

Quentin paced back and forth outside Hunter's bedroom.

They'd left the Vampire Clinic after sundown and come back to Quentin and the wolves' home. Quentin had been sure that, with his injury, Hunter would want to go back to the vampires.

He'd even gone so far as to call Bowden to tell him to come back home. Bowden had taken Hunter's spot with the vampires, and if Hunter was going to go back there, then Bowden could come back to the wolves. He'd especially be needed because Quentin had planned to go with Hunter. He didn't care what anyone said.

Hunter might not want to be with him the way he wanted to be with Hunter, but he couldn't shut off his feelings for the vampire. He wasn't going to let Hunter out of his sight until he was better or Bram was caught. Preferably both.

But, as soon as Quentin had made that phone call, Hunter had stopped him. He had insisted on going back to be with the wolves. He'd claimed he would be up on his feet soon, and he was more determined than any wolf to catch Bram.

Quentin didn't know how fast Hunter would really heal, but he couldn't fault the male for his need for vengeance.

So here Quentin was. Pacing outside Hunter's room. The house was quiet. Either everyone was working or in bed, but he was going to make sure no one bothered Hunter, so the vampire could get his rest.

Quentin reached the end of the hall and turned around to walk back the other way. Just before he walked past the door to Hunter's room, a pillow came flying out, almost hitting Quentin in the head.

He stopped and picked up the object that had nearly beaned him.

"I can hear you pacing," Hunter whisper-yelled.

Quentin peeked his head in the doorway. "I'm sorry. I just don't want anyone bothering you. You need your rest."

"You're bothering me. Every time you walk past, you mumble the same thing under your breath."

"Oh." Quentin hadn't realized. "Sorry." He put the pillow down on Hunter's bed. "No more pacing. I promise."

Hunter shoved the pillow under his head. "Thank you."

Quentin left the bedroom and walked out of Hunter's line of sight, but he didn't go very far. He sat down on the floor and rested his head on the wall. Now that he wasn't walking back and forth, he was having a hard time not fidgeting.

He was so full of emotions, and he didn't know what to do with it. He knew what he wanted to do.

He wanted to go into Hunter's room and take off both their clothes, pull Hunter to his knees, and push his cock inside the vampire. Being close to him and making them both come would go a long way in easing Quentin's raw nerves.

But that wasn't going to happen. Hunter had let Quentin know where he stood months ago.

Quentin rubbed the inside of his wrist where Hunter had fed from him earlier. The two tiny pinpricks were almost completely healed, much to Quentin's disappointment. But at least his blood was flowing through Hunter's veins. That was something.

"Quentin?"

He perked his head up. "Yeah?"

"Get your butt in here."

He scrambled to his feet. "Is something wrong? Are you okay? Are you in pain?"

Hunter sighed. "No. I can't sleep with your emotions going a million miles an hour. I can only block so much."

Quentin felt his face heat, much to his chagrin. He'd forgotten about the emotional connection through the blood he'd provided. He dropped his head. "I'm sorry. I'll go. Will you please call me if you need anything?"

"No."

That was kind of rude, but maybe he deserved it. "Okay. I understand."

Hunter sighed again. "No, you don't." He pulled down the covers on his bed.

It was dark in the room, but Quentin could still make out Hunter's smooth, muscular chest. And there was a hint of a cast on his lower leg. Quentin wanted to slide in next to him. He was hard, just thinking about it.

"Get in."

Quentin shook his head, trying to clear it. "I must be more tired than I assumed. I just thought you'd said—" He laughed at his own foolishness. "Never mind."

He turned to leave when Hunter spoke again, "You didn't mishear. I told you to get in."

Quentin slowly pivoted on the ball of his foot and stepped up to Hunter's bed. He'd already been able to smell Hunter, of course, but now, the vampire was even closer, and Quentin's dick was so stiff, it hurt.

"I don't think that's a good idea." He wasn't one to beat around the bush, so he fisted himself to show Hunter exactly what he meant.

"I want to see it."

That was the last thing he'd expected out of Hunter's mouth, and his hand froze.

"Pull off your pants. I want to watch you touch yourself."

Quentin couldn't decide if this was the best idea or the worst idea in the world. Hunter had been given some pain meds at the clinic.

As if he'd read Quentin's mind, he said, "I haven't taken anything more than ibuprofen for over five hours. Now, show me, Quentin. Show me how you touch yourself."

Not wanting to think about it any longer and just feel, Quentin quickly locked the door before returning to Hunter's bedside. He shoved his jeans down and kicked them off. Then, he pulled his T-shirt up and over his head.

Hunter groaned. "I forgot how beautiful you are. I love the color of your skin." Then, he said so low that Quentin almost missed it, "I still remember what you taste like."

Quentin growled and took his cock in his hand. He began to stroke it. Up and down, slowly so that Hunter didn't miss a thing. Quentin watched as Hunter's tongue licked his bottom lip, and his shaft was tenting the front of his nylon shorts.

Quentin closed his eyes and let his head fall back on his shoulders. If he continued to watch Hunter, he'd come embarrassingly fast, and he wanted this show to last.

When his breathing quickened and he felt the tingling in his spine and the tightening in his balls, he heard his name being called. He gradually raised his head and opened his eyes.

"Come here," Hunter said. "I want to finish you."

Quentin kept a firm hold on his dick as he sat next to Hunter, resting his back against the headboard.

Hunter slowly peeled Quentin's fingers off his cock. "Let me."

Quentin almost combusted just at the feel of the vampire's warm hand on him. God, he wished he weren't so close to coming. He wanted to feel Hunter touch him forever.

But Hunter couldn't hear his thoughts, and he stroked Quentin, increasing his speed and the strength of his grip, until Quentin had to shove his arm in his mouth to stop his shouts from waking the whole neighborhood.

The warmth of his seed erupted on his belly, but Hunter didn't let go.

It was only after Quentin grew too sensitive that he placed his hand over Hunter's to stop him. "Too much." Quentin reached for his shirt on the floor and wiped off his stomach. He bunched it up in a ball and placed it back on the carpet.

He looked over at Hunter, afraid he'd tell Quentin to leave, but the look on Hunter's face was one of pure hunger.

Quentin pushed any reservations out of his head again and leaned over to take Hunter's mouth. The vampire opened for him, so he swept his tongue inside.

God, he tastes as good as I remember.

Hunter grabbed on to his shoulders, and Quentin shifted down, so he was lying on the bed. He gripped Hunter's ass and pulled him close. Hunter's firm cock rubbed against Quentin's already-hardening one. He'd just come, and he was ready to come again. But then again, he was in bed with Hunter.

Hunter separated his mouth from Quentin's and began kissing down his face and neck. When Hunter reached the place where it met his shoulder, Quentin cupped the back of his head.

"Bite me."

Hunter shook his head but licked and sucked on Quentin's skin.

"Yes. I know you didn't take enough earlier. Feed from me. I want to feel you drink from me."

"You once told me that I couldn't put myself inside you until you put yourself inside me."

That had seemed like a lifetime ago. He'd wanted Hunter to feed from him the first time Quentin pushed his cock inside him. But things had changed since then.

"That was before you were injured. I know you need this. And I already fed you at the clinic." And Quentin didn't think he'd ever get to have sex with Hunter the way he wanted to anyway. No holds barred, no reservations, no hiding. "Feed."

Hunter's willpower seemed to be as weak as his own, and he sank his fangs into Quentin.

Quentin's hips shot out toward Hunter as he groaned. There was no way to explain how it felt to have the person you cared about feed from you.

Hunter rubbed their cocks together, and Quentin slid his hand under the waistband of Hunter's shorts, fisted his length, and squeezed.

Hunter ripped his fangs from Quentin's neck. "Holy fuck."

That was what Hunter had said the first and only time Quentin gave him head.

Hunter leaned forward and licked Quentin's neck to close his wounds, he assumed, and then he dropped back on the pillow, pulling an arm over his eyes. "God, that feels incredible."

If Quentin's hand felt incredible, then he couldn't wait to make the vampire feel even better.

Quentin clutched the waistband of Hunter's shorts with both hands and pulled them down.

Hunter lifted his head and looked down just as Quentin sucked his magnificent cock into his mouth. He tasted even *better* than Quentin remembered.

"Holy shit," Hunter said and thrust his hips. "I'm not going to last long."

Quentin reached up and touched Hunter's chest to tell him that it was okay. He would take what he could get.

Quentin placed open-mouthed kisses all along Hunter's dick and then sucked the head into his mouth.

Hunter barked out a moan and exploded in Quentin's mouth.

Quentin sucked and sucked, wanting to take every last drop of Hunter down his throat.

It was only after Hunter's body relaxed that Quentin released him. He moved up his body and looked into Hunter's face.

Not wanting anything to ruin the moment, Quentin placed a finger over Hunter's lips. "Go to sleep now."

Hunter grabbed on to Quentin's hand and put his head on Quentin's shoulder.

Quentin pulled him close just as a soft snore slipped from Hunter's lips. He knew this moment wouldn't last, but he was going to enjoy what he could get.

Chapter Twenty-Four

Zane entered the bedroom to see his mate on the bed, sprawled out and naked under the ceiling fan going at full speed. The bedroom lights were off, but the shades were open, so the Vegas strip shone through the window.

She looked so beautiful to him and smelled incredible, but he knew she was lying like that because she was hot, not because she was ready for him. Besides, there was going to be plenty of sex in their future.

Zane sat down next to her. "Ranulf and Chase found an available security company, and Reid confirmed they were reputable. They'll start in the morning." He put his hand on her arm. Her skin almost felt feverish. "Are you okay? You were quiet through dinner."

She looked at him for the first time. "Something Tegan said had me thinking."

"What's that?"

"She said I was a feminist."

"Oh God. The horror. No mate of mine can be a feminist."

She smiled at his joke. "I've never really thought of myself that way, but maybe I am. I want to empower women, especially the young girls I teach. I want them to know they can do anything a male can do." She looked at the ceiling again. "So, how did I end up with someone like Bram? I've thought about it a lot over the last few months, and I always have excuses, but I feel like a fool. How can I teach girls to be strong when I was so weak?"

"Hey." He hated to hear her being so hard on herself. Zane kicked off his shoes and stretched out beside her. "You're not weak."

She turned her head to the side. "How do you know?"

"Because you're here. Now. With me." She still looked skeptical, so he suggested, "Why don't you tell me about it? And then I'll give you my full opinion on the situation."

Isabelle sighed and looked up again. "I met Bram at a coffee shop. My first instinct was that only nice guys went into coffee shops." She held up a hand, as if to stop him from saying something. "Silly, I know."

He took her hand in his. He didn't want to interrupt her, but he wanted her to know that he didn't think she was silly.

"We were in line. He accidentally bumped into me, and we got to talking. He was so nice and friendly. I remember thinking he had the best smile." She snorted. "What a joke. It was all fake, fake, fake. Of course, I didn't know it then, but it still pisses me off, how I fell for it."

He squeezed her hand.

"So, after we picked up our coffee, he asked if he could sit with me. He was so polite and cute, so I thought, *What the hell?* We sat and talked for an hour. We had so many of the same interests and liked the same things. When he asked me out on a date, I said yes. Things started out so slow. He didn't pressure me or push me into doing anything. In fact, I was the one who started to want more."

Zane hated hearing how she wanted to be with another male, but he didn't say anything. He didn't want her to stop talking because he was jealous.

"I found out later that the reason he didn't ask me for sex was because he was getting it somewhere else."

Zane squeezed his eyes shut for a second. How anyone could cheat on Isabelle, he would never understand.

"After we had sex, I think that's when things gradually started to change. I don't know if he felt like, once we did the deed, I was his or if he thought that I wouldn't leave him, but that's when he started to show his true colors. The smiling, friendly guy I'd met in the coffee shop wasn't so happy anymore. At first, he nitpicked about things, and then, before I knew it, I couldn't do anything right."

Zane kissed her hand.

"It went from him wanting to wait for us to be intimate to him accusing me of cheating on him. Meanwhile, he was cheating on me. I often wondered if that's where the accusations came from or if he did it to put me off guard. Probably both. But that's how he ended up almost living with me and why I didn't protest. If I was with him, then I couldn't be cheating on him, so I was relieved when he was with me."

She used her other hand to hit the bed.

"I played right into his hands. He used me and manipulated me to do what he wanted. And I did it. I didn't even fight him."

A tear slipped from Isabelle's eye and rolled down to the pillow. Zane kissed the spot where her tear had fallen and got up on one elbow. He let go of her hand to brush the tear from the other side of her face.

"Guys like him are master manipulators, Isabelle. That's why everything happens so slowly. He crossed one little line, but it's okay because it was just one. And then he crossed another and another and another. All over a period of time, so it doesn't seem like much. It isn't until you look back that you realize that where you started is so far away." He brushed his lips against hers. "Please don't beat yourself up. He tricked you. And, when you realized it, you got out. That's all you can do."

He kissed her again, keeping his hands on her face even though he wanted to touch her all over.

"Thank you for telling me. Thank you for trusting me. You know that I will never hurt you like that, right?"

She nodded. "Yes, and no."

He frowned. "Yes, and no?"

Isabelle pushed at the furrow in his brows with one finger and smiled, her hazel eyes filled with humor. "I know you would never control me like Bram did. And I will never be afraid of you like I was him." She met his eyes. "But you have the ability of hurting my heart, Zane. I think that's why I left two years ago. I think that's why I got involved with Bram."

"What are you saying?"

"I knew I would never fall in love with Bram. I thought I could love him but not be in love with him. Does that make sense?"

He nodded.

"But you…I knew that you could take my heart, and I'd never get it back. It scared me."

"Oh, Isa." *Doesn't she know that it's the same for me with her?*

Zane kissed her again, but this time, he didn't stop himself from touching her. He thumbed her nipple and pinched it, tugging on it until she moaned in his mouth.

He trailed his hand down her stomach and in between her legs. She immediately opened herself for him, and he pushed his middle and ring fingers inside her.

"Damn, Isa, your pussy is so wet."

She was also swollen and hot. The spongy part inside her was at least twice as large as normal. He rubbed his fingers over the area, and she came on his hand, flooding him with her scent and arousal.

"Holy shit." He'd never seen anyone get off that fast. Not even himself when he had been a teenage boy.

She clutched at his shirt, almost blindly, trying to tear at it.

"Isa, Isa, hold on."

He got up on his knees and pulled his shirt over his head. Before he was even done, Isabelle was reaching for his jeans.

She seemed uncoordinated though. She couldn't get the button through the tab, and her eyes were feverish. He put his hand on hers to still it.

"It's okay. I'll get it. It's okay."

"Hurry, please."

Zane backed up until his feet hit the floor. He pushed his jeans and boxers down and kicked them off. He grabbed her legs and rotated her to face him. He clutched both her thighs in his palms and pulled her toward him when her scent exploded all over the room.

He took a step back from the force of her hormones surging.

Isabelle moaned, a combination of pain and arousal, and Zane watched as her wetness leaked down her pussy and over her the inside of her thighs. His own cock was hard as stone, and pre-cum leaked out of him and dripped down his shaft.

He whipped his head up toward the door as he heard someone yell, "*Holy shit,*" from the other room, and then there was the sound of glass breaking.

As if in slow motion, Zane looked back at Isabelle.

Her heat was here.

He stepped back between her legs and dropped his hands on either side of her face.

She blinked up at him, almost as if her eyes hurt even though the lights were off in the room.

"Your heat's here, Isa. I'm giving you one chance to turn back. Are you sure you want me to take you?"

She dropped her knees to the side. "I'm sure, Zane. Take me. Make me yours."

Chapter Twenty-Five

Isabelle gasped and fisted the comforter as Zane pushed his thickness inside her. She had never been so horny in her life. Not even when she'd gone through her previous heats.

Her body felt like it was a thousand degrees, her vagina felt engorged, and she couldn't stop her wetness from escaping her body.

She threaded her fingers through Zane's dark blond hair. "Oh God, please don't stop. Oh God, please don't stop." There was a burning ache inside her that could only be cured when he came.

"I wouldn't dream of it." He planted a kiss on her mouth. "And you can call me Zane."

Isabelle laughed at the age-old joke.

"Holy shit, Isa." His sea-green eyes were wide. "Just when I thought you couldn't get any tighter, you laugh."

She smiled up at him. "That is your goal though, right? To make others laugh?"

He dropped down onto his elbows. "But, now, my goal is to make you and only you laugh."

Her body buckled as a cramp squeezed her lower body. It was as if it were telling them to hurry up.

Zane brushed her hair off her face. "That hurts you, doesn't it?"

She took a deep breath and pushed it out through her lips. "Yeah, a little," she fibbed. She didn't want him to know how bad the pain was.

"Don't worry; I'll take care of you." He hooked his arm under her knee, bringing it almost to her ear. He thrust inside her, pushing deep and as far as he could go.

"Oh, yes." She clawed at his back. "I love feeling you inside me."

Zane kissed her, their kiss sloppy as he pounded in and out of her pussy. He pulled away and met her eyes. "I love being inside you."

At his words, her orgasm hit her hard and out of nowhere, just like the last time. She clamped her free leg around his back. "Please come," she begged. She knew that, if he didn't orgasm soon, the pain would be even greater.

Zane arched his back as he did exactly what she needed. His normally hot seed felt like a cooling balm flooding her pussy, telling her just how heated her body was.

She was aware of his barbs burrowing into the walls of her vagina as he continued to empty himself inside her.

He let go of her leg and collapsed on top of her, holding her close.

While her orgasm had been quick and fast, his was long and drawn out.

She held on to him, soothing him now, as she felt him swell, and another pump of semen was released into her.

Every time his cock throbbed and pumped, he would give a small moan, and she couldn't tell if he was enjoying what his body was doing to him or if he was now the one in pain.

And she couldn't believe he was still coming. He had already filled her, and his seed was now spilling out between them.

She suddenly had an idea, but she didn't know if it would work.

Isabelle pushed at him. "Zane."

"What?" he said breathlessly.

"I need you to pull out of me."

He raised his head. "Huh?"

"I need you to pull out of me. I don't think you're going to stop while you're still inside me."

He dropped his head and groaned as he swelled and emptied inside her again. When he had a second of peace, he picked his head back up.

"But my barbs. That'll increase your chance of getting pregnant. We never fully discussed if it was okay."

She rubbed his back and looked him right in the eye. "I'm telling you to pull out of me."

Zane hesitated for a few more seconds but then withdrew from her body. He did it quick, like pulling a bandage, as if he was afraid it would be distressing if he didn't.

His barbs grated against her inner walls, and she screamed as a painful orgasm swept over her body. Her pelvis clenched, but deep inside, it felt as if something was opening. Her cervix. It was expanding to try to take in Zane's seed.

He fell down on the bed next to her. "I'm so sorry."

She grabbed on to his bicep. "It's okay." Her orgasm had been strong, but it was already fading. "I'm okay."

He toppled back on the bed. "We're never doing that again."

Isabelle laughed and touched his still-hard penis with her finger. "I think Zane Junior begs to differ."

She circled his head, disappointed she'd missed seeing his barbs, and he flinched.

"Yeah, well, he doesn't know what's good for him." He swung his head toward her. "Or you. You scared me at the end there."

Isabelle pulled on his arm to get him to roll toward her. "Come here. I want to show you something."

Despite his proclamation about never doing that again, his eyes lit up with curiosity.

She brought his hand down between her legs and pushed his fingers inside her. "Ah," she said and closed her eyes when they touched her tender flesh. She opened her eyes and looked at him. "Do you feel that?"

He shook his head. "I don't know what I'm supposed to be feeling. Except for how silky your pussy is."

"Okay, how about what you don't feel?"

He gasped slightly. "My cum. You should be bathing in it, for how much I came inside you."

She wrinkled her nose. "Kind of gross, but I get your point." She pulled his hand away from between her thighs and put it low on her pelvis.

"It's inside me now. I took it into my body. Into my uterus. And, hopefully, one of your little guys will find its way to my egg." She smiled. "In theory anyway. Who knows if I will even ovulate? Or if your guys can find what they're supposed to?"

Zane sat up and pointed a finger at her. "Hey now. My guys are not little, and they sure as shit are going to find their way to your egg. Your *little* egg won't know what hit her. She'll be bombarded by so much sperm."

His blond hair was sticking up all over the place from her hands, and it was hard to take him seriously.

She raised her brow. "You do know that's not how it works, right? One egg. One sperm."

He scowled. "I know that." His frown lessened. "But I didn't realize the other stuff," he said, pointing to her crotch. "You said you'd never done this before. How did you know?"

"I'm a teacher. I make it my business to know things. I do have at least one shifter student every year, and I let them know that I'm available to answer any of their questions since there's no shifter anatomy or shifter sex education in school."

He cupped the back of her head and kissed her. He touched his forehead to hers. "You're amazing."

She blushed. "I don't know about that."

Zane grinned at her. "Does this mean we can play strict teacher and naughty student?" He turned his back to her and pushed his butt out. "Ms. Talon, I've been a bad boy. I cheated on my paper, and I gave Saxon a swirly. I think I need a spanking."

Isabelle rolled her eyes, but it was impossible not to laugh. "Oh my God, you're incorrigible."

He looked over his shoulder and wiggled his eyebrows. "So, how many spanks does that earn me?"

She smacked his butt with a little more force than necessary. "One."

"Ow." He rubbed his ass cheek.

"You asked for it." She laughed.

Zane turned around and pinned her arms over her head. "You're going to get it now, Ms. Talon. You might be my teacher, but I'm bigger and meaner."

That was the second time he'd called her Ms. Talon instead of Ms. Rand. Both times, she felt a warmth in her belly.

She pretended to try to buck him off her. "I'm so scared. What are you going to do to me?"

"I'm going to fuck you until you can't see straight."

Too late. Her future was already a blur where Zane was concerned.

"I can't wait."

Her insides squeezed as another cramp took hold of her. She tried not to wince for Zane's sake and forced out a chuckle.

"I guess my body can't wait either."

He let go of her arms. "Don't worry, Ms. Talon; I'll take good care of you. You are my favorite teacher after all."

And take care of her he did.

Chapter Twenty-Six

Quentin woke with a jolt and an unawareness of where he was. It took him a second or two to realize he'd fallen asleep in Hunter's room.

The vampire was currently lying on top of him, the leg without a cast slung over one of his own.

This revelation did not help his morning wood, but he didn't dare wake Hunter for any fun and games.

One, Quentin didn't know how Hunter would feel about what they'd done the night before after a long, hard sleep. And two, if Hunter had slept for several hours at night—a time when he was normally awake—then he needed his rest.

Quentin wished he could stay and enjoy being close like this with Hunter, but he probably had an hour at most before the house came alive. It was a damn shame, too, because he probably wasn't going to end up back in Hunter's bed anytime soon.

Before Quentin rolled Hunter off him though, he ran his fingers through the vampire's dirty-blond hair a few times and kissed him on the forehead. He wished he could figure out what was so special about Hunter, so he could fix it in his mind. Being infatuated with someone you couldn't have sucked.

Quentin slowly slid from Hunter's bed, put on his jeans, and picked up his dirty T-shirt. He lightly padded to the door, giving Hunter one last look, and slipped out the door.

Quentin had thought that maybe his fascination with Hunter was because he couldn't have him. But Quentin wasn't like that. He'd been interested in other males in the past who were taken, weren't interested in him in return, or weren't ready to come out of the closet. Quentin had moved on with ease.

But something about Hunter had stuck with him. And he hated it.

When Quentin reached his room, he threw his dirty tee in his hamper and grabbed clean clothes.

He was supposed to work last night, but he had called in because of Hunter's injury. Rather than taking vacation time, he had told his captain that he would work the day shift. He still had a couple of hours before he had to leave the house, but he might as well get ready. He wasn't going to go back to sleep now.

Quentin showered, got dressed, and went downstairs to find some breakfast. He was a little surprised to find Damien already up and in the kitchen.

"Morning," Quentin said.

"Hey." Damien nodded toward the counter from his seat at the table. "I made coffee already."

"Thanks." Quentin poured himself a cup and raided the fridge for something to eat. He was starved, and it occurred to him that he hadn't eaten much in the last twenty-four hours. "What was for dinner last night?"

"Pot roast."

"Who cooked?"

They took turns cooking dinner, but not everyone had the best kitchen skills.

"Payton's mom."

Quentin's mouth watered at those two words. Mrs. Llewelyn was one hell of a cook, and she enjoyed doing it. Everyone loved when she came over to make dinner for her only daughter and the wolves as well. The cat-shifters were one lucky bunch.

Quentin began pulling out all the leftovers from last night and loaded up his plate with food before sticking it in the microwave. "I wish she were looking for a job."

Damien pulled a second chair closer to him and put his bare feet up on it. "I would hire her in a heartbeat."

"Maybe we should look into actually hiring someone to come and cook for us. He or she could have the bedroom downstairs, so he or she would have their own space."

"I've been seriously thinking about it. Especially at a time like this when we're down shifters. I can eat takeout for only so many days."

"Agreed."

Damien sighed. "But I also don't want to put anyone in danger. It's a tough call."

His alpha did have a point, but Quentin hoped Damien wouldn't dismiss the idea completely.

The microwave beeped, so Quentin grabbed his food and silverware and took it to the table.

"You work today, right?"

"Yes. I hope that's okay. I had to trade because of last night."

Damien shrugged. "We'll make do."

Quentin swallowed his bite of food. "First thing, I'll see if I can get an update on Bram."

Damien nodded. "Good, good. Let's hope the asshole stays where he is for now. I still haven't figured out how to deal with him. Everyone wants a piece of him."

Quentin thought he should slit the fucker's throat for hitting Hunter with his car. He grunted in response because Damien didn't want to hear his idea.

Damien traced the outside rim of his coffee cup. "How is Hunter doing?"

"Pretty good. Healing well. He was able to come home last night after having surgery. I don't think they would have let him if they'd had any concerns."

Damien nodded, still looking at his coffee. "I noticed you didn't sleep in your room last night."

How did—

Damn it, he'd left his door open last night. All anyone had had to do was walk by and see it was empty.

Quentin set his fork down and sat back in his seat.

Damien looked up, meeting his eyes. "Don't fret; I'm the only one who knows."

Quentin blew out a breath. That was a relief.

"How involved are you? Is it going to get in the way of your work?"

Quentin laughed.

"Complicated, huh?"

"Very." Quentin picked up his fork again. "We're not really involved. Hunter has just realized he has feelings for…other guys. He doesn't think the other vampires will understand, and he's worried about losing his position as a Guardian." He shoved a big bite of food in his mouth.

"So, he wants to date in secret?"

Quentin shook his head and swallowed again. "He's so scared that he doesn't even want to do that, which is fine by me. I've dated a couple of guys in the closet, and it sucks. And, after hiding it from your father for years, I'm not going back."

"I don't blame you."

When Damien had first gotten involved with his mate, the wolves and cats had still been at odds with each other. If anyone knew how Quentin felt about hiding a relationship, it would be Damien even if the situations were quite different.

"So, last night…" Damien asked.

Quentin chuckled. "A fluke, I suspect. He was injured. I was concerned about him."

Damien nodded in understanding.

"You won't say anything to anyone about Hunter, will you?"

"No. It's his secret. And, as long as he does good work and no one gets injured or killed, then it's his personal business."

"Thank you."

And thank the universe for giving them Damien as their alpha. His father, Dwyer, had been a dictator. Damien always asked their input on things, and while he made the ultimate decisions, he trusted his sentinels to think for themselves.

"Since no one knows, if you ever want to talk, I'm here." He took a drink of his coffee. "And my mate gives pretty good advice, too, if you ever want a woman's perspective."

"But can she keep a secret?"

A knowing smile came over Damien's face. "Oh, yeah."

Quentin laughed awkwardly. He did not want to know what Damien was thinking. "Good to know."

Damien shook his head, as if to clear his thoughts. "Just know the offer stands."

"Thank you."

Quentin finished his plate and resisted going back for seconds. He might need to stop and pick something up on the way. His shifter appetite was not satisfied.

He rinsed his plate, put his dishes in the dishwasher, and looked at the time. "I might as well go to work." It was still early, but he didn't have anything else to do.

"Avoiding the morning after?"

Quentin laughed. "I didn't even think of that. But it might be better this way. I don't feel embarrassed, but Hunter might." He cleared his throat. "Will…will you check on him every once in a while? And try to get him to move around? I know you have enough to do, but I'd appreciate it."

Sympathy filled Damien's eyes. "Don't worry about Hunter; we'll take care of him."

"Thank you. And I'll fill you in on what I find when I get to work."

Damien nodded his appreciation, and Quentin took off for work. He took one last look at Hunter's bedroom window. He hoped the vampire wasn't mad about last night because Quentin didn't regret a single second.

Chapter Twenty-Seven

Tegan trudged out of bed and into the kitchen. She was hot and uncomfortable and cranky. Her heat would be upon her very soon, and she didn't know what she was going to do about it. If only she could run away from her own body.

No one was in the living room this morning, which was good because she didn't feel like saying hello. She walked into the kitchen to get a glass of water and turned to lean against the counter while she sipped from her cup.

She was wondering where everyone was when Zane walked into the room in only a pair of boxers with an exhausted expression on his face.

"Wow. You look like you've been through hell."

He grunted and went to the fridge. "I need food. I need protein."

"I only grabbed a few things at the store last night for breakfast. You're probably going to have to order room service." She remembered something. She walked over to the fridge next to Zane and looked inside. "We should have some leftovers from last night."

Zane slowly rotated his head and looked at her. "I need you to go over there. I don't have the energy to run away from you."

Tegan straightened. "What did I do?"

"You're giving me a fucking boner, and it's creeping me out."

"*Ew*," she said and backed away.

"My sentiments exactly. I can fucking smell you, and even though my dick is about to fall off, it's still getting hard."

"Time out. TMI." She did not want to think about Zane getting hard, especially because of her.

He shrugged and grabbed last night's dinner from the fridge. "I'm just telling you the way it is. I don't like it any more than you. It's your hormones. I can't help it."

Knowing he would need more room to make his food, she backed out of the kitchen. She stood, so she could still see him without encroaching on his space.

"Is Isabelle still sleeping?"

"Yes. She needs the rest."

"I bet you do, too."

"I do, but my stupid stomach woke me up. I'm hoping to eat something and then go back to bed. It's going to be a long day."

"Are you sorry about what you're doing for Isabelle?"

Zane looked up from the food he was preparing like she was crazy. "No way. I feel…special, honored. It's just a lot of work. I'm not quite sick of sex, but I'm getting there, and that's saying something." He wrinkled his nose. "It's just kind of weird."

"Hmm."

Movement caught her eye, and she saw Chase and a couple of guys she'd never seen before come into view through the sliding glass door. The two men had a security logo on their shirts. Chase must be showing them around. But Reid wasn't there.

A cold flash went through her body. What if he'd left?

But then the three of them turned and looked behind them, and a second later, Reid came into view. The cold that had invaded her bones a moment ago was replaced with warmth.

She noticed he was wearing one of the T-shirts she'd bought him, and it made her smile.

He lifted his arms—it looked like he was telling a story—and his shirt went with him. His jeans were riding low on his hips. So low, she could see his V and the very top of his pubic hair. No one else seemed to notice. They were all laughing at what Reid had said.

But she couldn't stop staring. She wanted to tackle him to the ground, strip him naked, and push him inside her.

"Are you going to let Reid take you during your heat?"

She looked over at Zane. "I don't know what's going to happen," she honestly told him. "I don't even know if he wants to."

After all, he'd done the heat thing before with someone else. That surprise revelation had sure made her green-eyed monster make its presence known.

"He is your husband," Zane pointed out.

"Yeah, but not my mate."

Reid's wedding ring glinted as it caught a ray of light. It wasn't the same as seeing her mark on his neck, but it still made her feel pride to see her ring on his finger.

She was in over her head. "Everything is moving so fast."

Zane lifted his brow. "Maybe that's what you need."

Maybe, but she wasn't sure.

A hot flash, so strong that it caused her to suck in a breath, swept through her. A bead of sweat rolled down the side of her face, and she wiped more off her upper lip.

"I'm going back to bed," she told Zane.

She didn't want to be where everyone could see her when her heat hit.

She just made it into the bedroom and shut the door when her insides squeezed, and she almost dropped to the floor.

"Oh, fuck."

She crawled over to the bed and climbed on top. She scanned both nightstands, looking for the medicine she'd gone out to buy last night when she realized what was going to happen.

Both tables were empty. She hadn't even been sure that she would take them, but now that she couldn't find them, she panicked.

She flopped back on the bed as another cramp racked her body. She needed to figure out what she was going to do before the pain became too much.

The bedroom door opened, and Reid walked in, determination on his face.

"You should have told me," he said.

"I-I..." she stuttered. She really didn't know what to say. She didn't know why she hadn't told him about her heat. She didn't even know what to think.

Reid reached behind him and pulled off his shirt. Then, his jeans and underwear went next. His monster cock bounced out, hitting his stomach, and wetness coated her thighs.

Reid climbed onto the bed and nudged her legs apart. He gripped the bottom of her T-shirt nightgown and pulled it over her head.

"God, you smell incredible. It's like nothing I've ever smelled before."

"Not even when you had sex with another female in heat?"

Reid raised a brow, and Tegan snapped her mouth shut.

Jeez, I sound jealous.

"How many times do I have to tell you that no one compares to you?"

She shrugged. "A lot?" she suggested.

Reid picked up one of her legs and placed it over his hip. "I'm going to fuck you now, Tegan. I'm going to mark you. I'm going to make you mine. I will be the last one to ever touch you like this again. And I'm going to put myself deep inside you where I'm going to release my seed, and I'm going to fill you with my young."

Holy shit. The dirty talk coming out of Reid's mouth was so hot.

"I'm not going to make you do anything. I will leave you alone. I will go and get your meds and take care of you the best I can. If that's what you want."

She swallowed. "And what if I want you to have sex with me but not mate with me?" she asked more out of curiosity than anything.

Reid shook his head. "I'm sorry. I can't do that. I can't be with you like this, during your *mating* heat, and not be your mate. I'm sorry."

A cramp seized her body, and they both waited for it to pass.

"How do you know that I'll have your baby? You know how hard it is for our kind to get pregnant."

He smiled. "Because your body has been waiting for me." He closed his eyes and inhaled. "And you're ovulating, Angel." He looked at her again. "I want you to know that it's killing me to sit here and not have sex with you. But I need you to know how important this is to me."

Tegan reached out and grabbed Reid's cock. "What about now?"

Reid groaned and shook his head. "Nope. I want all of you or none at all."

"You're so selfish," she teased as she stroked him from base to tip.

"Damn right I am." He looked her in the eyes. "When it comes to you, Tegan, I want everything."

It was irrational to even be considering this. She'd known Reid for years, but she hadn't even dated him, and he wanted her to be his mate.

"What if things don't work out?" she whispered.

"That's the least of my worries because I know we're meant to be together."

"You're crazy," she said.

"I believe I said the same thing to you at the wedding chapel."

She smiled up at him and pulled her other leg up to her chest. "Fuck me, Reid. Make me yours."

He growled. "God, I thought you would never ask."

He grabbed hold of his shaft and swiped it through her wetness a couple of times, and then he slowly sank inside her. His self-control was making her go insane. She wanted him to lose control and fuck her.

When he bottomed out, he tilted his head to the side. "Mark me, Tegan."

"Me first?"

"Yes."

"Why?"

"Because, when I mark you, there will be no holding back."

Tegan pulled Reid down and sank her canine teeth into his neck as she clenched her internal muscles around him.

He was hers now. Reid was hers.

And she was never giving him back.

Chapter Twenty-Eight

"**B**ram Varg?"

Bram jumped up from the filthy bench in the jail. "Yes?"

"You made bail."

About fucking time.

He'd called Stan and Larry twenty-four hours ago. He'd needed to get out of there before anyone found him. After he'd been thrown in jail for bullshit charges, he'd known that hitting the vampire was a mistake. If he was the reason his father got into a war with the Minnesota vampires, he'd never be able to go home to Illinois. Of course, if the vampires killed him, he'd have nothing to worry about.

The officer opened the cell door and took him through his paperwork to get him out of there. They were almost finished, and he was basically free to go when he remembered his vehicle.

"How do I get my car?"

The man looked at something on the computer. "It's been impounded."

"What the hell?"

The officer gave Bram a look.

Bram cleared his throat. "Does it say why?"

"Nope."

The man was clearly lying. Bram wanted to reach across the desk and wrap his hands around the officer's neck, but he wasn't that stupid or impulsive.

"Fine. Can you at least give me the information on where I can pick it up?"

The officer handed him a card. "Here you go."

Bram picked up the card, his wallet, and the keys, and then he exited out to the waiting room.

Larry and Stan stood as soon as they saw Bram.

"What the fuck took you two so long to get here?"

"We had to drive from Mankato," Larry said.

Do these two idiots think I'm stupid?

"It doesn't take you twenty-four hours to make a two-hour drive."

They both started stammering.

"Just shut up and get me out of here. I need a shower."

Bram needed to wash the filth of jail off of him and track down Isabelle. The fucking cunt was going to pay for everything he'd been through the last few days.

Sabrina—not her real name, of course—walked into the brightly lit hotel and headed straight for the suite number she'd been given.

She'd been hired to spend the next twelve hours with her clients. She was making a killing today, but she never knew if it was worth it until her shift was over.

She had no idea what would be waiting for her on the other side of the door. She knew she had two clients, which meant she was going to be one tired woman in twelve hours, but she only hoped that, if they could afford a place like this hotel, they were clean.

After many years in the escort business, she'd stopped caring if her clients were young or old, good-looking or ugly, sweet or assholes. All she cared about was if they showered or not.

She enjoyed sex and didn't have to fake it a lot in her profession, but she still struggled with it when her clients smelled. It was amazing how many professional businessmen didn't wash themselves on a regular basis, thinking a thick layer of cologne would make up for it.

Sabrina knocked on the door and heard movement on the other side. The door swung open, and a very good-looking man around her age stood on the other side. His hair was dark blond, and his eyes were a beautiful sea-green. He only wore a pair of boxers, which outlined an impressive package, and his chest and arms were very well-toned.

His hair was messy, and his eyes had bags under them, but she just might enjoy herself today.

When he'd opened the door, he'd looked excited, but upon seeing her, his face fell.

"Damn it, I thought you were room service. I need to eat."

She had to laugh at that. Most men were happy to see her. They weren't usually disappointed that she wasn't food.

From her position at the door, she could see a living room straight ahead with a sliding glass door to an area in the back. Right in front of her was a hallway that went right and left, and from the left, she heard footsteps before a woman appeared, wearing an oversize T-shirt.

She was blonde, too. Not as good-looking as the man in front of her, a little plainer, but she looked clean, so Sabrina was fine with that. She'd thought her two clients were men, but she must have misheard, or the receptionist had.

Whatever. It didn't make any difference to her as long as she got compensated. She was still paying off her student loan debt for a career that paid pennies compared to being an escort.

The woman stepped in front of the man and wrapped herself around him. She stood up on her tiptoes and sucked on the man's neck. When the woman pulled away, that was when Sabrina noticed the bite mark there.

Shit. She hadn't been told the clients were into biting.

"Who's this?" the woman asked, looking at Sabrina over her shoulder. The woman had a clear stay-away-he's-mine look on her face.

The man draped his arm around the woman and said, "Beats the shit out of me. I thought she was my room service."

"Mmm…food. Did you order some for me?" the woman asked.

The man kissed her. "Of course. You need your strength more than I do."

"Excuse me?" Sabrina said. She was very confused. "I was told to come to this hotel room. I was told I had two clients to meet. But you two seem to have no idea why I'm here."

There was a knock on the open door beside her as room service arrived. The man who had answered the door practically pushed Sabrina out of the way to get to his food. The attendant set the plate on the entry room table and lifted the lid, and then he was tipped and sent on his way.

It was all bacon and sausage.

The woman picked up a fork to feed herself, but the man started shoving the sausage in his mouth with his hands.

Another man's voice came from the right side of the hall. "Did I hear someone knock on the door?" He came into her line of view, and his shoulders dropped. "Damn. It's just your food." He grabbed his crotch. "I am dying here."

The female looked up. "Sorry."

What is she sorry about? Isn't she with the first guy?

About the same age as the first man, the second guy had tan skin, dark hair, and the most unusual orangish-yellow eyes. He, too, was shirtless but had on shorts at least. His muscles were bigger than Guy One.

He spotted her in the doorway. "Hey. There you are." He grinned. "We've been waiting for you."

Finally.

She held out her hand. "I'm Sabrina."

Guy Two took her hand and pulled her into the room. "Hey, Sabrina. I'm Chase."

He reached behind her and closed the door. She noticed he smelled wonderful.

He stepped back. "You like?"

"I'm sorry. Like what?"

"How I smell." He raised his hand and looked up. "It's all the hormones in the air." He looked back at Sabrina and grinned. "They make you want to have sex with me."

She'd heard a lot of lines in her day, which was ridiculous because she was a sure thing. If they paid, they got laid. Yet her clients hit on her all the time.

But he was right. She was actually getting turned on from just being close to this guy. That stuff didn't happen anymore.

Chase grabbed her hand when there was a bang to her left.

She and Chase looked over. The lid of the plate had hit the ground. The woman jerked out an arm and clutched Guy One's shoulder. She made a noise, as if she was in pain.

"Shit, Isa. You need me again?" Guy One asked.

She nodded.

He threw down the piece of meat he'd been eating and picked the woman up. She wrapped her arms around his neck as he started walking away from them toward what looked like a bedroom from Sabrina's view.

She noticed he had scratch marks across his back. *Damn.* Those two must like it a little rough.

The woman kissed the man as he used one hand to push up her shirt and pull down the front of his boxers. Sabrina was completely surprised and turned on as she watched the man thrust inside the woman.

The couple hadn't hired her, but they had no reservations about having sex in front of a stranger. For a second anyway.

They walked through the door, and the man kicked it closed with his foot.

"Don't worry, honey; Ranulf and I will take care of you."

"Huh?"

Chase rubbed his nose behind her ear. "You smell good, too." He stepped away and pulled her with him to the last door on the right.

He pushed it open, and Sabrina saw another man coming out of what had to be a bathroom. This guy had light-brown hair, bluish-green eyes, and only a towel covering his muscular body.

"This is Ranulf. Ranulf, this is Sabrina."

"Thank God," Ranulf said as he threw the towel in the bathroom behind himself.

She turned to look at Chase. He pushed his shorts off and kicked them in the corner.

"Where did you guys come from?"

All three men were muscular and hung.

Chase pulled her into his arms and began to kiss her neck while unbuttoning her shirt. "It's part of our job."

Ranulf came up behind her and kissed the other side of her neck.

"It's part of your job to be hung like a horse?"

Both men laughed, and Chase said, "No, I was referring to our physique." He pushed her shirt off, and Ranulf unhooked her bra. Both fell to the floor. "Beautiful," he said and cupped her breasts.

"Are you guys in the military?" How she was having a conversation she didn't know because all their touching felt incredible. But she was so curious about them.

A sound of ecstasy came from behind the wall.

"Don't worry," Ranulf said. "That's Reid and Tegan."

There are more of them?

Ranulf pushed off her skirt and her thong. "Keep the high heels on," he said in a low voice.

Chase moved his mouth up to hers and pushed his tongue past her lips. She normally didn't kiss her clients, but he knew what he was doing with his mouth, and she didn't have the willpower to stop him.

It felt too good.

She grabbed on to him as Ranulf pulled her ass back and pushed his cock inside her.

A gasp escaped her throat, both men making her feel insane with pleasure.

Maybe the next twelve hours would be worth it after all.

Chapter Twenty-Nine

Quentin's cell rang. "Hello?"

"Hey, Rawling. I need you to come back to headquarters," his captain said.

Quentin pulled the phone away and looked at it as if it would show his captain's face. He put it back to his ear. "Okay. What's this about, sir?"

"I'll tell you when you get here."

That didn't sound promising.

"Okay, I'll be there in about ten, give or take a few minutes."

"Sounds good. Oh, and, Rawling? That guy you put in jail yesterday? A Bram Varg?"

"Yeah."

"Peterson said you were keeping track of him?"

"I am," Quentin answered hesitantly but honestly. He doubted this was why his boss was pulling him back to the station since he'd said he'd tell Quentin when he got there. But the captain didn't like it when they took too much of an interest in the criminals they'd arrested.

"Yeah, well, it looks like he made bail this morning."

Fuck. Fuck, fuck, fuck.

Quentin had to bite his lip from cursing out loud. There was no way he'd be able to explain who and what Bram was to him.

He cleared his throat. "Thank you, sir."

"You're not going to go out and hurt him, are you?" His captain phrased it as a question, but Quentin knew he was partly serious.

Quentin laughed. *I won't.* But he couldn't promise no one else wouldn't. "No, sir."

"Good to hear. I'll see you in ten."

As soon as his captain hung up, Quentin called up his other boss.

"Quentin, what's up?"

"I just found out that Bram got out on bail."

"Shit."

"That's pretty much what I said."

"I'll get Lachlan to look into him. Hopefully, the asshole used credit cards or something, so we can find him. I didn't want to go after him with two men down—four if you count Zane and Hunter. And I want to keep the vampires out of it. I understand their need for justice and vengeance, but if Bram's father finds out that he was killed by vampires rather than punished by shifter law, we could end up with a war on our hands."

"Damn. I didn't even think of that. I guess that's why you're the alpha."

Damien laughed, but he didn't sound like he thought the situation was funny. "I knew there was going to be politics involved, but I had no idea the extent."

"Good luck, man. If you need me to do anything, let me know."

"I always do, Quentin."

A surge of pride went through him at his alpha's words.

"Are you going to tell the vampires?" he asked.

"Yes, because, if the situation were reversed, I'd want to know."

"You're a good man."

"You might have to tell the vampires that."

"Say, my captain called me back to the station. I don't know what's up because he won't say until I get there, but I don't have a good feeling. I'll let you know if something has come up."

"I'll have my phone on. I'm going to go find Lachlan. We'll talk later."

"Later."

By the time Quentin hung up with Damien, he only had a few minutes left before he got to the station. He went straight to the captain's office and knocked on the door.

"Enter."

Quentin pushed open the door and was shocked to see his parents sitting on the captain's couch.

The captain stood up. "I'll be right outside."

Quentin turned to his parents. "What's going on?"

His mother's brown eyes filled with tears, and she dropped her head into her dark hands. His father put his arm around his mother, his own green eyes full of sadness. His father's light skin was paler than normal, and his mother's shoulders shook as she sobbed.

Quentin dropped his knees to the floor. "Mama, what's wrong?"

His father looked at him, and it hit him.

"Larissa," Quentin said, answering his own question.

His mother raised her head. "Your sister is in the ICU. She overdosed. They found her in an alley with a needle in her arm while-while-while—" She hiccuped from her crying and looked at her husband.

"Two men were having sex with her, son," his dad finished.

Quentin jumped up. "*What the hell?*" He put a fist in front of his mouth, afraid he was going to throw up. The thought of his sister being violated while she was dying made the breakfast he'd eaten that morning feel like a rock in his stomach. "Oh, Larissa." He swung around. "When did you find out?"

"This morning," her father said. "Your mother tried calling her phone. They didn't even know who she was. They had her listed under Jane Doe."

"Are you sure it's her?" Quentin asked.

Drug addicts lost stuff when they were high or traded things to get their next fix.

"We went there this morning," his mom said. "We went there first before we came to you."

"I need to see her." It killed Quentin that his sister struggled with drugs. "I don't understand. She was doing so well. How many months had she been sober this time?"

His parents stood.

"Two," his mother said. "I was worried when I hadn't talked to her for a few days. I had no idea it would be this-this-this bad." She started crying again.

Quentin opened the door and looked down the hall for his captain.

When the captain saw him, he came back to his office. "Take as long as you need, Quentin."

Quentin nodded. "Thank you." He turned to his parents. "Let me get changed. I'll be right back."

When he met up with his parents again, they were standing by the elevator, and they had obviously been talking.

Quentin hit the down button on the wall. "What's going on?"

His parents both turned to him.

"We've been discussing some things. We found a treatment facility."

The elevator door opened, and they stepped inside.

"She's gone to a treatment facility before," Quentin pointed out. Several in fact.

"This one is in Switzerland," his father said. "It has a very high success rate, especially with Americans."

Quentin was still skeptical, but it was better than watching his sister die. "How much does it cost?" he asked.

"No more than the facilities here."

Quentin sighed. His parents had spent so much money, trying to help his sister get sober. It wasn't fair. "That's something at least."

His parents exchanged looks.

"Is this when you tell me there is a *but*?"

His father nodded. "A family member has to go and stay with her."

"What for?"

"With foreign patients, they want someone to participate in therapy and work on what life will be like when they're done. Also, they want someone there in case of emergencies."

"That seems kind of weird."

"They have a high success rate, so they must be doing something right."

Quentin cursed. "How are you going to manage that?"

His parents owned a franchise of a very successful fast food restaurant chain. They needed to be here to run the business. It was too much for one person.

His mother shrugged. "We'll manage somehow."

He wasn't sure if that was true.

Chapter Thirty

Zane flipped through the channels on the television. Isabelle was asleep on top of him as the two of them lay on the couch. Night had fallen, and Zane had needed a change of scenery.

It was a shame they were in Vegas and couldn't experience any of the things that tourists got to do. But having sex with his mate over and over was nothing to scoff at.

He turned his head and kissed her, inhaling at the same time. He loved how much she smelled like him. Mates always smelled a little like each other, but after a female's heat, it was obvious who she belonged to. Or who she'd been with if she wasn't in a relationship. It was as if the female's pores had opened up and sucked the male's scent into them.

Biology was a crazy thing, but he liked it. He lifted his free arm that held the remote and sniffed. He smelled like Isabelle, too, but not as much as she smelled like him. So, biology was a little sexist.

The good thing was, if—*when*—that fucker Bram showed up, there would be no mistaking that Isabelle was Zane's. She wore his ring on her finger, his mark on her neck, and his scent on her body.

That was enough to tell any male to stay away. Unfortunately, from the way Isabelle had described him, it would probably only infuriate Bram into doing something drastic.

A crash sounded as a bedroom door opened and slammed against the wall. The woman who'd knocked on the door that morning appeared in the front hallway. She looked like she'd gotten run over by a truck. Her skirt was wrinkled, her blouse's buttons didn't line up, and her hair was a mess.

He realized now that she was probably from an escort service. At least someone was enjoying something Vegas had to offer.

"Are you okay?" he asked her.

She stopped to lean against the wall. "I have no idea."

"Can I help you with anything?" He felt bad for the way he'd practically ignored her that morning. He'd been so hungry that all he was able to think about was food.

She looked at Isabelle sleeping and shook her head. "Don't get up. But, if you had an ice pack, I'd take it."

He pointed toward the kitchen behind him. "You can check, but I doubt it." He frowned. "Are you hurt?"

She walked past him, saying, "Just my pussy. I didn't think those two would ever stop fucking me."

The door to the freezer opened and closed, and then she came back. "Any luck?" he asked.

She shook her head. "I'll find something."

"Are you okay to drive? You look…" He couldn't say *like hell*.

"Like crap? I know. I'll be fine. I'm going to go home, take a long bath, and crash." She looked toward Chase and Ranulf's bedroom. "They're both sleeping. Will you tell them my time was up and that I left?"

"Sure will. Sorry if they treated you badly," he added as she walked to the door. He felt a little like he was responsible since it was his mate's heat that had caused everyone's hormones to multiply.

The woman turned and smiled at Zane. "Oh, they didn't treat me badly at all. That was some of the best sex I've had in a long time. I would even do those two for free." She winked, opened the door, and was gone.

Zane chuckled at her last comment. He thought about telling the two wolves what she'd said but decided their egos were big enough already. Besides, by the screams and moans he'd heard coming from the room earlier, they probably already knew.

Isabelle stirred in his arms and looked up at him with sleepy eyes.

"How long have I been sleeping?"

Zane looked at the time. "About an hour."

She laid her head back down. "No wonder I'm still tired."

"How are you feeling? Is it time to go back in the bedroom?"

"I'm okay for right now. It's weird. I can tell another wave is coming, but I don't know how to explain it. Either way, it's not here yet. I just want to lie here and relax."

He rubbed her back. "Sounds great to me."

"Was it my imagination, or were you talking to someone?" Isabelle asked, changing the subject.

"Do you remember the woman at the door this morning?"

She didn't answer.

"When our food came?"

"Oh, yeah."

Zane grinned. His mate had been thinking about food, too, at that time. Didn't she realize how perfect they were together?

"She was here for Ranulf and Chase. They hired her. She just left."

Isabelle laughed. "They actually hired a prostitute?"

"Kind of smart, if you ask me. They don't have to go searching for a one-night stand. And she's a professional. She's probably seen some weird shit we can't even dream up. Way stranger than a hotel suite full of shifters having sex."

Isabelle looked at him. "You're so right."

"Say that again. But wait until I get my phone. Just in case this is the only time you ever say it."

She rolled her eyes and laid her head down again. "How much longer do you think we'll be here?"

"I have no idea. But at least until your and Tegan's heat ends. Why do you ask?"

She shrugged. "I just feel like it's putting off the inevitable. I'm going to have to confront Bram sooner or later, and while I don't want to, wouldn't it be better to get it over with?"

Zane squeezed her, letting her know he was there for her. "I totally understand where you're coming from. And who knows? Maybe our alphas will ask us to come back soon. But I don't want you anywhere near him while you're still in heat. If something happened and he tried…"

"To have sex with me?"

"If he tried to *rape* you. I don't know if I could handle that, Isabelle. I don't think you should have to either."

She shuddered. "I don't want to even think about it. And if he got me pregnant."

She shuddered again, and Zane growled.

"Don't even talk about a hypothetical baby of his inside you." His voice came out stern, a little mean. He took a deep breath. "I'm sorry. I didn't mean to sound like a dick. Just…I can't." He took another breath. "Nobody—and I mean, *nobody*—is putting a baby in you but me."

"Okay," she said.

"Are you laughing?"

"No," she denied, but Zane could hear it in her voice.

"You think this is funny?" he asked, surprised.

She met his eyes. "Not at all. I know it's serious. But I can't help but smile at your alpha attitude. All you need to do is pound your chest and throw me over your shoulder."

He raised a brow. "Okay then. How would you feel if I had sex with another female and got her pregnant?"

Isabelle's eyes darkened, and she scooted up his body to get in his face. "I would rip her face off. And, if you ever touch another woman the way you touch me, I will go full wolf on her ass. Not to mention, what I'd do to you."

Zane tried really hard not to, but a grin burst from his face. "Hot damn, Isa. You're fucking hot when you get all possessive."

She narrowed her eyes at him.

He held up his hand with the remote. "Hey, I'm not going to do anything. I was just trying to prove a point."

She looked at him out of the corner of her eye. "Okay. As long as you're sure."

"I'm sure."

She moved back to her original spot. "And I see your point."

He wished he could tell her that he'd been sure about her for two years, but he wasn't certain if she was ready to hear that. Things were going well between them, but he was worried it was because of the situation they were in. He couldn't deny that he liked her possessive, jealous attitude toward him, but what was going to happen when Bram was no longer a threat and she was no longer in heat? It could be the hormones talking. They were kind of in their own little world here, in Vegas. He wondered if she would still feel the same once reality set back in.

He supposed only time would tell. And he was going to try not to worry about it right now. Instead, he was going to enjoy his time with Isabelle, his mate.

Zane hugged Isabelle close and kissed her on the head.

If things didn't work out between them, at least he would be able to say, *We'll always have Vegas.*

Chapter Thirty-One

"Oh God, right there. Please, Reid, don't stop."

Tegan was on the bed with Reid behind her as they lay on their sides. He had her top leg under his arm and was slowly thrusting in and out of her.

She noticed that he really liked to take his time. He was methodical in his lovemaking, wringing every ounce of pleasure from her body.

She wrapped an arm behind her, around his neck. "Reid, please, I need you to come." Her insides burned. She needed his seed to ease the pain.

This was the first time she'd gone through heat without any medication, and everything was amped up to a ten. She couldn't believe how much more she felt things when she didn't try to mask her symptoms.

Reid put his mouth against her ear. "Only after you do, Angel. I want to feel you squeeze me tight as I plant my seed inside you."

Tegan moaned. She had to hand it to Reid. He was the best dirty-talker she'd ever been with. She could orgasm just from some of the things he said to her.

He slipped a hand between her legs and rubbed her clit.

"Oh God. I can't...I can't...I can't handle it. It's too much."

Reid shoved his cock inside her, right against her cervix, and she exploded. As she came, so did Reid. She could feel his cum flooding her insides, but her orgasm made sure that her body tried to take in everything he gave her.

Reid pulled out of her body almost as hard and fast as he had pushed inside her, and his barbs triggered a second orgasm. Reid shoved his hand between her legs and pushed his fingers inside her.

"That's right, Angel. Keep coming. I love feeling you throb around me." He nuzzled her neck and then bit down, slowly increasing the pressure of his bite.

For someone who wasn't sure how she'd feel or if she'd be mated, she loved when Reid marked her. It made her feel things she'd never felt before with anyone she'd dated in the past.

Slowly, her body stopped pulsating, and Reid let up on her neck. She let all the tension go from her muscles, and she relaxed back against him.

He slowly withdrew his hand from between her legs and brushed his fingers over her lips. She tentatively darted out her tongue and licked the tips of his fingers. He took his hand from her mouth, and she followed them with her eyes. She turned her head to watch him suck the rest of their lovemaking off with his own mouth.

He fell back on the bed, and she went with him.

His eyes were closed, and he seemed to be deep in thought.

Troubled by the stiffness in his body, she rolled over, so she faced him. "Are you okay?"

"Never better."

"You don't sound very convincing."

She didn't understand. *What just happened that caused a sudden attitude change in Reid?*

"I'm scared."

This caused her alarm. *Reid? Scared?*

He was so logical about things. He analyzed situations and came up with solutions. She'd never seen him scared. Worried maybe. Concerned, of course. He wasn't heartless; he just didn't let emotions rule him normally.

She put a hand on his chest. "What's wrong? I have never seen you scared before. Are you worried about Bram? Did you find something out the last time you got on your computer that you haven't shared with the rest of us?"

Reid bunched up a pillow and put it under his head. He looked over at her. "No." He shook his head. "I didn't find out anything about Bram other than what we discovered this morning."

Dante had called to tell them that Bram was out of jail. The bad thing was, nobody had been able to locate him. The good thing was, he hadn't bought a plane ticket to Vegas either.

Tegan breathed a sigh of relief. As much as she tried to embrace Isabelle's mantra that she was strong because she could have babies, she still felt vulnerable in her heat. She didn't want Bram to hurt anyone because she wasn't one hundred percent at her best.

She put her hand on Reid's chest. "Why are you scared?" she whispered.

"I'm scared this isn't going to last. I'm scared you're going to change your mind. And I'm scared you're going to regret everything we've done together." He brushed a finger back and forth on the mark he'd left on her neck. "I know I've wanted you for a long time, but now that I have you, I realize exactly how much. I know I'm not your usual type. I analyze too much. I'm kind of a nerd. You're so beautiful and wild and free. What if you decide you don't want to be tied to me?"

"And what if you put a baby inside me?"

"That's the worst part. I'm selfishly using a potential child to keep you tied to me." He looked down at her belly. "Don't get me wrong. I would love the little shifter like no other, and I would love to be a father, but it doesn't make it right."

"Oh, Reid." She moved up his body and took his mouth.

He groaned and rolled toward her and cupped the back of her neck. He licked the seam of her lips, and she opened for him. Reid tilted her head, changing the angle of their kiss, and gently pushed his tongue into her mouth. He kissed like he made love. As if all his energy was focused on her.

Tegan pushed him on his back and climbed on top of him. She reached between them and grabbed on to his penis. She put his head against her entrance and gradually sank down on him. She slowly rotated her hips over his as they continued to kiss.

Reid moaned into her mouth, and she swallowed his sounds of

pleasure.

Maybe sex wasn't the answer he was looking for, but she wanted to show him that she wanted to have sex with him, not just because she was in heat. She didn't need him right now. She wanted him.

She broke their kiss and sat up, still riding him.

Reid brought his hands up and touched her all over. Her face, her mouth, her shoulders, her breasts, her stomach, and her hips.

When she felt like he'd gotten his fill, she got on her knees, dragging him out of her.

Reid gasped. "Wh—"

She stopped him from saying anything more by taking him in her mouth. She tasted herself on him, but that didn't bother her. She loved knowing it was her juices that were all over him. Her scent, her taste…her mate.

As she sucked Reid's impressive cock to the back of her throat, she realized that she hadn't gone down on him yet and vice versa. They had so many more things to explore with each other, and it only ramped her up more.

Tegan had always liked sex. Males, females, shifters, humans. She'd slept with a couple of vampires before Vaughn and Naya got together and changed the two species dynamic with each other. She'd liked the naughtiness of it all.

Reid was right about her being wilder than him, but that didn't make her better or anything.

She tasted pre-cum from Reid, so she released his shaft from her mouth. It popped out from between her lips, and he grunted. She saw another drop appear, and she sipped it like he was fine wine. To her, he was better.

She felt him throbbing under her hand, and despite all their previous sex in the last half a day, she knew he wouldn't last much longer. She just had to decide how she wanted him to finish. It was tempting to ride him again, but they'd had plenty of him coming inside her, and there would be more of that until her heat was over.

She could take him into her mouth and swallow, but that had been done before. She wanted to show him how much she wanted all of him in a different way.

She sucked just his head into her mouth as she used her fist to pump him. He barked out a groan, and right before he came, she took her mouth away and stroked him until he finished on his beautiful stomach.

She kept her grip on him as she licked up all his seed from his abdomen. She placed kisses on his belly in between swallowing his drops. When she had cleaned him up, she sucked on his tip once more to make sure she hadn't missed anything.

He hissed and jerked but didn't push her away from what had to be his now-sensitive penis. She kissed his tip and released him from her grip. She slid back up his body and rested her head on his shoulder.

Neither of them said anything for a few seconds.

"That was…wow. I have no words."

She smiled and kissed his chest. "You're welcome." She shifted, so she could get up on one elbow and look at him in the face. "You didn't force me into anything. You didn't trick me into anything either. I'm here with you because I want to be. I wouldn't have mated you just because of my heat. I could have easily told you to bring me the medicine." She ran her fingers through his auburn locks. "I think my heat just sped up the process of our courtship. A couple of days ago, you were my friend, and now, you're my mate." She held his face in her hand. "But I have no regrets." She placed a gentle kiss on his lips. "And, if we have a child together, it would make my year. So, no more beating yourself up. No more being scared. I love you, and I'm not going anywhere."

Reid grinned. "Oh, thank God. I've been wanting to say this forever." He cupped her cheek. "I love you, too, Angel."

Chapter Thirty-Two

Quentin dragged his feet up the stairs to his bedroom. It was after midnight, and he was trying to be as quiet as possible, but it had been a long day.

He'd sat at his sister's bedside all day. Because she'd been found unconscious in an alley, the ambulance had taken her to a human hospital. There wasn't a way to move her since she was in such critical condition. But a shifter doctor had come to visit them today to give his own opinion, and he'd said the humans were taking good care of her.

Quentin had done some digging. His sister had been found outside of Minneapolis, so he'd had to call another police department, but he'd had connections there. The amount of drugs in her system would have killed a horse and definitely a human. She was lucky to be alive.

And the two men who had been raping his sister? They were lucky they were in jail. Quentin was lucky, too, as he wouldn't do his sister much good if he were in prison for two counts of murder.

Quentin dropped off his things in his bedroom, grabbed a clean pair of shorts, and went to the bathroom. He took a quick shower and brushed his teeth. He thought he'd heard something over the sound of his electric toothbrush and air vent running, but he was so tired; he couldn't rely on his senses at the moment. Still, he opened the door and sniffed the air.

No unusual smells, but one particular scent was strong. Of course

Quentin's nose would zero in on Hunter.

Quentin spit out his toothpaste, rinsed his mouth, grabbed his dirty clothes, shut off the light and vent, and left the bathroom. It took his eyes a second to adjust to the dark hallway, and he looked toward Hunter's room.

He should go check on the vampire. He wanted to, but his emotions were so raw at the moment; he didn't know what would happen if he did. He had no idea if Hunter regretted last night, and Quentin just couldn't hear something like that right now. And if Hunter acted like nothing had happened? Well, he couldn't handle that either. Quentin was afraid he'd do something he'd regret, like say things he could never take back.

So, Quentin walked to his bedroom instead. Damien had promised to look after Hunter and hadn't reported anything to Quentin all day. He would just have to go to bed with the knowledge that Hunter was okay.

Quentin pushed open his bedroom door and shut it behind him. When he turned around, he practically jumped when he saw a figure sitting on his bed.

"I waited for you all day," Hunter said. His crutches were against the wall. That was probably what Quentin had heard a few minutes ago in the hall.

"Sorry." Quentin had asked Damien not to say anything to anyone about his sister, so it wasn't a surprise that Hunter didn't know he'd been preoccupied with family stuff.

"You were out late," Hunter said, fishing for information.

Quentin desperately wanted to go to Hunter, drop to his knees, and lay his head in Hunter's lap. And then he wanted to strip Hunter naked and bury his problems for a while as he buried himself in Hunter's body.

But Quentin stood strong. He didn't need rejection now.

"I was." Quentin didn't have the energy to fight, and he didn't owe Hunter any information. He had once told Hunter about his family and his sister, but he didn't want Hunter's sympathy or judgments. "If you came here to tell me last night was a mistake, can we talk about it tomorrow instead?"

Hunter shook his head and looked down at his hands. "Were...were you out with someone?"

Really?

"Not that it's any of your business—your choice, not mine—but no, I was not out with anyone." He thought about saying he was with his family but decided against it. Let the vampire think what he wanted. "I am beat, so I'm going to bed."

Hunter looked up but didn't move.

Whatever. He didn't have the energy to kick Hunter out. He barely had the energy to talk to him.

Quentin dropped his shorts and walked naked to the side of his bed, pulled down the covers, and got in. He put an arm over his eyes, and surprisingly, he started to fall asleep right away. Despite his fatigue, he'd figured his worry for his sister would keep him awake.

He'd barely nodded off when he felt the bed sag. He pulled his arm from his eyes and saw Hunter lying next to him. He was on top of the covers though, which was good. Even though Quentin was tired, seeing Hunter lying there made him want to roll the vampire over, pull down his shorts, and fuck him.

Quentin growled, "What are you doing?"

Hunter flinched but didn't back away. "Something is bothering you. You're not normally an asshole. I know you're being curt with me because something is wrong."

Quentin turned on his side, away from Hunter. "I don't want to talk about it."

The bed shifted, and Hunter's arm wound around Quentin's waist.

"What are you doing?" Quentin asked, horrified to hear a break in his voice.

"Comforting you."

No, no, no. He couldn't handle Hunter's comfort right now.

Quentin rolled over and faced Hunter. He pulled the vampire's face toward him and took his mouth. He trailed his fingers down Hunter's six-pack and shoved his hand in Hunter's shorts. He grabbed on to Hunter's dick and squeezed harder than necessary.

Quentin pulled his mouth away. "If you want to comfort me, then take off your clothes and let me fuck you. For real."

Quentin moved his hand down, past Hunter's balls, and rubbed his anus. Quentin pushed the tip of his finger into Hunter, and the vampire gasped.

Hunter's eyes widened, and his body stiffened.

Quentin pulled his hand from Hunter's shorts and rolled away from him again. "That's what I thought. Go to bed, Hunter."

Quentin knew he was being an asshole, but it was for both their sakes.

He heard and felt Hunter get up, and part of Quentin was immediately sad and a little depressed. He knew it was for the best, but the situation sucked.

He squeezed his eyes shut and tried to think of something good. He needed to block out the sound of Hunter leaving the room. Maybe if he pretended things were different…

He pictured coming home and going to the bedroom he shared with Hunter, who would be lying in bed, waiting for him with open arms. Quentin would lie next to Hunter and tell him all about his sister and how much it'd hurt to see her lying in the hospital bed like that.

And, despite his sister's condition, Hunter would know exactly how to make Quentin feel better. Hunter would pull down Quentin's pants and grab on to him.

If only it were true.

Quentin rolled onto his back for real and spread his legs, pretending that he needed to give Hunter more room to work. He relaxed and imagined he could let Hunter do whatever he wanted to him.

It was almost so tangible that he swore, he felt the coolness of the night as the sheet was pulled down from his body.

That was the good thing about being so tired. The line between reality and imagination blurred. It was almost as if he were dreaming while awake.

Hunter would grab on to his cock.

Quentin groaned at the almost-vivid sensation of Hunter's touch.

Damn, he might need to do this more often when he was tired. It felt like Hunter was actually touching him.

When a wet tongue swiped over the head of his cock, Quentin jerked and opened his eyes.

Hunter was really there. He was kneeling beside Quentin's bed with his hand on Quentin's dick.

Quentin sat up, ripping Hunter's hand from him. "What are you doing?"

Hunter stood up, putting his weight on his good leg. He was naked and very aroused. "Being here for you. You were there for me when I got injured the other morning. Now, I want to be here for you."

For a second, he'd thought that Hunter cared about him the way he cared about Hunter. But, no, Hunter just felt like he owed him.

Hurt and angry, he pulled Hunter down to the bed, onto his hands and knees. "You want to be here for me? Stay like that," he commanded.

Quentin reached into his drawer for his lube and poured a nice amount onto Hunter's ass. He threw the bottle on the floor and pushed a finger into Hunter.

Hunter moaned, so Quentin added another. He scissored his fingers, opening Hunter up. Quentin was big, and Hunter was going to be sore after the first time he fucked him.

Quentin kneaded Hunter's prostate gland, and Hunter shuddered and moaned.

"You like that, huh? It's going to feel even better when it's my cock rubbing it. I'm going to get you off just by fucking you."

Quentin rubbed his dick through the lube on Hunter's ass and pressed forward.

Hunter froze, and reality slammed into Quentin.

What the fuck am I doing?

He dropped down onto the bed and covered his eyes. He was a horrible person.

The bed shifted beside him, and Hunter put his hand on Quentin's chest. "What's wrong? Why did you stop?"

Quentin pulled his arm away and looked at Hunter. "I can't fuck you when I'm angry. Not the first time at least. It's wrong."

Hunter frowned. "Why are you angry?"

"Because I want you to be here, and I don't want you to be here. I want you to *want* to be here for me, not because you feel like you owe me."

Hunter opened his mouth, and Quentin put a finger on his lips.

"It's okay. I understand." Quentin dropped his hand and looked away. "I'm kind of emotional right now, and I shouldn't take it out on you. My sister is in the hospital. She overdosed." He looked at Hunter again. "That's where I was all day. She's in a coma, and they don't know when she's going to wake up."

Hunter's eyes filled with sympathy and something more, so Quentin rolled away.

Hunter put his arm around Quentin again. "Please, just let me hold you again."

Quentin nodded, and much to his horror, he started to cry.

Hunter squeezed him tight and soothed him with tender words.

Quentin cried himself to sleep in Hunter's arms.

When he woke the next morning, Hunter was gone.

Chapter-Thirty-Three

The hotel door opened, and Bram looked up to see Larry walking in.

He waved a piece of paper in his hand. "We got something."

"About fucking time." Bram had been stuck in that hotel for two days now.

He'd forced Stan to get a hotel under his name while he told Larry to hire a private detective.

Bram didn't want anyone to find him and wanted nothing traced back to him. He couldn't go home until he knew neither the shifters nor the vampires were coming after him. And he wasn't going home without Isabelle.

While he'd been sitting in jail with nothing more to do than think, he'd realized why he found it odd that the Minnesota Pack alpha didn't want him near his mate. Isabelle had told Damien about him. That meant that Damien had been lying about seeing Isabelle.

This had pissed Bram off, but he'd calmed down after he found a cheap prostitute and beat the shit out of her. He'd given her a thousand bucks, so he didn't feel guilty. She'd have a couple of hot meals—when she was able to walk correctly.

After that, he'd decided he needed to hire someone to look into Isabelle. He was okay on the computer, but he was no hacker. Tweedledee and Tweedledum couldn't even find the Enter key on the computer.

Finally, they'd gotten some results.

Bram stood and took the paper from Larry. "What does it say?"

He read through it as Larry spoke, "Your girl bought a plane ticket to Las Vegas three days ago. She went with five other people. At least, all the tickets were bought at about the same time. Different cards were used, but the PI said it was suspicious. And two of them got a hotel suite for six people."

"Who the hell are they?"

"Turn the page," Larry said. "The PI said he gave you their info and addresses. Three of them live at the same place, and the other two live with that alpha you went to see the other day."

Bram's head whipped up. "What now?"

Larry grabbed the paper from Bram and turned a couple of pages. "Yeah. Some guys named Chase and Ranulf. They live at the same place you went to visit." Larry listed off an address. "Is that it?"

Bram ripped the paper away from Larry. He had to look at it with his own eyes.

"Motherfucker. That asshole lied to me!"

Larry's eyes lit up. "What are you going to do to him, boss?" He flexed his fingers in and out. "You want me and Stan to have a *chat* with him?"

Yes. But that would only cause problems. "No."

Larry's face fell.

"I want you to buy us all plane tickets to Vegas."

Larry scratched his head. "Won't they be able to find out you bought a ticket, just like you found out Isabelle had bought one?"

Maybe Larry wasn't as stupid as he looked.

"Yes, but we're going to catch the next flight out of here. They won't know we're there until it's too late."

The door to the hotel opened, and Stan walked in with lunch. "What did I miss?" he asked.

"We're going to Vegas," Bram told him with a smile.

"Damien, Damien!" Lachlan yelled as he came running into the kitchen where Damien was having lunch with Payton.

Lachlan didn't get excited unless there was something to get excited about, so Damien knew something was up.

"What's wrong?"

"I finally got an alert on Bram. He just bought a ticket to Las Vegas."

Damien jumped up from his seat at the table. "Shit! We have to call Zane. They have to get out of there as soon as possible."

They'd been keeping track of Bram. He thought he was clever for renting a room under one of his goons' names, but he wasn't smart enough to remember that Isabelle knew both of their names. They'd been keeping an eye on them until everyone was home, and Damien could confront the shifter with a full staff. He had no doubt that Bram would fight any sort of prosecution. Damien was also trying to get a conference call with Bram's father to gain his full support. He didn't want to make an enemy out of the Illinois Pack alpha.

"Should I buy them plane tickets home?"

Damien shook his head. "Reid can buy them. That's why Vance sent him."

Payton, who was still sitting, grabbed his hand. "Honey, what about Tegan? She's still in heat."

At first, Damien had told the group to stay in Vegas, and then the two females had gone into heat. It would be unbearable for them to fly home in that condition. He'd also considered telling them to drive, but by the time they drove that many miles, they'd probably get home the same time as if they'd waited and flown.

Chase had reported that morning that Isabelle's heat had ended sometime in the night. She was tired, but at least she'd be able to get on a plane. Tegan, however, wasn't done yet. She was going to be miserable, but it was better than Bram finding them. Damien doubted he would just go after Isabelle. After what Bram had done to Hunter, he obviously had no regard for life.

Damien squeezed his mate's hand. "She'll have to medicate herself, baby girl. It's too risky for them to stay there, and we can't leave her there, alone. Bram has figured out that Isabelle went to Vegas. He had to have.

Otherwise, why would he go there now? It's not a coincidence. If he hasn't already, he's tracked down their hotel room, too."

"I feel so bad for Tegan."

"I know, baby girl." He'd seen his mate through several mating heats, and he knew how they affected females. Tegan was going to be miserable. And so would every male on the plane. "Let's just hope that Reid finds the shortest flights with no layovers, if it's possible."

"Do you need me to do anything?" Lachlan asked.

"Email Reid the flight info for Bram. We have to make sure that they buy their tickets when it's too late for Bram to find out they're coming home. I'd hate for Bram to be waiting at the airport for Isabelle."

"Anything else?"

"Once Reid emails you their flight info back, plan to pick them up from the airport. Then, with everyone home, we're going to have to form a game plan. There's no doubt, Bram will be coming back, and this time, we'll be waiting for him."

"Is that it?"

"No, I need you to send Reid one more thing."

Chapter Thirty-Four

Zane sat on the bed in his hotel room, enjoying that he could sit and relax.

Isabelle's heat had ended during the middle of the night. The two of them had slept until almost eleven o'clock in the morning. He hadn't slept that late since he was a teenager. It was the best sleep they'd gotten in the last few days. Eight hours of uninterrupted sleep.

The water shut off in the bathroom, and Zane waited for Isabelle to come out. After spending hours together, they had both agreed it would be nice to bathe alone. Isabelle had let Zane go first, and now, he was waiting for her to be done with her turn.

Even though her heat was over, he wanted to make sure she ate and stayed hydrated.

As his mate walked out of the bathroom, the reason for his concern was right in front of him, directly in his line of view.

"Hey, you're not dressed yet," she said, using a towel to dry her hair.

He crooked a finger at her. "Come here."

She raised her brow. "You can't seriously be wanting to have sex again?"

Zane laughed as she walked over.

He pulled her close and kissed her distended belly. The place where his child could be growing.

"You keep touching me there," she said with a smile.

She was right. He held her close, wrapping as much of his hand around her belly as he could.

"I'm fascinated by it." He looked up at her. "At your body."

At the crescendo of her heat, she'd doubled over in pain, and Zane had felt lost for a moment. He'd wanted to hold her to make her feel better. Having sex with her had seemed wrong even though he knew that was what she needed.

When she'd taken him inside her body that last time, he couldn't believe how swollen she'd felt. He'd been convinced that he was hurting her until she cupped his ass and pulled him deeper inside her.

God. Then, when he'd come in her, she'd gripped him tighter than ever before, as if her pussy were trying to suck his dick off his body.

The amazing part had been when she continued to orgasm, and every climax she'd experienced triggered one in him. He'd watched her belly grow before his eyes. He knew it was just his seed right now. But that seed had the chance to meet with her egg and make a little Isabelle or little Zane.

It was a miracle.

He kissed her stomach again and rested his head against it. "Do you think you're pregnant?"

She ran her fingers through his hair. "I have no idea. I'll only know when I either get my period or not."

Zane pulled away and looked at her. "Your period?"

She laughed. "I work with a lot of human women. I meant, I'll know when I either bleed or not."

"Females talk about that stuff?"

She gently yanked on his hair. "Get the disgusted look off your face. It's natural, and yes, we talk about everything. Even farting."

Zane gave her a horrified look. "Females don't fart."

Isabelle laughed. "Yes, they do."

Zane furiously shook his head back and forth. "Nope, nope, nope. I refuse to believe it."

This only made Isabelle laugh harder.

"Why are you laughing, woman? Females don't fart."

She was laughing so hard that he had to pull her into his lap, so she didn't fall down.

He didn't think he was that funny, but he loved to see her so carefree and happy.

His phone rang, and he leaned over to pick it up.

It was Damien, which was a little odd.

Did something happen to Chase's and Ranulf's phones?

"Zane here."

Isabelle put her head on his shoulder, and he wanted to hang up the phone and cuddle her close.

"Zane, it's Damien. I need you to get packed right away. And I need you to tell Reid to check his email."

Zane's entire body went on alert.

Isabelle lifted her head. "What's wrong?"

"Bram just bought tickets to Las Vegas."

Isabelle's eyes filled with fear, and Zane squeezed her to let her know he wouldn't let anything happen to her.

"Lachlan sent the information and instructions to Reid," Damien continued. "He needs to buy all the tickets home right when Bram's flight is scheduled to take off. We need to make sure he is in the air and won't turn around because he knows you're coming home."

"Okay. I'll tell everyone to pack." He looked at Isabelle, who nodded her head and got up from his lap to get dressed.

Zane went for his clothes as well while Damien finished talking, "Call me if you run into any problems."

"Got it." Zane hung up the phone and turned to Isabelle. "Pack. I'm going to tell everyone else they need to get moving. And I need to tell Reid to get on his computer."

Isabelle's hand flew to her mouth. "What about Tegan?"

Zane's heart went out to Tegan. "Meds." He shrugged. "It's the only way. She needs to go home." He walked over and gave Isabelle a kiss. "She'll survive. She's tough."

He left the bedroom and knocked forcefully on Tegan and Reid's door. "Time to join the Mile-High Club. You need to get your butts moving." He kept walking to Ranulf and Chase's room, again knocking with force. "You two need to start packing. Damien called."

Both bedroom doors flew open at almost the same time, and there were four sets of eyes on alert, looking at him.

"Damien called. Bram's coming to Las Vegas. We have to go home." Zane looked at Reid. "You're supposed to check your email. The directions from Lachlan are in there."

Reid nodded and walked out of the bedroom and into the living room.

"Sorry, honey, it's time for you to go," Chase said.

A female appeared. She was pulling her shirt down and finger-combing her hair. "I'll get my full fee, right?"

"Of course," Ranulf said.

The female kissed both males on the mouths. "It's such a shame I have to go early. I was thinking about giving you two boys a little extra time for free."

"Ah, man." Chase looked up at Zane.

"No."

Chase looked back at the woman. "Sorry, honey."

She shrugged. "Whatever. Call me when you boys are back in town."

As she walked toward the door, Tegan grabbed her middle.

"Oh. Are you okay?" she asked Tegan.

Zane mouthed, *Get her out of here*, to Chase and Ranulf.

Ranulf took the woman by the shoulders and steered her toward the door. "She'll be fine. She's got IBS," he said with a completely straight face.

Despite the seriousness of the situation, Zane had to laugh because Tegan straightened her spine as best as she could and said, "Hey."

Chase came up next to her and put a hand on her shoulder. "It's nothing to be embarrassed about."

Tegan knocked his hand away. "Don't touch me."

Reid came back just as Ranulf shut the door to the hotel behind the escort.

"Okay, so I found a flight. I haven't bought the tickets yet because we don't want Bram to find out we're coming home." He narrowed his eyes at the corner of his computer. "I can theoretically buy them in twenty-five minutes. That means, we all need to get packed and get out of here because it's going to be a close call. And we're going to be spread out, but it's the first flight out of here in the next couple of hours. After that, we'd have to wait four to five hours to get out of here."

Tegan grabbed on to the doorframe and clutched her middle again.

Reid shoved his computer into Zane's hands.

"Shit, Tegan, what are we going to do?"

"Meds," Zane said.

Tegan lifted her head and nodded. "I'll be okay. Just help me get packed, will you?"

"Of course." He started to lead her into the room and then turned around at the last second. "Computer," he said.

Zane gave it back to him. "Okay. We'll get ready as soon as we can." He went back toward his bedroom when he saw movement outside. "Damn it. I forgot about the security team."

"I'll tell them they are free to go as soon as we take off for the airport," Ranulf said.

"Thanks," Zane said and went back to Isabelle.

She was zipping up her bag as he walked in the door. Her expression read anxious and scared.

"We're leaving ASAP." He pulled her into his arms. "But, remember, I won't let anything happen to you."

She held him tight. "I know."

The good thing was, he knew she meant it.

Chapter Thirty-Five

The plane was fucking crowded, and Tegan was miserable.

She pulled her T-shirt away from her body and tried to fan herself with it.

They'd taken off only twenty minutes ago, and she and Reid had had sex right before they left the hotel, but she could tell the end of her heat was coming. The worst of it. And she was trapped on a plane. She had no idea how she was going to make it home.

Reid kept glancing back at her. They were both sitting in aisle seats. He was several rows up and adjacent to her. She tried to smile every time he looked at her, but it was hard to be sincere. Plus, Reid wasn't dumb. He could probably smell her.

The couple next to her had started making out about five minutes ago, and Tegan wasn't sure they wouldn't get naked right there in front of everyone.

A male came down the aisle, and as he neared, Tegan could smell that he was a shifter. A cat. She groaned because the man's eyes were zeroed in on her.

He stopped right at her seat and knelt down. "Hey, honey. You need someone to help you with your little problem?"

"Perhaps you need to get your nose checked," Reid said from right above them. "She already belongs to someone."

The shifter stood.

"I would appreciate it if you left my wife alone."

Reid had used the human word for mate, but the shifter understood.

He looked back at Tegan. "Let me know if you change your mind, honey," he said before walking back to the front of the airplane.

Reid grabbed her hand and pulled on it. "Let's go."

She stood. "Where are we going?" As soon as the words left her mouth, a cramp hit her so fast and strong, she doubled over in pain.

Reid wrapped an arm around her waist and helped her walk to the back of the plane and into the restroom. Thankfully, their seats were toward the back, so it was a short trip.

"You didn't take any medication, did you?" he said, obviously not happy with her.

She shook her head. She hadn't wanted her senses to be dulled. What if something happened, and she just sat in her seat like a lump of worthlessness? Too bad her heat was so bad that she wasn't any good to anyone anyway.

She'd never gotten to the end of a heat without medicine. Big mistake.

Reid closed and locked the door and spun her, so she faced the sink. He pulled her yoga pants down to her knees. She heard the sound of his jeans shifting and his zipper being pulled down.

He pushed on her back until she had no choice but to bend over. She clutched the sink as he thrust inside her. He clutched her hips and hauled her back to him. Over and over, he drove inside her until she snapped and came. Her orgasm hit her so hard; she had to bite her arm to keep from crying out.

Reid jerked her hips back one more time and poured himself into her. The rush of his seed hitting her was such a relief that she thought she might pass out. Instead, she came again.

And again.

Each time she came, so would Reid.

He put an arm around her, pulling her close and keeping their bodies together. He used his other hand to pull her hair away from her neck and kissed her shoulder. "You okay?"

She grabbed on to his arm and nodded. "You?" she gasped out as she climaxed again.

"I'm okay," he said and nuzzled her neck.

She tipped her head. "Will you mark me? Please?"

He pushed her shirt aside with his nose. "Of course, Angel." He kissed her first and then sucked on her skin, and right as her next orgasm hit, he bit down.

She clenched her jaw tight so as not to cry out, but it was hard to do when her orgasm went on and on. Every time she contracted around Reid, he would grunt and pulsate inside her. Her belly had already started to grow since they went in the restroom, and she started to wonder if she'd leave the lavatory, looking like she was six months pregnant.

One more long contraction, and then it was over.

It was the strangest feeling, but it was as if her whole body went from stone to jelly. There was a residual ache from her muscles cramping so much, but the sharp pain was gone.

She took a deep breath and relaxed against Reid.

Sometime during their last mutual orgasm, he'd let go of her neck. It was sore but a good sore.

He enveloped her in his arms. "Give me a minute, Angel, and I'll pull out of you. I don't want to hurt you any further."

She knew he meant his barbs. They'd been buried in her tender flesh for the last fifteen minutes, keeping Reid against the opening of her cervix. She now felt them recede, and she gasped from the sensation.

He slowly withdrew from her body, and she appreciated him going slow. Her body didn't seem to want to let go of him, and there was a slight tug as he pulled out.

Reid pulled up her pants and helped her straighten her shirt, and then he went to work on his own clothes. She should turn around and help him, but she was suddenly so tired that she was using all her energy to stand.

She heard his zipper go back up just as there was a knock on the door.

"Excuse me. You two need to come out of the restroom right now." Whoever was on the other side did not sound happy.

"Come on, Angel," Reid said and pulled her to his chest. He opened the door, and Tegan didn't even attempt to move from the warmth of his body. "Sorry, miss. My wife doesn't feel good. I didn't want her to be sick in here, alone. I'll take her back to her seat now."

The flight attendant stepped back. "Oh, I'm sorry, sir, ma'am. We've just had an unusual amount of couples trying to have sex in the restrooms on this flight. It's the strangest thing."

Tegan felt bad, but she couldn't help smiling at the situation. The humans would never know the reason for the weird spike in sexual arousal.

"Look at that," Reid said. "You made her smile. Thank you."

The flight attendant blushed at his praise.

"I think I might fall asleep, standing up," Tegan said.

"Oh, sorry," the flight attendant said. "Yes, go sit down."

"Thank you, miss."

Reid led her back to her seat and helped her sit. He knelt next to her and ran a hand over her hair. "You going to be okay?"

"Yeah. I'm going to try to nap. Don't worry about me. The worst is over. We'll be home soon."

He looked at her, and she could tell he didn't want to go.

"Really, Reid. It's okay. I'll be fine." She cupped his cheek, astonished by how fast their relationship had changed. She would have always been sad if something happened to him, but now, she didn't know what she would do if she lost him. "The worst is over, love."

This made him smile at least. "Okay." He looked at his seat. "I'll be right over there, okay?"

She nodded and watched him walk to his seat. Her eyes were closing, but she wanted to make sure he made it back to his seat and got buckled in. He reached his chair but didn't sit down. He was talking to someone. Either the person he was seated next to or the window-seat person.

Reid came back to Tegan with a smile on his face. "The guy next to me offered to switch." He took her hands and helped her stand. "Come on, Angel."

They passed the nice man on the way to Reid's aisle. "Thank you," she said to the older gentleman.

"You're welcome, miss. I was married once. I understand."

Reid let Tegan sit in the middle, and then he took his chair on the end. He pushed up the armrest between them and took her into his arms.

She fell asleep almost at once and didn't wake until the plane's wheels touched down. She jerked up at the sensation of landing. "*Oh.*" She looked at Reid.

"We're home," he said.

She turned to the window and saw the familiar sights of the Minneapolis-St. Paul airport. "It feels good to be back," she told Reid. "Even if it's colder here."

He grabbed her hand. "I think we'll all appreciate a little less heat in our lives right now."

She smiled at his pun and kissed him.

After waiting for the doors to open and for everyone at the front of the plane to exit first, they finally made it off the plane. Zane, Isabelle, Chase, and Ranulf were all waiting for them when they came out of the tunnel.

"You okay?" Isabelle asked.

"Yeah. Just tired. You?"

She smiled. "The same."

Tegan looked at Zane, who had a sly smile on his face.

"What, Zane?" Tegan asked.

"I told you that you were joining the Mile-High Club today."

Reid hit him on the back of his head.

"Ow."

"This was about necessity, not fun."

Zane gasped. "Did you hear that, Tegan? Reid just said having sex with you wasn't fun."

Tegan socked him in the stomach.

"*Ooph.*"

"Quit trying to start fights." Tegan looked at Isabelle. "Remember, once Bram is gone, you can leave this loser."

Zane put his arm around Tegan and gave her a noogie. "Who's trying to start fights now?"

Tegan pushed him away. "You are such a turd," she told him, but she was laughing.

Even with the threat still hanging over them, it felt good to be home.

Chapter Thrity-Six

$\mathcal{B}$ram walked up to the counter at the hotel, alone. He'd left Stan and Larry outside. They were intimidating to some people, and he needed to get Isabelle's room number.

"How can I help you this evening, sir?"

Bram smiled. "I'm looking for my girlfriend. She came here with a group of friends, and I want to surprise her. I was originally supposed to work, but I got the time off. So, rather than calling her, I thought it would be fun to show up."

The lady smiled. "That does sound like fun."

Bram chuckled. "More than you know."

"What's the name the room is under?"

Bram gave the name from the report he'd been given from the private investigator.

The woman typed a couple of things into the computer, and a puzzled expression came over her face.

She looked up at Bram. "I'm sorry, sir, but they checked out already."

Stay calm. Stay calm.

Maybe they had switched hotels. He would call the PI and ask for an update.

"Can you tell me when?"

She squinted at the screen. "It looks like it was a little over three hours ago."

Bram managed one last smile. "Okay. Thank you."

"I'm sorry your surprise is ruined."

"Huh?"

"You'll have to call her now, so she'll know you're here."

"Oh. Yeah, yeah." Bram turned and walked away.

"Sir, is your name Bram?"

A sense of trepidation came over Bram. He pivoted on his heel. "Yes, it is."

"I just saw a note in the computer. Someone left a letter for you. I'll be right back." She walked into an office and came back a minute later with an envelope. She showed him the front. "Is this you?"

He nodded.

She smiled. "It looks like she knew you were coming after all."

Bram wanted to rip the envelope from her hand but restrained himself from making a scene.

"Good luck, sir," the female said as she handed it over.

Bram wasn't even listening anymore.

He tore open the envelope as he walked outside to find Larry and Stan.

He reached them as he pulled out the note inside.

BRAM—

IF YOU'RE READING THIS, YOU'RE TOO LATE.

ISABELLE WANTS NOTHING TO DO WITH YOU. SHE HAS FOUND A GOOD MATE. THEY WERE MARRIED IN VEGAS, AND SHE MIGHT NOW BE PREGNANT WITH HIS CHILD.

I'M SORRY YOU CAME ALL THE WAY TO LAS VEGAS TO FIND ISABELLE, BUT SHE DOESN'T WANT TO BE FOUND. NOT BY YOU.

I AM GIVING YOU THE OPPORTUNITY TO LEAVE MINNESOTA. YOU

NEED TO STAY AWAY FROM MINNEAPOLIS-ST. PAUL MOST OF
ALL. IF YOU MAKE YOUR PRESENCE KNOWN, YOU WILL BE TRIED
AND PROSECUTED FOR YOUR BEATING OF ISABELLE RAND AND
THE HIT-AND-RUN YOU MADE ON HUNTER ESMUND.

THESE ACTIONS WOULD NOT NORMALLY UNPUNISHED, BUT IF
YOU STAY AWAY, WE HAVE ALL AGREED TO TAKE NO FURTHER
ACTION TOWARD YOU.

PLEASE CONSIDER THIS YOUR LAST WARNING.

—DAMIEN LOWELL

MINNESOTA PACK ALPHA

Bram crumpled up the note in his fist, wishing it were Damien Lowell's head.

"*Ahh!*" he screamed out in anger.

Larry and Stan exchanged looks.

"Uh…boss? People are looking at you," Stan said.

"I don't fucking care," he said and slammed the letter on Stan's chest. While Stan and then Larry read it, Bram paced back and forth.

"What are you going to do?" Larry asked.

"I don't know exactly. But I know I need to make them pay." He stopped and looked at Stan and Larry. "That fucking bitch let some other male service her during her heat." He jammed his pointer finger into his own chest. "That was my heat to service. She's my bitch to take. I'm going to kill the motherfucker who put his hands on her. She's supposed to be pregnant with my baby, so I could take her back to my father." Bram punched the wall and screamed, "She's ruined everything!"

"Boss, I think we should get out of here before someone calls the police," Stan suggested.

"Fine."

The three walked away from the hotel to find a cab.

"So, where are we going to go, boss?" Larry asked.

"Minneapolis."

Larry and Stan stopped walking.

"Uh…but you were just told not to go there. What if they kill you?" Stan replied.

Bram stopped and turned around. He smiled. "They're not going to kill me because I'm going to kill them first." *After I cut that fucker's offspring from that cheating cunt's belly*. Bram would make the guy watch, too. Then, he'd slit the fucker's throat and fuck Isabelle while her mate bled all over them.

No one—*no one*—told Bram Varg what to do. Not even his father.

Damien Lowell was going to wish he'd never set eyes on Bram because he was going to kill him, his mate, and all his sentinels. It was just too bad the alpha wouldn't be alive to learn his lesson.

Chapter Thirty-Seven

"Do you think Bram will stay away?" Isabelle asked Zane.

He snorted. "Hell no. A guy like that has an ego the size of Europe. There is no way he's walking away with his tail between his legs. And Damien knows it. The only reason he told Bram that he'd be free if he left Minnesota was because Damien knows Bram won't do it." He grabbed her hand. "Does that disappoint you?"

"To be honest, yes, and no. If I never had to see him again, that would be wonderful. No one would get hurt—more than they already have. But, if he was out there, I'd always wonder if he'd show up out of the blue." She rubbed her swollen belly. "What if he took my kids out of revenge?"

Zane squeezed her hand. "I would never let that happen."

Isabelle turned and looked out the window of the Suburban. The sights of the Twin Cities passed by them, and she couldn't help but feel anxious about Bram finding her. The last few days with her heat and being in Las Vegas, she'd felt safe in that little world even though they were just as vulnerable there—actually, more so. It just felt so much more real now that they were back.

She sighed. If only she could go back and tell him no when he asked her out on a date. Then, none of them would be in this mess.

"Hey," Zane said, pulling her attention back to him. "We'll be at the wolves' place soon. Besides, there's no way Bram has flown back yet."

Chase leaned forward, on the opposite side of Zane, and said, "Zane's right. You'll be safe at our place."

"Thanks, Chase." She looked at Ranulf in the front passenger seat, and he nodded his agreement. She was a little surprised by this. The two males hadn't hidden their displeasure at her arrival, but now, they seemed to have changed their minds. It felt good to know she had more support.

"He's right," Quentin said from the driver's seat. "Bram would be a fool to come after you with so many sentinels around."

She hoped so, but Bram wasn't always rational when he was upset.

A loud snore came from the backseat behind her, and Isabelle looked over her shoulder.

Reid was leaning back against the seat with his arms spread out. Tegan had her head in his lap and was sleeping.

"That's Tegan's way of saying she agrees," Reid told her.

Isabelle smiled at this and relaxed a little.

When they pulled up to the wolves' home, everything seemed normal. The outside porch light was on. Lights were on in the house. It didn't look scary or intimidating or like someone was hiding and waiting for them.

There were several vehicles in front of the house, telling her the house was full of shifters. Quentin had told them they were having a meeting with the cats, so right now, Isabelle felt extra safe.

"Tegan, time to get up. We're here," Reid said.

She rubbed her eyes and sat up. "I fell asleep?"

"You needed it," Isabelle told her. Isabelle was lucky that her heat had ended, and she'd gotten some sleep before they had to get on a plane.

"Let's go in," Zane said.

The group of them unloaded themselves from the big SUV and went into the house. Not only were the wolf-shifters and cat-shifters there, but so were some of the vampires, too. The same ones from the last meeting were present either because of their living situation or because of who they were mated to, but Isabelle still felt like they were staring at her.

She tried to read their faces for outright signs of hate and loathing, but most were unreadable.

The female vampire mated to the cat-shifter's son smiled at Isabelle in sympathy.

The large vampire with the yellow eyes straightened when he saw them. But not because of Isabelle. His eyes were on the couple behind her and Zane.

When Reid reached them, he said, "Are we going to have a problem?" to the vampire.

"Nope," the vampire answered, and Tegan breathed a sigh of relief.

Isabelle was curious about what that was all about, but it wasn't any of her business, so she blocked out their conversation.

She turned her attention to the rest of the group and searched for one person in particular.

When she spotted Hunter, she immediately went to him. He was leaning against a wall with the leg in a cast crossed over his good leg, which held all his weight.

She gasped when she saw him, and Hunter turned to her.

He'd been talking to someone else and smiling, but all Isabelle saw was the broken leg.

"I'm so sorry," she said and started to cry.

She wasn't normally one to cry so quickly, but she was emotionally drained, and her hormones were all over the place. Not to mention, she felt horrible about what Bram had done to the vampire.

Hunter's eyes widened at her tears, which only made her cry harder.

She took a deep breath and tried to calm herself down. "Please, tell me if there is anything I can do to help you. It's all my fault that you were injured. I'm the reason Bram came here." She held out her wrist. "I know you need blood, and I would be more than happy to feed you."

Zane caught up to her then, wrapping an arm around her and growling.

Hunter held up his hand. "Isabelle, I don't blame you. It's not your fault that this guy is an asshole." He turned to Zane. "I don't need to feed from her. I'm good, man." He looked back at Isabelle. "Besides, that's probably not wise in your condition." He nodded to her belly where her shirt was fitted around the shape of it.

Isabelle was about to tell him that she might not be pregnant when Zane spoke up first, "Isa, why don't we leave the poor male alone?"

Isabelle went from feeling guilty to annoyed. She turned and gave

Zane a dirty look, but he was smiling. She looked back at Hunter, who was also smiling.

"Isabelle, really, I'm fine. I was at the clinic for only half a day. I'm already recovering. I really don't want you feeling guilty. That won't help with my recovery. Okay?"

She nodded. "Okay."

There was a sharp whistle through the crowd, and they all turned to see Damien clapping his hands to get their attention.

"Welcome back, guys," Damien said to the Las Vegas crew and waved his hands for them to come forward. "Mission accomplished? You got married?"

Damien already knew all this, but Isabelle assumed he was asking to make sure everyone else was up-to-date.

Isabelle and Zane held up their left ring fingers.

"Congratulations, you two," Vance said. "Lilith is ready to have a party whenever you are."

Damien looked down at Isabelle's abdomen. "And it looks like another mission was accomplished."

"The first part. We'll have to wait for the results though," Zane said.

The crowd laughed, and Isabelle's face heated. She didn't want everyone to know their personal business even though she understood why everyone needed to know. When Bram showed up, they couldn't be blindsided by anything.

Damien laughed at her red face and pulled her into a hug. "I'm happy for you, Izzy. You deserve a good mate. And I have to say, there is something special about being mated to a cat-shifter." He looked over at his own mate and smiled.

Damien let Isabelle go, and she looked at Zane. Damien's words suddenly made her and Zane's relationship a reality.

She knew Zane cared about her. She knew Zane had wanted to mate with her. But did he really want long-term? They'd talked about this being a temporary thing from the beginning even if she ended up pregnant. But did Zane want forever? More importantly, did *she* want forever?

Her relationship with Zane should be the least of her worries with Bram breathing down her neck, but again, her hormones were all over the place. Her wolf definitely saw him as hers. Truth be told, her wolf had formed an attachment to Zane's cat from the beginning. That was why she'd run away, scared. She'd come to help Damien two years ago, not fall in love. It had scared her and made her panic. It had been easier to run away.

But now…now, she was here with Zane. She was his mate—in shifter law and human law—but would they last? It'd happened so fast. Could they live with each other? Would they get on each other's nerves?

And they'd never talked about exclusivity. She was pretty sure that Zane hadn't been celibate since she last saw him two years ago. Not that she'd expected him to. But would she be enough for him now?

The thought of him fucking someone else the way he fucked her made her sick to her stomach. She couldn't handle it. It would be almost worse than all the things Bram had done to her.

And didn't that just tell her how she felt about the cat-shifter?

"Okay, everyone," Damien said, breaking her out of her thoughts, "Vance and I have a plan to approach this Bram situation." He looked at Lachlan. "What's the status on our good friend Bram?"

Lachlan was sitting on a chair behind Damien with a laptop. "It looks like he bought a ticket to Des Moines, Iowa," Lachlan said, surprised.

"He's trying to throw us off his trail. He knows we tracked him to Vegas, so he knows we can track him back here. How long does it take to drive from Des Moines to here?"

Lachlan punched in a few keys on his computer. "Four hours, give or take fifteen minutes to a half hour, depending on what route he takes."

"Okay, so he'll be here in the middle of the night, which is prime attacking time. But, in case he decides to wait until morning, we're going to be sleeping in shifts. We don't want him waiting until we're all tired before he strikes."

"So, what's the plan?" Zane asked.

"Pay attention because I don't want any details missed or forgotten."

Chapter Thirty-Eigth

Bram never showed up.

Not that night or the next night either, and by day three, Zane's mate was getting restless. As was everyone else, but at least they were able to leave the house. Everyone had thought it best that Isabelle stay inside where she was safest, but something had to give.

While she was in the shower, Zane rounded up everyone he could to discuss a plan to get Isabelle out of the house before her wolf went insane from confinement. He was hoping to surprise her with a simple picnic outside where she wouldn't feel so cooped up.

Everyone agreed, and he went to tell her the good news.

Zane walked into their bedroom just as she was getting dressed. "Hey, Isa…"

She was only in her bra and underwear, and Zane lost his train of thought for a moment.

She turned and looked at him. "Yeah?"

She was so beautiful to him, and he scanned her body, taking in everything, including her still-expanded stomach. She hadn't bled yet, but it didn't mean that she wouldn't. And he had to wonder, once she bled and Bram was no longer a threat, would she leave?

They hadn't discussed anything about their future. Everything seemed to be fine in the now. But he didn't know if he could handle her leaving him again.

"Zane?"

He shook his head and met her eyes. "Yeah?"

She smiled. "You sounded like you wanted to tell me something." She grabbed a shirt and pulled it over her head.

"Oh." He chuckled at himself for forgetting for a moment when it was his idea. "I thought you'd like to get out for a while today. I was thinking a picnic around lunchtime."

Her eyes lit up. "Really?"

"Really." He grinned. He wanted to make her that happy all the time.

She ran to him and threw her arms around his neck. "You have no idea how much this means to me. I'm going crazy."

He rubbed her back. "I can tell. That's why I wanted to do something special for you."

She leaned back and grinned at him. "You're the best."

God, he hoped she meant it.

He kissed her and proceeded to make her forget that lunch wasn't for a few more hours.

Despite Zane's delicious lovemaking that morning, noon couldn't come fast enough. When it finally came time to leave, she was so focused on getting out of the house that she barely noticed how empty it felt.

There were still plenty of shifters around, but there were fewer than there had been the last few days. So, when it was only her and Zane getting into the car, she was a little confused.

"No one is going with us?"

"I thought you might like it to just be the two of us. We haven't seen or heard from Bram. I figured a few hours alone might do both of us good."

She closed her eyes at the thought. "It sounds heavenly." Wolves were pack animals, but her human half needed some breathing room after being so closely guarded for so long. She opened her eyes and pointed to the end of the long driveway. "Let's get out of here."

She was a little concerned about Bram, but she put that out of her mind. She needed a break from everything, including worrying.

They should have probably headed to a public park, but Zane took her to a secluded riverbank with lush green grass and beautiful green trees that were just beginning to bud out in the country. It was still a little cool since it was March outside, but she didn't care. The crisp breeze was like heaven to her senses.

Zane spread a blanket out on the grass for them to sit and opened the picnic basket.

"Where did you find a picnic basket?" she asked with a laugh.

"From my alphena. She has everything."

"And I suppose she's the one who cooked our meal, too?" At least, that was what Isabelle hoped. She'd tasted Zane's cooking, and it was not good.

He laughed as if he knew her thoughts. "Yes, she did."

"Suddenly, I'm starving."

"You're funny," Zane told her.

"I've gotta keep up with you."

Zane smiled as he leaned over and kissed her. "You have no trouble keeping up with me."

"Well, well, well, isn't this fucking cozy as hell?"

Isabelle gasped and froze at the sound of that voice.

Zane's jaw clenched as he sat back on the blanket.

Bram walked closer from his position in the trees with a gun pointed at the two of them.

She hadn't had any indication that he was sneaking up on them. He'd been downwind and quiet, but she had always assumed that she'd have some sort of sixth sense when it came to detecting Bram.

"Do you know how long I've been waiting to get you alone, Isabelle? But you just wouldn't leave that fucking house."

"Gee, I wonder why."

Bram looked at Zane. "Did you teach her to talk like that? She knew better than to smart off when she was with me. Don't you know how to control your woman?"

Isabelle was afraid that Zane wouldn't have any teeth left from the force of his grinding.

"Unlike you, I don't want a mate who's a doormat."

If Zane had hoped to prove a point to Bram with his comment, it didn't work. "Yeah, well, you should try it sometime." He looked at Isabelle. "Of course, now, I'm going to have to retrain this bitch to keep her mouth shut again. I should shoot you just for that."

Isabelle hung her head. She was ashamed to admit that Bram was right. He'd put her down and degraded her so much that she started to keep her thoughts to herself.

Zane grabbed her hand and squeezed.

She looked up at him, and he shook his head. She knew he was trying to tell her not to beat herself up.

With Zane's strength and support, she finally asked Bram something that had been bothering her, "Why me, Bram? I'm nobody special. I'm a plain Jane. Why don't you just find someone else?"

Zane narrowed his eyes at her. She was confused because her question wasn't meant to provoke Bram.

Bram laughed. "That's exactly why. I need the perfect mate to take back to my father to show him I've changed. If I took someone too important, he'd know it was a calculated move. If I took someone too pretty, he'd accuse me of thinking with my dick. Your lack of status and looks make you the best choice. That, and I've planned to knock you up to show my father that I'm going to be a family man."

Isabelle felt like she'd been slapped. She knew she wasn't the prettiest person, but to have it put out there like that was humiliating, especially in front of Zane. But worse than the insults was the thought of carrying Bram's child.

She clutched her middle and tried not to imagine how horrible it would have been to be with Bram during her heat instead of Zane. She literally felt nauseated, but she feared throwing up would be too much for Zane to handle.

She raised her chin instead. "What are you going to do with us?" She couldn't imagine Bram would want her now. Not after she had mated with Zane and could possibly be carrying his child.

Bram pointed to Zane with his gun. "Him I'm going to get rid of. I have no need for your stupid cat-shifter. But you, you're coming with me."

Fear traveled down Isabelle's spine, and she shivered. "Why?"

"Because, at first, I was very angry. Very angry, Isabelle," he said, narrowing his eyes at her. "I thought you had figured out what happened when someone left me, and I decided your punishment should be death."

Zane made a move to get up and attack, but Isabelle clutched his hand and pulled him back. She knew Bram well enough to know that he wouldn't hesitate to shoot Zane.

Bram snickered. "Pussy."

Zane growled.

"Anyway," Bram continued, "I decided this situation was even better for me. I'm going to explain to my father that we broke up for a while, and you hooked up with some loser who got you pregnant and left you."

Zane growled again.

"Oh, shut up," Bram told him. He looked back at Isabelle. "I'm going to tell my father that I love you so much that I don't care that you're pregnant by another male." He laughed. "It's almost too perfect. After getting kicked out for my jealousy, what better way to show my father I've changed?"

"And the baby?" Zane asked.

Bram scratched his head. "Well, it'll be a shame when it dies in its sleep now, won't it? Everyone will feel so sorry for me."

Isabelle gasped and put her knees up, as if that would protect the potential life inside her.

"You are one sick bastard," Zane said.

Bram shrugged and smiled. "I guess I am," he said as if it was something to be proud of.

"Did you get all that?" Zane suddenly shouted.

Chapter Thirty-Nine

Isabelle jumped from the boom in his voice. "What?" she asked, not understanding what was going on.

Several shifters stepped out from behind Bram, who turned around at the noise. "What the fuck?"

"Got it," Lachlan said, giving Zane a thumbs-up.

Zane grinned. "While you were waiting for Isabelle to leave, we were waiting for you to show up. We finally decided that you were too much of a *pussy* to show up with so many shifters there. We had to do something different to draw you out." Zane spread out the hand that wasn't holding Isabelle's. "And it worked." He leaned forward. "We got every word recorded, so when you end up dead, your father won't question our actions."

A cold dread hit Isabelle, and she yanked her hand away from Zane's.

Had he just used her? Had he used her to draw Bram out, knowing she could get hurt? Her and their possible unborn child.

Zane looked at Isabelle, confusion on his face. She wanted to give him the benefit of the doubt, but then why hadn't he warned her?

But she didn't say anything. Bram was still standing in front of them, holding a gun. And, now, he probably felt trapped and pissed off that he'd been tricked.

"You forget that I'm still holding a handgun, cat. What's to stop me from shooting you?"

Despite Isabelle's hurt that Zane had used her, panic flooded her. Bram had everything to lose now, and she had no doubt he would do just as he'd threatened. She only had one card to play in this situation because she didn't want the male she loved to be hurt or killed.

She stood and squared her shoulders. "I'll go with you."

Shock came over Bram's face, and Zane leaped from the blanket.

"What the fuck, Isabelle? You cannot go with this guy."

"If it means you won't be hurt, I'll go."

"No way." Zane stepped in front of her, keeping his front to Bram even though he was talking to her. "Over my dead body."

Bram shrugged. "Okay," he said and pulled the trigger.

Zane staggered back and fell to the ground. "Not again," he said as blood bloomed all over his white T-shirt.

All rational thought left Isabelle, and instinct took over. In a split second, she shifted into her wolf and attacked. She aimed right for Bram's throat and clamped down with her teeth. She heard a loud noise and then felt a burning pain, but neither deterred her focus on stopping Bram.

She bit down harder, and soon, Bram lay limp under her. But she still didn't let up. Every horrible thing he'd said to her reverberated in her mind. The first time he'd slapped her. And the time he'd beaten her for leaving him when she needed some time apart.

He was never going to hurt her or anyone else ever again.

Slowly, she became aware of Damien saying her name and trying to pull her off Bram.

"Izzy, he's dead. You can let go now. He's dead."

Isabelle released her teeth and growled at Bram. She nudged him with her nose, and his head flopped to the side, his throat a bloody mess.

She looked over at Damien, who was stroking the back of her neck.

"He's dead, Izzy," he said again.

Isabelle took a step back, and a piercing pain in her leg had her collapsing on the ground. Damien rolled her over.

"Shit. Isabelle, you've been shot."

It took almost all her strength, but she shifted back into her human form. She raised her own arm. It was covered in blood, and there was a large chunk missing from her bicep. She cringed. That was going to leave a mark, but at least Bram hadn't hit anything vital.

"Isa, Isa," she heard from behind her. "Let me up, asshole. I need to see if she's okay."

"Zane, you've been shot, too. You shouldn't be moving," she heard someone say to him.

For a moment, adrenaline had made her forget why she'd attacked Bram in the first place. She rolled over and used the last of her strength to crawl to Zane, using only her good arm.

Relief came over his face when he saw her, and he started to cry. "Isa, Isa, don't leave me. Don't leave me. Please, don't leave me."

She sat down next to him and cupped his face. "Shh...it's okay. He's gone. Bram's gone."

She looked up at Chase, so he'd confirm her words to be true and reassure Zane, but he shrugged, not understanding what she wanted from him. She looked over at Ranulf, who was holding his shirt on Zane's chest where he'd been shot.

"We have to get him to the infirmary ASAP," Ranulf said.

"Isa."

She looked back at Zane.

"You're naked."

She laughed as she tried not to cry. It was so unimportant at a time like this. "Yeah, my clothes got ripped when I shifted."

"Oh, shit," Chase said. "Here, I can give you my shirt."

"Do it and die," Zane said.

Isabelle chuckled again. "It's just a shirt."

Zane raised a bloody hand and brushed a thumb over Isabelle's cheek. "No other male's clothes are going to touch the body of the woman I love, except for mine."

Isabelle gasped, and tears welled behind her eyes. *He loves me?*

At the same time, Raven came over and handed Isabelle her coat. "Here, hon. It won't hide everything, but it's better than nothing."

"Thank you," Isabelle said, taking the jacket from the female and slipping it on, being careful of her wounded arm. Her adrenaline was starting to drop, and she was getting cold. "I'll try and get it back to you clean."

"It's no big deal," Raven said. "Good job on killing that fucker. Turns out, you didn't need us after all."

Isabelle blushed from the praise. "Thank you."

Zane coughed, and blood showed at the corners of his mouth. "Where is the ambulance?"

"Two minutes out," Damien said as he came up behind her. "I just talked to them."

Two minutes felt like forever when the male you loved was bleeding out.

She suddenly felt exhausted.

Isabelle lay down beside Zane. "Please don't die." She started to cry. "Please don't die," she said again.

I can't lose him, was the last thing she thought before she passed out.

Damien watched the shifter ambulance pull up a minute later. They hauled Zane and Isabelle into the back and took off. The EMT said that Isabelle was probably just in shock and would be fine. It was Zane who was touch and go. Damien really hoped the cat-shifter would be okay.

He looked to the group of them who was left. They were all covered with blood and looked like hell.

"What are we going to do about the body?" Chase asked.

"I'm going to call Quentin and tell the police the truth. He was attacked by an animal. He'll send the right people out to pick up Bram and investigate."

Quentin was at the hospital again with his sister. He'd wanted to stay, but Damien had insisted he go.

"And where's the wolf?" Ranulf asked.

Damien shrugged. "Who knows? Probably ran off into the woods, far away from here, after Bram tried to shoot it."

"And the other blood on the ground?" Raven asked.

"Zane and Isabelle got attacked, too, when they tried to stop the wolf from killing Bram."

"Damn, Damien, you make me think it's the truth," Chase said.

Damien looked his sentinel in the eye. "I don't know what you're talking about. It is the truth."

Chase smiled. "Got it. Remind me never to cross you."

Damien raised an eyebrow. "Were you considering it?"

Chase's eyes widened. "Never."

Damien smiled. "Good," he said. Then, he pulled out his phone and called Quentin.

Chapter Forty

Later that night, Quentin returned home from spending the day in his sister's hospital room.

Things were looking up. Bram was dead, and Quentin's law enforcement colleagues had taken Damien's word and classified it as an animal attack. Of course, animal control was never going to find the wolf that had killed Bram, but that was okay.

Bram's father had been given the recording of what had happened and said he had no ill will toward the Minnesota Pack. It helped that Damien had talked to Bram's father before Bram died. Damien had explained that he was going to give Bram a warning to stay away, and if he cooperated, nothing would happen. It wasn't Damien's or Isabelle's or the other Minnesota shifters' faults that Bram had come after them. Damien had later told everyone he suspected Bram's father was partly relieved that he wouldn't have to clean up after Bram anymore.

Quentin's sister had opened her eyes that afternoon, and they had removed her breathing tube. It looked like she might make a full recovery. Their parents had broached the subject of the recovery facility in Switzerland, and amazingly, his sister had agreed to go.

He had seen the worry on their faces, so after talking to Damien and his captain, he had told them that he was going to be the one to go with Larissa. Damien had promised his position would be waiting for him when he returned home, and it would be good for Quentin to get out of town anyway.

He hadn't seen much of Hunter since he cried in front of him several nights ago. When Quentin had woken up alone, he hadn't been surprised, but he had been hurt. He'd known that Hunter wouldn't want anyone to know he'd slept in Quentin's room, yet he had thought something had changed between the two of them that night.

He had been wrong.

Hunter would never come out of the closet, and Quentin didn't want to be anyone's secret. It was too hard, and in the end, it wasn't worth it.

Once he reached his bedroom, Quentin pulled out his largest duffel bag and started packing his clothes. He wanted to take as many as possible so that he wouldn't have to buy clothes. The nice thing was, he would have his own little furnished apartment to live in, so clothes and personal belongings were the only things he had to worry about. Everything else he'd leave in Minnesota.

Quentin heard the sound of Hunter coming down the hall. He was pretty easy to distinguish with his crutches and cast.

Quentin paused in his packing to listen. He waited to see if Hunter would go to his room or come down to Quentin's. Quentin's door was partly closed, so he couldn't see anything, but when he heard Hunter keep moving, he held his breath.

But it was for nothing because Hunter stopped at the bathroom instead.

Quentin wanted to beat his own head in. Hadn't he just told himself that nothing would come of him and Hunter? Yet his stupid heart had hope. Lame.

He was pathetic.

Quentin plugged his phone into his stereo on his dresser and turned on some music. Then, he would be able to block out Hunter walking away.

Quentin sat down on his bed, facing the wall, and opened up his nightstand drawer. He had something he wanted to take with him to Switzerland, but he had to go through the items first.

A few minutes later, he was deciding if he should bring his stack of books or buy them as e-books when the music was turned down.

Quentin spun around on his bed. "Hey, what…" He trailed off when he saw it was Hunter in his room.

"I wanted to talk to you," Hunter said.

"Oh. Okay."

Hunter pointed to the duffel on the other side of the bed. "You're packing."

"Uh…yeah. I'm going to help my sister for a while."

"How long are you going to be gone?"

"A year."

Hunter's face drained of color.

Oh, shit.

Quentin was an asshole. Hunter was standing there on his injured leg. He jumped up and went to Hunter.

"Hunter, man, I'm sorry. I'm not a very good host." He helped Hunter over to his bed, so he could sit.

Quentin knelt before Hunter and inspected his leg the best he could. It was pretty hard to do when most of the lower half had a cast on it. The part he could see didn't look red or swollen though. But that didn't mean there wasn't a problem.

"Are you okay? Are you in pain? Is there anything I can get you?" Quentin straightened. "Do you need to feed?"

Hunter reached out and touched Quentin's mouth. "Do you know how many times I've dreamed of you kneeling before me?"

"No," Quentin said breathlessly and then chided himself for such a stupid response.

"I do," Hunter said. "I can't seem to forget about you." He shook his head. "And I've tried."

Quentin picked up Hunter's hand and kissed it. "I've thought about you, too. Except, in my fantasies, you're doing a lot more than kneeling."

"Are you really leaving?"

"Yes. I'm going to Switzerland with my sister for a year. It's something I need to do for my family."

Hunter swallowed. "Switzerland. That's so far."

"I know. Believe me, I know. I'm going to miss it here." *I'm going to miss you.*

Hunter leaned forward and kissed Quentin. It was just a brushing of his lips, but it was the sweetest kiss Quentin had ever received.

"I want you to make love to me before you leave. I want to feel you inside me," Hunter whispered against his lips.

Quentin sucked in a breath. He should say no. He needed to say no. But he couldn't say no.

"Are you sure? I want that more than you know, and I'm afraid I won't be able to stop like I did the other night."

"I don't want you to stop," Hunter said.

Quentin stood and looked down at the vampire. *Am I really going to do this?*

Hunter looked up into his eyes.

Fuck yeah, I am.

"Take off your clothes," he told Hunter and went to close and lock his door. Then, he went to his other nightstand that didn't hold his books. It was the one that held his lube.

He came back to Hunter, who was almost naked but struggling to get his shorts off his cast.

Quentin knelt down again. "Here, let me help you." He got the piece of clothing off and threw it to the side. As he did so, he couldn't help but notice that Hunter was already at full mast.

Quentin stood, pulled off his T-shirt, and shucked off his jeans. He took a step closer to the bed. "Suck me, Hunter."

He'd only felt the vampire's mouth on him once. It was the most amateurish yet best blow job he'd ever received, and he wanted to feel Hunter's mouth on him again. And, if he shied away from this, then Quentin would know he wasn't ready to have sex.

Hunter cupped Quentin's balls in one hand and took his cock in his other. Hunter licked the outside of his head and then sucked it into his mouth.

Quentin groaned at how good it felt.

This must have encouraged Hunter to go further because he swallowed more of Quentin, and when he hit the back of Hunter's throat, he thought he might bust his nut early.

He gently pushed Hunter away. "Lie back and scoot up the bed."

The sight of Hunter splayed out on his bed like that was something Quentin hoped he'd never forget.

He put one knee on the bed and crawled halfway up, stopping when he reached Hunter's shaft. He licked the spot where Hunter's balls met his dick and then moved up his cock until he could take all of him in his mouth. Quentin was hungry for the vampire and didn't waste any time in taking all of him.

Hunter's shaft jumped in his mouth as Hunter moaned, and it was a beautiful sound. "Oh God, I don't think I'm going to last long."

Quentin loved on Hunter with his mouth a little longer and then released him. "We can't let that happen yet." He got up on his knees in between Hunter's legs and stroked himself. "Have you ever done this before?"

It was funny because, the other night, he remembered thinking he didn't want Hunter's first time to be when Quentin was mad, but he'd never even asked. He'd just assumed that he'd be Hunter's first.

"Had sex?"

Quentin nodded.

"With a female. This will be my first time with a male."

A smile took over Quentin's face. "God, I love knowing I'm your first." Quentin grabbed the lube, squirted some on his cock, and rubbed it all around to make sure he was coated.

Hunter started to roll over, and Quentin stopped him with a hand on his hip.

"What are you doing?"

"Getting on my hands and knees. Isn't that the way?"

Quentin held in his smile. "It can be. But it doesn't have to be. I want to watch your face the first time I push into you."

Hunter lay on his back again, and Quentin moved closer, pushing Hunter's legs up.

"Are you nervous?"

Hunter nodded. "A little."

"Scared?"

This time, he shook his head. "No."

"Good."

Quentin took more lube and rubbed it on Hunter's entrance. He pushed a finger into him. Then, he put another in and then a third when he felt Hunter was ready.

He knew it was still going to burn a little, but there was nothing to prevent that, and hopefully, it would be a good burn for Hunter.

The moment came, and Quentin placed himself at Hunter's entrance. He slid his hands down Hunter's chest and gripped on to his thighs. With one strong thrust, he pushed into Hunter.

Hunter exhaled a big breath.

"Are you okay?"

Hunter nodded.

That was a relief because Quentin was ready to come from the tightness of Hunter's body. He couldn't believe they were really doing this.

He waited for Hunter to relax before he started to move. He went slowly at first and gradually began to pick up speed. Quentin grabbed Hunter's cock in his hand as Quentin stroked in and out of his body.

Quentin wanted them to come at the same time, and he shifted his body so that he could hit Hunter's sweet spot better. When a long moan escaped from the back of Hunter's throat, he knew he'd accomplished his goal.

"Are you going to come soon? I want you to come with me," Quentin said.

Hunter touched Quentin's chest and was now rotating his hips on Quentin's shaft. "Yes, I want that, too."

Quentin stroked Hunter faster. Just as the vampire's orgasm hit, Quentin pulled out, and they both came on Hunter's stomach.

It was the best good-bye present Quentin had ever received.

Chapter Forty-One

Zane woke up from the hardest sleep he'd ever experienced. He was groggy as shit and felt like he'd been run over by a truck. It felt an awful lot like when Gerald had shot him.

He lifted his head and looked down to see his bandaged chest. "Fuck me," he said, his voice raspy.

He'd been shot again.

Stupid fucking Bram.

At least the fucker was dead. He did remember hearing that.

Oh no!

"Isabelle?"

"I'm here. I'm here," she said.

He looked over his shoulder to see her sitting in the corner of his infirmary room. "Come here."

She hesitated.

"Please."

She took a deep breath and came to his bedside.

She seemed like something was bothering her. He should talk to her about it, but right now, he was going to be selfish, so he pulled her down to lie beside him.

He nuzzled her hair, her ear, and her neck. Her smell comforted him.

"I'm so glad you're here. I don't know if I could take getting shot again and not seeing you."

She got up on her elbow so fast, she bumped him in the nose.

Ow.

"You were shot before?"

He rubbed his sore sniffer. "Yeah." He cocked his head. "You mean, you didn't know?"

"*No.* Where?"

"My upper chest." He pointed to it. "It healed really well."

"Wow. I noticed the scar, but I had no idea it was from a gun. When did this happen?"

"Two days after you left." He looked away. "I kept hoping you'd come back once you heard I was injured."

"I didn't know," she whispered.

He met her eyes. "You would have if you had known?"

"I have no idea."

He laughed. "At least you're honest."

"Did you want me to?"

Zane lifted his head. "Isabelle, haven't you figured out that I'm crazy about you? Yes, I wanted you to come back."

"I don't understand. Why me? You're…" She gestured with her hand at his feet to the top of his head.

He didn't get it. "I'm what?"

"You're…gorgeous. You're a sentinel." She looked down. "And I'm me. I'm just a plain schoolteacher. You could have anyone you want."

Zane tilted her chin up, so she would look at him. "I never took you for someone who lacked confidence."

"That's because I am confident. But I'm also a realist. I know I'm a good catch, and Bram didn't deserve me, but I also know you can do better. You could have someone beautiful, like Payton."

"Payton's taken."

She gave him a look. "I know that. And you know what I mean."

"You forgot one thing."

She raised her brow. "And what's that?"

"I don't want anyone else. I want you." He pulled her down to him and thoroughly kissed her. "You think I go around, volunteering to marry every mate with an abusive boyfriend?"

"Well…no. But—"

He shook his head. "There is no *but*. I love *you*, Isabelle. No one else."

Her lower lip quivered. "You love me?"

He nodded his head and smiled. "Oh, Isa. I have for over two years."

She dropped on top of him and cried.

He winced as she hit his gunshot, but he didn't say anything.

Zane felt like he was out of his element, but he just rubbed her back and said soothing things. When he'd told Isabelle he loved her, he hadn't thought she'd bawl her eyes out.

No wonder she'd left two years ago without giving them a chance. He was horrible at this romance stuff.

Her body stopped shaking. Her hiccups slowed, and so did her sniffles. She shifted, so she could look down on him again. "You really mean it?"

"Yes," he said with a laugh of disbelief. "You know I'm telling you the truth right now because you look like shit from crying, and I haven't kicked you out of bed."

She smiled and rolled her eyes. "Oh, Zane."

"Why the tears?"

"Because it's too good to be true."

He laughed. "You realize, we are lying in a hospital bed after your ex-boyfriend shot me, right?"

"You know what I mean." She leaned down and kissed him. "I love you, too."

"Then, why do you look like you ate a sour grape?"

"Because it was kind of scary to say out loud. I think I was scared to let myself love you."

"Ah, Isa, don't be scared." He grabbed her arms. "I won't—"

She winced.

He knew that wince. She was in pain.

"What's wrong?" *Please don't say the baby*, he prayed.

"My arm," she said, pulling it back. "It's nothing."

"Isabelle."

She rolled her eyes. "Fine." She lifted her shirt, and she had a white bandage wrapped around it. "I might have gotten shot, too."

"*What?* How did I miss this?"

"You were kind of bleeding out."

He put his arm over his head. "I failed you."

"Zane." She pulled on his arm. "Zane."

He looked at her. "What?"

"You didn't fail me. It was just my arm. I'll have a scar, but it was just skin and muscle. Unlike you. They had to save your lung."

He touched his lower chest. "Is that why it hurts so much?"

She chuckled. "Yeah." She ran her finger over his chest. "So…you weren't worried about me yesterday, knowing Bram could show up?"

That was an odd question.

"Of course I was. That's why I took as much backup as possible."

"Why didn't you tell me what you had planned?"

"Because I had no idea if Bram would show up. And you needed some time away from everyone. I didn't want to ruin our picnic by worrying you, especially if he never showed up. I wanted you to enjoy the day."

"So, you weren't using me to lure Bram out?"

A light dawned on him. He remembered her pulling away from him yesterday by the lake. And she'd been a little distant when he first woke up just now. She'd thought he'd used her.

"Well, Isa, I suppose I did a little, if I'm being honest. But I knew I would do anything to protect you. And something had to give. We couldn't leave Bram out there to strike when he felt like it. He needed to be taken care of. I'm sorry I didn't tell you."

"It was probably a good thing," she admitted. "My surprise led him to thinking we were alone and him blabbing his big mouth. His ego and overconfidence were what got him in the end."

The door to his room opened then, and a female walked in with a stethoscope and a name tag that said *Dr. Gordan.* Behind her walked in a male with his own stethoscope and a name tag that read *Dr. Leed.*

"You're awake," Dr. Leed said.

Isabelle slipped off the bed. "I'm sorry. I should have come to get you."

Dr. Leed smiled. "Let's just take a look at you, okay?" he said to Zane.

After a thorough examination, Dr. Leed announced that Zane looked good.

"You can probably go home tomorrow."

"That's a relief." He didn't want to be there any longer than necessary.

"You're going to have a bigger scar than your last wound. This one needed surgery."

"That's okay. Scars are sexy, right, Isa?"

She smiled at him. "Whatever you say," she teased.

"Isabelle, I wanted to talk to you about your test results," Dr. Gordan said and gave a wary look toward Zane.

Isabelle grabbed his hand. "It's okay. You can talk in front of Zane. He's my mate."

The doctor looked back and forth between the two of them and then said, "Your test came back positive. We won't know if everything is okay for a few more months because the baby is too small right now. But that's also the reason the baby will probably be fine. It's cushioned inside you, being very protected."

Isabelle's free hand flew to her mouth. "I'm pregnant?"

Dr. Gordan smiled. "You are."

Isabelle started crying again, and Zane pulled her down to him.

"Isa, this is good news."

"I know. That's why I'm crying."

Zane looked at Dr. Leed, who shrugged.

Zane was never going to understand women, but he'd try his best to understand this one for the rest of his life.

Chapter Forty-Two

Tegan was just finishing up breakfast when she felt it.

She ran to the bathroom, and there was the evidence right in front of her.

She wasn't pregnant.

She had known there wasn't a guarantee, but a part of her had thought that she was going to have a baby.

She got in the shower and watched the evidence of her empty womb go down the drain.

It was kind of silly to be so upset. Two weeks ago, she had been a single female, going along, doing as she pleased. Now, she had a mate whom she loved more than anything and a sadness that she wasn't pregnant.

Go figure.

Life was strange.

Tegan got out of the shower and toweled off. Thankfully, she had work to do today. She needed to keep busy and her mind off of things.

She went to her room to get dressed.

After coming home from Vegas, the cats had stayed with the wolves a few nights until Bram was caught. After they'd come home, she'd been sleeping with Reid. All her stuff was still in her room though, and she was grateful she didn't have to face her mate at the moment.

Along with being a sentinel, Tegan worked at L & L Construction. And, due to her being out of town and trying to capture Bram, she was behind on her work. She had a full day ahead of meeting with clients.

After getting dressed, Tegan walked silently down the hall and past Reid's room. His door was ajar, and she heard the click-clack of his keyboard going. She should say good-bye to him, but she couldn't face him right now. He'd be so disappointed.

Work did take her mind off her failed heat, especially with a couple of difficult clients who consumed all her mental energy. But, by late morning, when she was chatting with one of the polite ones, a cramp had her wincing.

"Are you okay?" her client asked.

Mrs. Auch was about Tegan's age, and her husband had already stepped out of the room to take a phone call.

Tegan found herself telling the truth. "Just cramps."

"Ooh...those are the worst. I have some ibuprofen or Midol if you need it."

Tegan held up a hand. "No, that's okay. Thank you, but I do have some in my drawer."

Mrs. Auch smiled. "It helps to have that stuff on hand, doesn't it? I keep hoping I'll grow out of them, yet every month, they nearly have me in tears."

Tegan paused in horror. "You go through this every month?"

Her client laughed. "Yes, don't you?"

Uh...

"No, they usually aren't this bad," Tegan lied.

"Count yourself lucky. Mine always are."

Tegan was grateful she was a shifter and only had to endure this every six months, although she had been honest when she said it wasn't normally this bad. At least, it felt worse than usual.

"Well, I'd better get going. Thanks for everything," Mrs. Auch said, standing.

Tegan got up from her chair and held out her hand. "Thank you. Call if you have any questions. I don't work every day, but I'll try to get back to you as soon as I can."

The client shook her hand and left.

It was lunchtime, and Tegan wouldn't have another client for over an hour. She picked up her phone for the first time since she'd come into work. Truthfully, she'd been avoiding it and put it on silent the minute she arrived at her office.

Reid: You left without saying good-bye. Everything okay?

Reid: It's been a couple of hours. I haven't heard from you. Are you alive?

Reid: All joking aside, please call me when you get this. I need to know you're okay.

The last text had been twenty minutes ago.

But there was no way she was calling him. She'd didn't want to lie and tell him everything was fine, and she didn't want to tell him there was something wrong and leave him hanging about the details until she got home.

She took the chickenshit way out and messaged him back.

Tegan: Sorry I left without saying good-bye.

Tegan: I've been super busy, playing catch-up all morning. We'll talk when I get home. 😊

Tegan's afternoon was just as full as her morning, and again, she avoided her messages. But, after work was over, she was shocked to see that Reid hadn't responded at all.

She drove home with mixed emotions. Maybe they could avoid the whole subject of her bleeding. She knew she'd have to eventually tell him, but if she could wait a few days, that would help. Of course, she'd have to come up with a really good excuse to avoid sex since she'd been jumping Reid's bones every night.

She was also a little sad that Reid hadn't replied back all afternoon. Maybe he wasn't as worried about her as she had thought, which kind of hurt her feelings.

"Stop being such a girl," she said to herself and then winced at her callousness to females everywhere.

There was absolutely nothing wrong with being female or girlie and being emotional. She was learning to not push her feminine side away all the time, thanks to Isabelle, but it was going to be a slow process.

When Tegan got home, the only one there was Ram, and that was most likely because the sun was still up. Well, this was going to be awkward, but it was probably time they stopped avoiding each other.

"Hey," Ram said when he saw her. He was sitting at the counter, eating an apple.

"Hey. So, how are you?"

Ram laughed at her question. She didn't blame him.

"Good. And you?" He lifted a slice of apple to his mouth and bit it with his fang.

She lifted a shoulder. "I'm okay."

Ram looked down at her pelvis. "Sorry about your heat. I accidentally overheard you talking about wanting a baby."

Her eyes widened. "How did you know?"

He raised an eyebrow. "I'm a vampire. I can smell blood."

She laughed nervously. "Oh."

"You don't have to be embarrassed. It's natural. And I'm not going to attack you."

She straightened her back. "I didn't think you would."

Ram smiled. "I know. I just didn't want you to be embarrassed."

"Thanks. I guess."

"Are you worried about telling Reid?"

"I am a little, yeah. Stupid?"

"Nah." He took another bite of his apple. "But I wouldn't concern yourself. He's crazy about you. While you're worried about him, he's going to be worried about you."

"Thank you."

Of all the people she'd expected to get advice from, Ram was at the bottom of the list.

"Do you know where everyone is?"

Ram shook his head. "Not everyone. Reid had to go do something for Vance though."

"Okay, thanks." She took a step toward her room and stopped. "Even though it was kind of awkward between us, I hope that you find yourself a good mate."

The corner of Ram's mouth ticked up. "I'm not looking, but thanks."

Tegan nodded and continued to her room. She sent Reid a quick text, now eager to see him.

Tegan: I'm home. When will you get here?

There was no answer the rest of the evening, and Tegan finally had to give up waiting and go to sleep.

She didn't know how long she'd been out when she felt the side of Reid's bed dip behind her, and an arm came around her waist.

"Hey, Angel."

Tegan snuggled back against her mate. "Hey, yourself."

Reid's hand wandered her body in a loving touch but stopped when he got to her underwear. "You're wearing panties."

She rolled onto her back and ran her fingers through Reid's auburn hair. "I started bleeding this morning."

"Are you okay?"

"A little sad. Worried about disappointing you."

Reid leaned over and kissed her. "Aw, Angel. Don't worry about that. I'm sad, too. But we have the rest of our lives to be with each other. And we'll have fun trying again in another six months."

"I love you."

"I love you, too." Reid pulled her into his arms, and Tegan fell asleep on his chest, feeling like the luckiest female in the world.

Chapter Forty-Three

"Baby...baby...can you hear me? It's your daddy."

"Zane, the baby is the size of a grain of rice. It doesn't even have ears yet."

"Shh. I'm talking to my baby."

Isabelle rolled her eyes and let Zane do his thing. She was sitting on her parents' couch in their family room, waiting for them to come home from visiting her sister. Zane was lying on the couch with his head in her lap, talking to her stomach.

It was the same size as when her heat had ended. The doctor had told her she wouldn't notice any significant size changes for a while, which had actually disappointed Zane. Apparently, he wanted to see her big and round.

God, she loved her mate for his weird idiosyncrasies.

Isabelle heard the garage door open and pushed at Zane. "Get up. They're here."

She'd met his parents a few days ago, and they'd seemed to love her, saying they'd thought their son would never settle down.

Zane didn't protest and was up on his feet in two seconds.

"Okay, let me go talk to them first, and then I'll introduce you."

When her parents had left, she'd been dating Bram. Now, she was mated and carrying another male's child. They were going to wonder what the heck had happened while they were gone.

Her parents came through the garage door into the kitchen where Isabelle was waiting.

"Isabelle. You're here," her mother said.

"I told you I'd be waiting for you when you got home."

Her father came up behind her mother. "Hey, Isabelle. Why didn't you pick us up from the airport?"

"Dad, you told me not to."

"I know. I was just teasing you." He set down the suitcases he'd been holding and held out his arms. "Are you going to give us a hug?"

Isabelle knew her parents would smell her, but she couldn't resist. She ran to her parents and threw her arms around them. "I missed you."

"Oh, baby, we missed you, too," her mother said.

A few more squeezes, and Isabelle stepped back.

Her father put his hand on his hip. "So, you want to tell me why you smell like a male cat?"

Her mom grabbed her hand. "And why you smell like you're with child?"

Isabelle's jaw dropped. Her scent shouldn't have changed that fast. "How did you know?"

Her mom patted her cheek. "I'm your mother, dear. I have your scent memorized. When you were little, I knew the second you were coming down with something. Now, tell us, who is this male?"

"And where the hell is he?" Her father looked around. "And what happened to Bram?"

Isabelle held up one finger. "One second." She ran to the family room to grab Zane. "Hey, I was waiting for you—"

She stopped at the doorway and sighed.

Zane had turned on the Minnesota Wild game and wasn't even listening to her. She hadn't even known he was a fan. She guessed they were going to have fun, learning all these things about each other.

She walked into the room and stood in front of him. "Zane, my parents? They're waiting to—"

"What the hell kind of call is that?" Her father's voice boomed behind them. "That penalty is bullshit."

Zane sprang up from his seat. "Uh…hello, sir."

"Dad, this is Zane. Zane, this is my father, Jack." Isabelle's mom came in at the same time she was making introductions. "And this is my mother, Elizabeth."

"So, you're the one who knocked up our daughter?"

"*Dad.*" She knew he was just trying to put Zane on the spot.

But her mate wasn't going to be deterred. He put his arm around her. "Not before I mated and married her though."

She tried to hide her smile, but Zane got her dad on that one.

"So, what happened to Bram?" her mom said, not really showing how she felt about Zane one way or the other. Her mom was like that. She reserved her judgment until she heard all the facts.

Isabelle put her head on Zane's chest as he pulled her tighter to him. "Bram's dead."

"Oh, thank the Lord," her mom said.

Isabelle lifted her head. "What?"

A tear slipped from her mom's eye. "I never had a good feeling about him, Isabelle. Never."

"Why didn't you say anything?"

"Because you seemed to like him. And you never came to us with any issues."

"That's because I didn't want to involve you. He wasn't a good man, Mom."

"I was afraid it would take something extreme to get him out of your life." Her mom stepped closer to Zane. "Are you the reason he's dead?"

Zane smiled. "No, ma'am. That was your daughter's doing. She took him down herself."

Isabelle blushed. "It was only because he'd shot you. Otherwise, I don't know if I would have had the courage."

"You were shot?" her father asked.

"Yes, sir." Zane put his hand on his left side. "But they say I'll make a full recovery."

"So, tell us the whole story," her mom said. "I want to hear everything."

Isabelle told her parents everything that had happened, leaving out her heat. Her parents could put two and two together to figure out how she'd become pregnant. They were alarmed when they heard she'd been shot, but she was quick to reassure them that it was nothing compared to Zane's injury.

"I can't believe I'm going to be a grandmother again," her mom said to her when they left to go pick up dinner, leaving the two males to finish watching the hockey game.

"Are you okay with it?"

Her mom grabbed her hand. "Of course, honey. I remember when you came back from helping Damien. You've obviously had a thing for Zane for a long time."

Isabelle smiled. "I agree. It just took me a while to realize it."

When they got home, her mom called out to the guys to come and eat. After waiting five minutes with no sign of them coming into the kitchen, Isabelle went to find them.

Her father and Zane were in a deep discussion about the game. Isabelle watched them go back and forth a few times. Zane had obviously won him over right away, but that was her mate. He was really hard not to like.

"Hey," she said as she walked into the room. "Dinner is here, and it's getting cold."

"Sorry, son, I have to go fill this empty tank," he said, rubbing his belly. "I haven't had anything since the airplane." As her father walked out of the room, he kissed Isabelle on the cheek. "I like him."

"Thanks, Dad," she whispered.

Then, it was just the two of them. Or the three of them if you counted the TV.

"Zane, come on. It's time to eat."

"Just give me one more second," he said, holding up a finger, his eyes glued to the screen.

"Okay, I'll sit and wait. I don't mind watching a little Jason Zucker, Charlie Coyle, Marcus Foligno, Nino Niederreiter, and let's not forget Zach Parise. I mean, he's not the same since he took a puck to the face, but scars are sexy." She put a hand out and rubbed his back. "Right, honey?"

Zane turned off the TV. He slowly turned from his spot on the edge of the couch and looked at her. "We're never watching hockey again."

She shrugged innocently. "Whatever you say."

He shook his head. "Whatever I say, my ass."

Isabelle grinned at him, and Zane pulled her down to her back and started tickling her.

"Please stop," she said between laughs. "Please."

"Not until you tell me I'm better-looking than those guys."

"You're the ho-hottest male I know."

Zane stopped tickling and lay over her. "Don't think I didn't notice the 'I know' part of your little declaration."

She wrapped her arms around his neck. "You have nothing to worry about. You're the only one for me, Zane Talon."

He kissed her then, taking her mouth leisurely but sweetly. He licked inside her mouth, and she tightened her hold on him. She could feel herself getting wet and almost forgot she was at her parents' with them in the other room.

She broke their kiss. "We have to go eat," she said against his lips.

"I know."

Zane moved off her and gave her a hand to help her up. "By the way, how do you know who all those hockey players are?" he asked as they walked to the kitchen.

"I live in Minnesota. Of course I know who the hockey players are."

He put his mouth right next to her ear. "As if I didn't think you were sexy enough before. Now, I know we can talk stats and watch games together."

"You just said we weren't going to watch hockey ever again."

"I decided we can only do it when I'm inside you." Zane pulled away from her, stepped forward into the kitchen, and clapped his hands. "What's for dinner, folks?"

Isabelle followed with a grin on her face.

Being claimed by Zane was the best thing that had ever happened to her.

Epilogue

NINE MONTHS LATER

Zane cringed as Isabelle squeezed his hand. *Damn*. His mate was strong.

She collapsed back on the bed as she tried to catch her breath.

Zane took the washcloth he held in his other hand and wiped her face.

"How much longer?" he asked the doctor. "This seems like it's been going on longer than it's supposed to."

Dr. Gordan laughed. "Zane, this is a process. It takes time."

Zane looked at Isabelle. Her hair was full of sweat, and she looked exhausted. He hated that she was in pain, and there was nothing he could do for her. At least, when she was in her heat, he knew he could do something to relieve her agony. Right now, he felt helpless.

"We're never having sex again," he told her.

"That's supposed to be my line," she panted.

He narrowed his eyes. "I'm serious, Isabelle. No more kids."

"You'll change your mind in several weeks after you haven't had sex for a while."

He shook his head. "No, I won't."

Isabelle laughed at him.

"I hate seeing you in pain."

"Oh, it's for a good outcome," she said right before another contraction racked her body.

He held on to her for dear life again and toweled off her face when the contraction was done.

He must have had a bad look on his face because Isabelle said, "Oh, Zane, I'll be all right. I promise."

He wasn't so sure about that because he knew he'd never be the same again.

"If you want to make me feel better, can we decide on names?"

Isabelle had been hounding him to pick a boy name and a girl name for their baby, but he was having trouble since he hadn't met him or her yet. But, if it would make Isabelle feel better, he was all for it.

"Okay, okay. What were your suggestions again?"

"I have new ones. How about Wulf with a U if it's a boy or Kat with a K if it's a girl?" She laughed.

"I don't know how you can make jokes at a time like this."

This made her laugh harder. "Now, you know what it's like, being mated to you."

Zane scowled. "Fine. Wulf if it's a boy and Kat if it's a girl. I agree."

"What? No. I was joking."

Another contraction took hold, and after it passed, he asked her, "What names do you really want, Isa?"

"I like Finn for a boy and Lydia if it's a girl."

"I'll think about it."

"*Zane.*"

"I'm sorry, Isa. I can't. I can't until I meet the baby."

She didn't get a chance to answer because another contraction hit.

"Okay, Isabelle, this is it. I think you can do it in just a couple of more pushes," the doctor said.

Isabelle grabbed on to his hand harder than ever before as she used all her strength to push.

After what felt like forever, the sound of a baby crying filled the room, and Isabelle and Zane both began to cry.

"It's a girl!"

About a half hour later, Zane carried his new daughter out to the waiting room.

After she'd been born, the doctor had placed her tiny body on Isabelle's chest, and Zane had been in awe.

Dr. Gordan and a couple of nurses had then taken their daughter away to assess her and clean her up. She'd started crying the second they took her from her mama, but she'd been back in her arms soon enough.

Their daughter weighed six pounds and twelve ounces. She wasn't very big, but the doctor had assured them she was perfect.

Zane now said soothing words to her as he carried her to see her new family and friends. She seemed to calm when she heard his voice. He'd have to gloat to Isabelle about how him talking to her belly had been worth it.

When Zane walked out from the hallway, the room erupted into cheers.

His daughter scrunched up her little face, and Zane held out a hand and lowered it to tell them all to be quieter.

"Everyone, I'd like you to meet Katlynn Elizabeth Talon. Kat for short."

Everyone cheered again but this time a little quieter.

"I knew you were going to have a girl, man," Chase said to him as he looked down at the baby.

"Oh, and how did you know that?"

Chase tapped his head. "I just knew."

Zane elbowed him. "Get out of here," he said with a laugh.

Both sets of grandparents came over to see their new granddaughter.

"Oh, Zane, she's perfect," his mother said. "Can I hold her?"

"For a minute. Isabelle is anxious for me to bring her back."

"Hello, little one," his mom said as soon as Katlynn was in her arms. "I'm your Grandma Eve. And I just love your name. Yes, I do."

Zane tried not to laugh as his father-in-law scowled.

"Sorry, Jack. It was Isabelle's idea."

Jack smiled. "It's fine. I'm just glad she's healthy."

After all the grandparents got a chance to hold the baby, he took her back to her mama.

Isabelle was sleeping when they came in, but she stirred right away and held out her arms.

Zane placed her in his mate's arms.

"What did everyone think?"

He sat on the bed next to Isabelle. "Everyone loves her."

She looked up at him. "What did our parents think of her name?"

"My mom loved it. Your father, not so much."

"Did you tell him we'll try for a Wulfgang next time?"

"Uh, no, because we're never doing this again. Remember?"

Isabelle laid her head on his arm and laughed. "We'll see."

"Ha. I'm stronger than you think."

She kissed his arm. "When it comes to me, you're not."

Zane put his arm around his mate and slid down. "You're right. I'm not." He sighed. "Okay, we can have another baby." He put his finger into Katlynn's fist. "She is pretty cute."

"That didn't last long."

"What?"

"Your resolve."

"That's because, when it comes to you, I have none." He kissed her on the head. "Thanks for giving me a daughter."

"You're welcome. Thanks for putting her inside me."

Zane smiled. "My pleasure."

"And that's why you didn't last long."

Zane looked down at his mate and daughter and felt more in love than ever before. Except, this time, it was for two females.

If you like the Forbidden Series, check out R.L. Kenderson's contemporary romance, *Dirty*!

Chapter One

*E*lise Phillips scanned the bar and grill as the door closed, leaving the June warmth behind her.

An arm toward the back of the room shot up, waving. Next, she saw her college friend's light-brown hair, and then Rachel Garwood's pixie face lit up as she beckoned her to the table.

When Elise approached, Rachel stood and squealed, her hazel eyes shining, as she held out her arms for a hug. Rachel had to step on her tippy-toes while Elise had to bend down. Elise was five-seven, but Rachel was only five-two.

"I'm so happy you're here," Rachel said. "I can't believe you get to come out with us whenever you want now."

About a month ago, Elise had moved back to the Minneapolis-St. Paul area, where she'd gone to high school and college. She'd found out her father was sick, and she wanted to be close to him just in case he didn't have much time left. Even though Rachel had also been born and raised in the Twin Cities, they hadn't met until they became roommates at the University of Minnesota.

"Me either," she said as she stepped back from her friend.

"So, how's the house-hunt going?" Rachel asked as she took her seat.

Elise sighed as she hung her purse on the edge of the chair next to Rachel and sat next to her. "Okay. I'm so glad my old house sold; that's a relief. I really like the realtor you referred, but so far, I haven't found something I really like and want to buy."

"I'm so glad you like Cara. She's great. And I know what you mean. Sean probably would have been happy with the ten other houses we saw, but I didn't have that I-could-live-here feeling." Rachel had just bought a home with her fiancé, Sean, about six months earlier. "I'm sure you'll find one you like sooner rather than later."

"I hope so. I can only live with my parents for so long before they drive me completely nuts. I'm twenty-nine, but sometimes, I think they forget that I've been living on my own for over a decade."

"Ah, they're sweet."

Elise snorted. "You don't have to live with them."

Her mother had always been protective, but her hovering had gotten worse ever since her father was diagnosed with colon cancer.

"Well, let's agree to disagree. I'm just happy you're home."

So was she. Elise had enjoyed living in Denver since finishing graduate school, but it felt good to be home. And, while she would miss it, she didn't regret coming back once she learned her father was sick.

Elise gestured to the four open seats at the table. "Who else is coming?"

"Do you remember Shelly and Joe Howard?"

"Hmm." Elise couldn't quite remember them off the top of her head. "Oh. Did I meet them one year at your Christmas party? Shelly teaches with you, and her boyfriend is Joe. Both redheads?"

"Yes, that's them. Although they're husband and wife now. Shelly is actually pregnant. They are going to have the cutest little ginger baby."

Elise chuckled. "That's so great for them," she said, meaning it even though she felt slightly let down.

When Rachel had asked her to have dinner and drinks, Elise had assumed it was going to be a girls' thing. While she remembered liking Shelly and Joe, they were a couple, which meant one of the six seats belonged to Sean. So, either it was a couples' get-together and Rachel was setting her up with someone or she was going to be the dreaded fifth wheel. Neither option sounded appealing.

"So, Shelly, Joe, and Sean are coming. Is the sixth seat someone you're trying to hook me up with?" she asked just as Rachel said, "Oh, look. There are Shelly and Joe now."

Her friend stood and waved to catch the newcomers' attention.

Despite the two of them speaking at the same time, Rachel had heard her question. She sat back down and cocked her head. "I wouldn't do that to you. I know how much you hate being set up on blind dates."

Fifth wheel, it was then. Elise didn't know whether to be relieved that she wouldn't have to fake interest in someone—because she really didn't have the energy for that tonight—or disappointed that she was going to be the poor single girl.

Turned out neither because Rachel then said, "No, the last seat is for Luke Long. Do you remember him?"

Elise's answer was a groan of irritation. Oh, she remembered him all right. So did every other member of the student body—at least, those with ovaries. Girls' IQs dropped when Luke was around. It almost made her embarrassed to be a member of the female sex.

Thankfully, Shelly and Joe walked up, so Rachel didn't hear her response because Elise knew Sean and Luke had been good friends in college. Greetings were made, and Elise was reintroduced to the couple considering it had been a few years since she last saw them. They talked about Shelly's ever-expanding belly. She was huge, but she still had seven weeks to go. Shelly was barely over five feet while Joe was a former football player and closer to six feet tall, and they joked about how she was going to have an enormous baby. Thankfully, the group's joking had Elise almost forgetting all about the previous conversation.

When the door opened, she was sure she could feel a breeze all the way at the back of the room as Sean and Luke walked in. The two of them contrasted each other. Sean was blond and blue-eyed and only about five-eight while Luke was over six feet with thick dark brown hair and chocolate-brown eyes. Sean was showing Luke something on his phone, and Luke threw his head back and laughed, catching all the attention in the room. Elise swore she saw drool on a couple of ladies' chins.

Barf.

To be fair, Luke wasn't a horrible person, and she hadn't seen him in years, since college, so he'd probably matured...hopefully. But, back in school, he'd been quite the man-slut. While he hadn't been truly arrogant—she'd known some conceited assholes, and Luke had never been like that—he was gorgeous, and he knew it. Girls had practically thrown themselves at him, and he'd had no shame, sleeping his way through the female student body and leaving a trail of broken hearts.

Elise hadn't been a saint. She'd had a few one-night stands and even a couple of exclusive friends with benefits, but she'd like to think she'd had some discretion. She certainly hadn't slept with every guy who had hit on her.

Luke looked at one of the girls—probably ten years his junior—who was staring wide-eyed at him, and he winked at her.

Elise rolled her eyes. She might have given him too much credit on the maturing thing.

Luke and Sean reached their table, and she realized that she had watched them walk through the whole restaurant. God, she was such a hypocrite. Her only defense was that she didn't have her tongue hanging out, and she'd never been dumb enough to hop into bed with Luke.

Sean leaned down and kissed Rachel before taking the seat across from her in the middle chair. Shelly and Joe were already sitting on opposite sides of the table, so all the girls were on one side, which only left the seat directly on the other side of Elise open.

Great. This was supposed to be a relaxing night out with friends. She really didn't feel like being near King Flirt all evening.

It wasn't that she thought she was some irresistible beauty. In fact, he probably didn't even remember her. It was just that the Luke she remembered flirted with everyone who had a vagina.

Case in point, Luke walked over to Shelly and kissed her on the cheek. "Hey, gorgeous. How's my baby doing?"

Everybody laughed, even Joe. Elise snorted.

"You wish, Luke," Joe said.

Then, Luke kissed Rachel on the cheek. "Hey, beautiful. When are you going to leave that loser over there and marry me instead?"

"Never," Rachel told him with a grin on her face. "But I'll keep you in mind for when he kicks the bucket."

"Hey!" Sean exclaimed. But he was laughing, too. "I'm never dying, woman. You're stuck with me forever."

Luke went around to his side of the table and sat down across from Elise.

Sean pointed to her as Elise held out her hand to shake. "Luke, I don't know if you remember—"

"Elise Phillips," Luke said as he met her eyes. Taking her hand, he kissed the back of it, his trademark cocky smile on his face. "Of course I remember her. How could I forget?"

Like she said, flirt.

Luke Long watched as Elise rolled her eyes, cupping the back of her hand where he'd kissed it, and he chuckled. He remembered that, back in college, it had always been easy to get a rise out of her, and it seemed things hadn't changed very much.

He knew she thought he was a dog, but it wasn't his fault that he liked sex and that women liked him. It wasn't as if he forced ladies to sleep with him. In fact, he usually waited for them to proposition him, and Elise probably wouldn't believe it, but he had said no a time or two.

But *she* had never been one of those girls. She'd never hit on him, and out of respect for his friendship with Sean, he'd never hit on her. Even though he knew she found him attractive. He'd seen the way she stared at him when he walked in the door today although she tried to hide it.

He always thought that one of the reasons she looked down on him so much was because there was unmistakable chemistry between them, and she hated it. While most girls had liked him back in college because he was a jock who played hockey, that hadn't seemed to impress Elise. This had only made him want to goad her more. Maybe it was the ten-year-old boy in him.

He could acknowledge that he might go a little overboard on the flirting, but flirting was fun, and he might as well drive Elise nuts since he couldn't sleep with her. Because, unlike her, he could admit he had wanted to—and apparently, still did.

She was pretty but not exceptionally beautiful, yet there was something about her. She was taller than most women, which he always liked since he was tall himself, and she was thin but not skinny. She had curves in all the right places, and she'd even filled out significantly more since college. She wasn't too big or too small. Like in *Goldilocks and the Three Bears*, she was *just* right. She had long dark blonde hair and large green doe-eyes. And big red lips that the guys in college had labeled DSL—dick-sucking lips.

He snickered, just thinking about it, and Elise narrowed her eyes at him.

Ha.

If she knew what he had been reminiscing about, she'd probably deck him. It was a good thing he wasn't going to tell her.

No, he wasn't going to say anything, and he'd do his best not to torture her tonight. He knew from Sean that she'd recently found out about her father's cancer, and she was busy moving and starting a new job. While Luke liked to provoke her, he'd like to think he wasn't a total asshole.

Yep, tonight was going to be nothing more than just a bunch of friends hanging out.

Chapter Two

*D*espite Elise's initial concerns, dinner had been enjoyable, and Luke hadn't flirted much. Maybe she was right, and he had matured.

Right now, he was in a heated conversation with Sean and Joe about politics. They were all on the same side, but the conversation was still fairly animated. The women were talking about Shelly's upcoming baby shower and birth, but Elise found herself catching bits and pieces of the things Luke had to say. She was impressed with his knowledge on the subjects they were discussing. He'd obviously done his research, and she was surprised. And rather turned on.

She'd always found intelligence sexy. Not that she didn't find muscles and a hard body sexy because she was a living, breathing woman after all. It was just that she'd always been attracted to wit. But, right now, Luke was showing brains, and he already had brawn. And she was horny.

Although she'd had two beers with dinner, so that was probably the alcohol talking. That, and the fact that she hadn't been with anyone for seven months, two weeks, and four days. Not that she was counting or anything, right?

God, she missed sex.

Thankfully, she wasn't drunk, just tipsy, and she planned to keep her skirt and underwear right where they were. On her body.

But it didn't stop her from stealing glances at Luke. His deep brunette hair was short and coarse, his coffee-colored eyes were round and large, and his lips were on the full side and naturally rosy. His eyebrows were dark and thick, as were the eyelashes that she would kill for because it would mean never having to wear mascara again. His skin had a beautiful golden tan that she couldn't help but notice whenever his biceps flexed under his tight T-shirt. He was half-Caucasian and half-Asian—Chinese, if she remembered correctly—and that was where he got his dusky features from. She'd always been a sucker for brown eyes and brown hair. That described almost all of her ex-boyfriends. But none of them had been as good-looking as Luke.

Ugh.

She looked away from him and down at her beer. She should really stop drinking. Otherwise, she was going to go home, feeling sorry for herself, and end up masturbating to images of Luke going down on her while she grabbed on to his short hair.

She looked to her friends to see if they could tell what she was thinking, but they weren't even paying attention to her. She turned to look at Luke, and he was staring at her with a smirk on his face. But there was no way he could know what she had been thinking, could he?

"Okay, enough talk about babies and politics. Joe and I don't have many more kid-free nights," Shelly said, turning Elise's gaze away from Luke.

"What are you thinking, babe?" Joe asked.

"First, everyone needs to get another drink since I can't."

"Works for me," Joe said as he raised his arm to catch their waitress's attention. "I'm going to enjoy having a DD for as long as I can."

"Uh…I'm not sure I should drink anymore," Elise said.

"Why not?" Rachel asked. "Tomorrow is Saturday, and this is the first time you've come out with us since you moved back. We should be celebrating."

Elise didn't answer because she couldn't tell the whole table her lame reason for wanting to cut herself off.

"Yeah, Elise, why not?" Luke joined in.

She couldn't tell if he was mocking her or not, but she didn't want to disappoint Rachel. Elise was certain she could stop thinking about Luke sexually, so she said, "Okay, order me another beer."

"Woohoo!" Rachel said. "That's the girl I remember from college."

Elise laughed as their waitress approached.

"Refills for everyone," Sean said. "And five shots of Jägermeister," he added, wiggling his eyebrows.

Elise groaned. "Oh God. Jäger was my go-to shot in college. I used to get so drunk off that stuff."

"And that is why I ordered it."

"Your fiancé is evil," Elise told her friend.

Rachel laughed. "Nah, we just want you to have fun with some reminiscing on the side."

Their server brought back their five shots along with one shot of Coke. "I didn't want you to feel left out," she told Shelly.

"Aw, that's so sweet," Shelly said. After their waitress walked away, she added, "Someone's getting a big tip." She picked up her shot, and everyone else followed. "What are we toasting to?"

"Good friends."

"Healthy babies."

"Getting laid."

"*Sean*," Rachel chided.

"What? I've been gone all week on business. You *know* you're going to be giving it to me later."

Rachel set her full shot glass on the table. "Yeah, but you don't have to tell everyone. I work with Shelly. I don't want her thinking you're a pervert."

Joe laughed. "Babe, you wouldn't think that about Sean, would you?"

Shelly shook her head. "Never." She put her free hand on Rachel's arm. "And, if it makes you feel any better, this baby was conceived in the back of Joe's SUV at his brother's wedding."

Everyone laughed, except for Joe, his face serious.

"Baby, we promised to never talk about that. If my mom ever finds out that I had sex in the church parking lot, she's going to make sure this baby is baptized the minute it comes out, and she'll make me attend confession every day for a year. At least."

Shelly stopped laughing. "You're right. She already thinks her Protestant daughter-in-law corrupted her Catholic son." She pointed her finger around the table. "Not a word to anyone. I can't even use the I-was-drunk-when-I-said-that, it's-not-true excuse."

Elise understood where Joe and Shelly were coming from. She hadn't grown up Catholic, but her parents were religious.

"Don't worry; we won't say anything," Rachel promised. She picked up her shot again. "Okay, where were we?"

"To good friends, healthy babies, and getting laid," Elise said.

Everyone repeated the words, and they all clinked their glasses together and downed their shots.

"Who wants to play pool? There's one table open," Sean asked after they all deposited their shot glasses on the table.

"I'm in," Joe answered.

"I'll take winner," Luke said.

The guys got up and headed toward the pool tables. Since their table was in the back of the room, the girls would have a clear view of the game without leaving their seats.

"How did Sean and Luke start hanging out again? I haven't seen him since, like, junior year or something, and I haven't heard you talk about him in forever," Elise asked.

Luke and Sean were two years older in school than Elise and Rachel. The girls had met the guys their freshman year, but Rachel hadn't started dating Sean until she was a sophomore. Sean and Luke had been roommates, and since Elise and Rachel were good friends, the four of them had seen a lot of each other. Both guys had finished their bachelor's degrees and stayed on for graduate school, but by that time, Elise had started dating Tyler. She was ashamed now by how much she'd thrown herself into that relationship. She'd barely even seen Rachel their senior year because she was so caught up with her boyfriend.

After Elise and Rachel had finished their undergraduate degrees, they'd both stayed at U of M for graduate school. Elise had been going to school full-time, working as many hours as possible, and moved in with Tyler, so she still hadn't seen Rachel that much although they both tried.

From what she remembered, the same thing had kind of happened with Luke and Sean. They had both gotten busy, seeing each other less and less, especially since Rachel and Sean lived together, until the two guys no longer hung out and then lost touch. Thankfully, that had never quite happened to Elise and Rachel, and they had remained friends, even when Elise moved to Colorado. It probably helped that Rachel was the shoulder that Elise had needed to cry on when she and Tyler broke up right before her move to Denver.

"I know. It's kind of crazy. Sean ran into Luke at our local Home Depot, of all places. Did you know that Luke works at Southdale? I was kind of surprised when I found out."

Elise knew Sean had gone to school for his MBA and worked for a big-box store. It wasn't hard to believe that Luke had graduated with a master's, too, and gotten a job at somewhere like Southdale Center, the mall in Edina. He was a womanizer, not an idiot.

She was just about to ask what Luke's role was when Rachel continued with her story, "Anyway, that's how we found out we only lived a few blocks away from him. Go figure. We'd practically been neighbors for about two years. After that, it was almost like the two of them had never been separated."

"Good for them," Elise said. "It doesn't seem like Luke has changed all that much."

Rachel laughed. "You mean, because he's a flirt and a half? Yeah, he's still kind of a man-ho. I swear, he dates a different girl every weekend. That's probably the only thing I don't like about Sean being friends with him. But Luke has never tried to push his singleness on Sean, and Luke seems genuinely happy that the two of us are getting married."

"Joe and I have gone out with him only a few times," Shelly said. "He is totally a flirt, and the women are always eyeing him." She nodded her head toward the guys. "Like now."

Elise looked over and saw a beautiful woman sliding up to Luke and getting as close as possible to him.

"But, to give him credit," Shelly continued, "he doesn't dog on women when he comes out with us. When he spends time with us, he spends time with us. I can't even blame all the girls who hit on him. He's hot. If I were single…"

The woman hitting on him put her hand on his arm. While Luke smiled politely at her, he was standing with his feet spread apart, and his hand on his pool cue, his body facing the pool table. Elise got the distinct impression that he wasn't interested. The woman slipped a piece of paper in his back pocket and walked away. As soon as she turned, Luke took the paper out and chucked it into the trash can in the corner of the room.

Elise was impressed again because the Luke she'd known in college probably would have ditched them all and walked out the door with the woman without a backward glance.

Luke looked up from the garbage, his eyes colliding with Elise's so swiftly that she turned back to the girls and took a couple of sips of her drink. She hoped he didn't think she'd been staring at him.

"I guess it's true that men can change," she said, almost forgetting what they had been talking about.

"Nah, we don't change that much," a deep voice said in her ear.

She jumped in her seat and turned. "Shit, you scared me." She hadn't heard Luke come up behind her.

He was way too close for her liking. He smelled wonderful, a natural muskiness with a hint of aftershave that was utterly male. She wanted to bury her nose in his neck and breathe him in.

Had she mentioned that she missed sex?

She tried not to lean too far away because she didn't want him to know that he affected her or how confused she felt when she was near him.

He tugged on a piece of her hair. "Another table opened up. Come play pool with me?"

She welcomed the distraction. Now, pool, she could definitely manage.

She raised her brow at him. "Are you sure you want to play against me?" she asked sweetly.

"Sure. You can't be that bad."

Elise just laughed.

"You kicked my ass." Luke sighed, surprise showing on his face. "And here I thought, I was good with *my* stick and balls."

Elise ignored his sexual innuendo and smiled. "I asked you if you wanted to play against me," she said in a singsong voice.

Luke narrowed his eyes. "That was when I thought you were bad at pool."

She shrugged innocently. "That'll teach you to assume things about women."

He snorted. "I didn't assume you were a bad player because you were a woman."

She put one hand on her hip. "Then, why did you think I was bad?"

"Because I remember you being kind of a fuddy-duddy."

"*What?* I was not. Just because I didn't fall into bed with you like every other chick does not mean I was a fuddy-duddy." She swept her hair over her shoulder and stepped closer to him, looking him in the eye. "I'll have you know, I had plenty of sexual conquests in college. You just didn't happen to be one of them."

He grinned down at her. "See, I know you're trying to make me feel inadequate because we didn't have sex, but all you're doing is making me hard."

She rolled her eyes. "You're hopeless."

"Nah. Wanna play again?"

"Sure."

She was actually having fun with Luke. She liked playing pool, and Luke was a good opponent.

"Do you want another beer first?"

She looked into her almost-empty glass. "That'd be great." After all, she was drinking for the pregnant lady, and she'd managed to keep her hormones in check so far.

"You set up, and I'll go get us drinks."

Elise grabbed the triangle and began racking the balls, putting them in their proper place. She grabbed the one ball and put it at the apex when Rachel walked over and leaned against the side of the pool table.

"Are you having a good time?" her friend asked.

"Yeah. I'm glad you asked me to come. I totally kicked Luke's ass."

Rachel smiled, but it was hesitant.

Elise stopped what she was doing. "What's wrong?"

Rachel stood up straight. "I think we're going to take off. I don't feel well. Shelly and Joe are leaving, too. Shelly's tired, and she wants to go home and put her swollen feet up."

"Are you okay?"

"Yeah," Rachel said, putting her hand over her stomach. "I think it was something I ate."

Elise narrowed her eyes and studied her friend. "Liar. You just want to go home and get laid."

Rachel blushed. "Guilty. I haven't seen Sean for a week." She stuck her bottom lip out.

Elise laughed. "I understand. Go have fun with your man."

Rachel looked around the room, as if she was calculating the situation. "What is it?" Elise asked.

"Nothing."

"Rachel, just spit it out. What's wrong?"

"I don't want to leave you here with Luke."

Elise shook her head. "I'll be fine. We're having fun. I'm not ready to go home yet."

Her friend looked over her shoulder to where Luke stood at the bar, talking to Sean. They seemed to be having a serious conversation. She looked back at Elise. "I just want you to be careful."

Elise tilted her head. "How do you mean?"

"It's been over six months since you and Jason broke up. I don't want to see you get hurt again."

Elise shook her head in confusion. "I still don't get it. Why would I get hurt?"

Rachel sighed. "Just don't sleep with Luke, okay? He's grown up quite a bit, but he's still Luke. I've never seen him get serious with anyone, and I don't want your heart to get broken."

Elise threw her head back and laughed. "We are just playing pool. Nothing's going to happen."

Rachel didn't laugh. "I know you haven't slept with anyone since before you and Jason broke up." She leaned in close and lowered her voice. "And I know how horny you get when you've been drinking. I also know that sex with Jason was mediocre, at best, so you're probably really jonesing for sex now. And let's face it; we both know that Luke probably fucks like a rock star."

Elise laughed again and shook her head. "Trust me, Rach, you have nothing to worry about. I am never going to sleep with Luke Long."

Chapter Three

*T*he next morning, Elise woke, flat on her stomach, disoriented, with a piercing headache that only came from a hangover. While she'd been living with her parents for about a month now, she'd often still wake up in confusion from forgetting where she was at first. It'd sometimes take her a minute to realize she wasn't in her house in Denver anymore. She opened one eye to check the time, but the alarm clock wasn't hers or the one in her parents' guest room.

She sat up, jarring her already-sore head, and let out a moan. Thankfully, dark shades were covering the windows, casting the room in shadows and hiding the evil sun.

What happened last night? Her memory was fuzzy, and it hurt to think.

She realized she was naked and pulled the sheet up to cover herself as she slowly looked around the room, recognizing nothing. Nothing but the sleeping naked male lying on the bed next to her.

Oh God. No! Panic raced through her body, and memories rose to taunt her.

She'd slept with Luke Long. She'd slept with. Luke. Long.

She whimpered and closed her eyes. She had managed to escape college without screwing the guy, only to have dirty, dirty sex with him last night. And that was only the stuff she could remember.

She was never drinking again.

If Rachel ever found out, she was going to give Elise so much shit— after she quizzed Elise on whether the whole fucks-like-a-rock-star thing was true.

Elise couldn't recall everything from last night after the rest of their friends had left the restaurant, and Luke and she had decided it would be fun to take a bunch of shots. But, now, she did know that, yes, Luke Long did indeed fuck like a rock star. Her sore vagina could attest to that.

I hate you, alcohol.

Luke shifted beside her, but the arm he had over his eyes remained where it was, and his breathing regulated and deepened again.

She really should get out of there before he woke up, but instead, she found herself staring at his beautiful body. *Why does he have to be so gorgeous?*

She moved her gaze from his face to his muscular chest and stomach and noticed a blemish of some kind. She leaned closer to look at the red mark directly above his hip.

Are those teeth marks?

A memory surfaced. She'd bitten him so hard that she bruised him…*after* she went down on him…*again*. She dropped her head in her hand. She was such a slut.

She looked again at the wound, and her gaze moved to the thin white sheet that was covering one leg and only part of his penis. God, even flaccid, it was thick and long. She remembered thinking it was perfect. She might have even told him that she wanted to mold his dick, so she could use it on herself when she was alone. She moaned softly with embarrassment.

"Jesus, would you stop thinking? You're making my hangover ten times worse."

Elise jumped. "Would you stop scaring me?"

Luke chuckled and moved his arm from his face. His brown eyes glittered with amusement. "Sorry," he said, but his tone indicated that he wasn't the least bit remorseful.

And, now, she was regretting not getting the hell out of there right away. She looked at the floor next to the bed and only saw a few items of clothing and nothing that looked like the shirt or skirt she'd been wearing last night. Nothing to cover her up so that she could make her escape. Then, she spotted them by the door on the other side of the room and winced.

She looked at Luke, hoping maybe he'd shut his eyes in an attempt to go back to sleep, but luck was not on her side this morning, and she found him watching her. It was making her self-conscious, knowing all the naughty things she'd done with him and to him last night.

"Can you please close your eyes, so I can get dressed?"

This made Luke laugh, but she didn't find it the least bit funny. She needed to get up and out of there before Rachel called her or her parents called Rachel. She really didn't need a lecture about sleeping with Luke right now—from her parents or Rachel. Especially after she'd told her friend it was never going to happen.

"I think that ship has sailed, Lise. I already saw everything last night, babe." He looked down at her crotch. "*Everything.*"

She fidgeted on the bed. First, she didn't know if she liked him shortening her name like they were close now or something, and second, she suddenly pictured him kneeling between her legs as he parted her and blew on her nether lips right before he—

Luke threw back the covers and sat up on the edge of the bed, giving her a clear view of his back. Even his back was sexy. Except for the red claw marks there.

Holy shit. Had she possessed any restraint last night?

Luke stood and walked to the door to retrieve her clothes. He didn't seem to care that he was naked because he didn't bother dressing. Of course, he had a world-class butt. Elise tried hard, but when he turned around, she couldn't help staring at his morning wood, and she grew wet between her legs.

"Can you put on some clothes, please?" Her tone was bitchier than she had meant it to be, but she really needed him to get dressed before she threw back the bedsheet and spread her legs for him, begging him to fuck her again.

He raised an eyebrow.

"I know, I know. We already had sex, so what's the big deal? And I'm sorry for being rude, but I'm finding it hard to think with you walking around..." *With your big, beautiful dick saluting me.*

Luke snickered as he tossed her clothes on the bed, as if he knew exactly what was going on in her head. But he didn't object as he went into his walk-in closet.

As soon as he was in there, she quickly yanked on her clothes, except for her underwear. She didn't see them anywhere, and since Luke would walk out at any second, she opted for going commando. It wasn't ideal since she was wearing a skirt, but at least she wasn't nude anymore.

Luke exited his closet, wearing a pair of nylon shorts and holding a T-shirt in his hand. The bite mark she'd left stood out against the light gray of his shorts. She considered just pretending like she didn't know it existed, but she was maturer than that. Or, at least, she wanted to think she was.

"I'm sorry—"

"If you apologize for fucking me…" Luke's lips were in a hard line, and his eyes had lost all humor. He almost looked hurt. "Look, we're both adults, both single, we used protection, and no one got hurt."

She sat on the side of the bed. "Well, see, that's not exactly true…" She waved her hand toward his lower body.

He shook his head, obviously not understanding. "What's not true? Are you trying to tell me you have a boyfriend?"

"No."

He frowned. "Are you saying, we didn't use protection? Because I might have been drunk, and you did almost jump the gun there the first time, but I distinctly remember using condoms."

Her cheeks got warm as she vaguely recalled pushing him down on the sofa, slipping her underwear off, lifting her skirt, and—

"Open your eyes and watch me while I fuck you, Elise. I want you to know whose cock you're riding."

She shook her head before she turned red, clearing the memory. "No, that's not it either."

"Okay, Lise, you're just going to have to spit it out then."

"Hurt. You're hurt." She pointed to his hip and sighed. "I hurt you."

Luke lowered his head and examined her bite mark. "Oh, yeah, I remember that." He looked up at her and grinned. "I never would have taken you for a wildcat in bed, but damn, I liked it." He shrugged and put his shirt on. "Besides, I sort of got you back." He waved his hand over his neckline.

She gasped and jumped up, bolting for the bathroom. "You didn't!" she yelled at him before she flipped on the light switch. She lifted her chin up and to the side, and there it was—a big ole hickey right on her neck. Thankfully, the top she'd worn last night had a low collar, so she should be able to find a more modest shirt to cover it for work, but she sure as shit didn't know how she was going to walk into her parents' house and not let them see it.

He came up behind her. "I'd tell you I was sorry, but then I'd be lying. If it makes you feel better, I don't remember doing it, and I didn't do it on purpose."

She angled her head to look at it again. "Fat lot of good that does me. It's there whether you meant to do it or not."

He leaned in closer to her, meeting her eyes in the mirror. "Well, at least I didn't bite you," he teased.

Embarrassed, she didn't reply. Instead, she worked on straightening her appearance. She finger-combed through her long hair to get the snarls out and used hand soap and water to get rid of the mascara that rimmed her eyes.

She almost forgot he was still there when he said, "I'm going to get coffee. I'll meet you downstairs."

She hurried up, trying to make herself look presentable, and quickly used the facilities before heading downstairs.

If she wasn't hungover and freaking out about sleeping with Luke, she would have taken the time to admire his beautiful home. But, at the moment, she wanted to forget that she had ever been there and get the hell home.

She quickly scanned the living room for her missing article of clothing, but with no luck, she met Luke in the kitchen where he handed her a glass of water and a couple of pills while the smell of coffee brewing filled the kitchen.

"Ibuprofen," he explained when she gave him a questioning look.

"Thank you," she said. Swallowing the medicine, she downed the whole glass in a few gulps. She hadn't realized how thirsty she had been until now.

She handed him the empty cup, and he put it in the sink. After he poured himself some coffee to go, he grabbed his keys off the counter.

"I rode with Sean last night, so my car's here. You need a ride, I'm assuming?"

"Yes, please."

"Do you want any coffee?"

She shook her head.

He reached for something else on the counter and handed it to her. It was her purse.

"Do you have everything?"

Everything but her underwear, but she wasn't going to tell him that. She slung her purse over her shoulder. "Yep, I'm ready."

ABOUT THE AUTHORS

R.L. Kenderson is two best friends writing under one name.

Renae has always loved reading, and in third grade, she wrote her first poem where she learned she might have a knack for this writing thing. Lara remembers sneaking her grandmother's Harlequin novels when she was probably too young to be reading them, and since then, she knew she wanted to write her own.

When they met in college, they bonded over their love of reading and the TV show *Charmed*. What really spiced up their friendship was when Lara introduced Renae to romance novels. When they discovered their first vampire romance, they knew there would always be a special place in their hearts for paranormal romance. After being unable to find certain storylines and characteristics they wanted to read about in the hundreds of books they consumed, they decided to write their own.

They both live in the Minneapolis/St. Paul area where they're a sonographer/stay-at-home mom/wife and pharmacist/mother by day and a sexy author by night. You can find them at http://www.rlkenderson.com, Facebook, Instagram, Tumblr, Twitter, and Goodreads. Or you can email them at rlkenderson@rlkenderson.com, or sign up for their newsletter here. They always love hearing from their readers.

29170603R00141

Printed in Poland
by Amazon Fulfillment
Poland Sp. z o.o., Wrocław